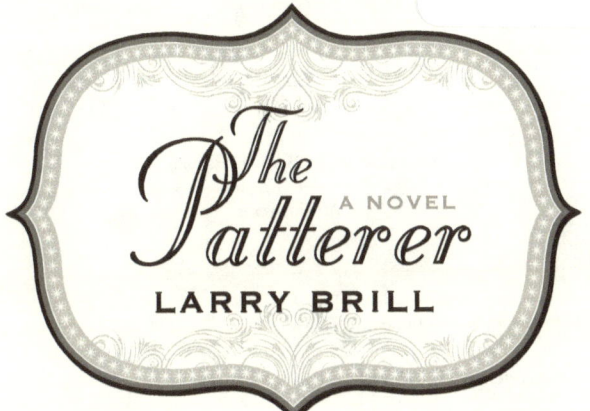

The Patterer

A NOVEL

LARRY BRILL

Black Tie
BOOKS

Black Tie
BOOKS

Published by Black Tie Books

Austin, Texas

The Library of Congress has catalogued the trade paperback edition as follows:

Brill, Larry

The Patterer / by Larry Brill

LCCN: 2013911572-edit

ISBN: 978-0-9888643-4-4

Printed in the United States of America

First Edition

10 9 8 7 6 5 4 3 2 1

www.larrybrill.com

Lar@larrybrill.com

Acknowledgements:

Thanks to a number of people who helped make *The Patterer* a reality. My wife and sounding board, Kim. George Zirfas for his technical wizardry, and Angela Smith, my trusty editor. But a special shout-out goes to my new best friends in London, Wendy and Bob Janes, the Brits who saved me from myself with their unselfish review and editing to make our story historically and logistically plausible.

This one is for Ginny and Chuck. Mom and Dad.

Especially for my father, who spent his life in a job
doing work he never cared for
so that I could do the work I love.

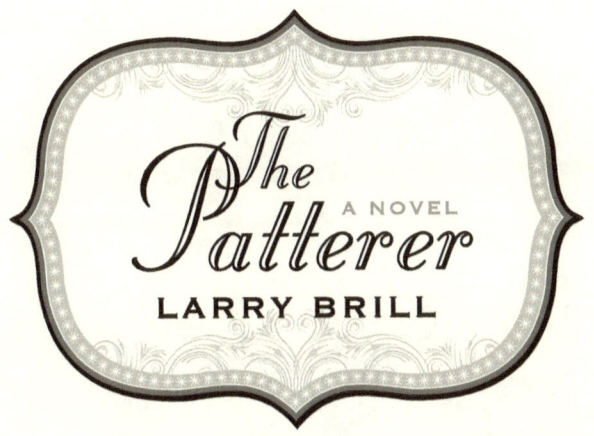

The Patterer

A NOVEL

LARRY BRILL

Chapter One

London-1765.

Blood and lust make the world go 'round, I say. You may argue that it is money—the pound or the pence, the farthing, the shilling, the crown, gold or silver—that makes it spin. God knows money is good. I will tell you straight away, I have personally found it quite handy when bartering for a wench or wine in those rare exquisite moments of self-indulgence. But if you believe that, you'd be as wrong as tits on a bull.

Ladies, forgive me. A crude turn of phrase, that. Men, you expect it. But I will, for the ladies' sake, attempt to rein in the crudeosity of my tale. It won't be easy what with britches dropping nearly as often as your jaw. What I offer is a tawdry tale of bullets flying and death-defying antics—but also a tale of love. Man on woman. Man on man. Camel on...well, let's have none of that here, shall we?

Mostly, this is a story about oral stimulation.

Wait! Don't run. No need to even blush. It's not at all what you imagine. Although your imagination did just have a go with you, now didn't it? Cheeky devils. Yes, you are my kind of crowd, and you have proven my point. Blood and lust make the world go 'round. Repeat it with me. That, in fact, is my world. And I offer it for sale to you. Got two pence and a halfpenny? Then step up even closer, and let's have at it. You see, I am a patterer. At your service.

That is my exceptional skill. It is also my curse, as you will surely see.

Now the first rule of a good patterer is to begin with the most titillating, scandalous or horrific story you can find. Flesh it out whenever possible with references to bodily fluids, and never, *never* let facts get in the way.

Actually, I have a saying, which I made up, entirely original, though you may steal it if you wish: "If it bleeds, it..."

"Leeds!"

That's me. Leeds Merriweather. The roar of my name as it rolled like thunder through the printer's shop yanked me rudely from a deep and dreamless sleep. A bellow this loud and spitting anger could have awakened Shakespeare himself. And this just in: Shakespeare is still dead.

"Leeds Merriweather, you lazy son of a raging git! The ink's dry an' a day's a-wasting."

Charles McNabb owned the dusty print shop where this story begins. He added an exclamation point to his roar with a kick to my ribs. I squinted up at him from the corner of the pressroom where

I had curled up for the night with a soft pillow and a hard floor. It seemed as if I had only just closed my eyes before being subjected to the indignity of McNabb's boot. I know for a fact that it was nearly dawn when, like a weary tomcat, I padded in and settled down with a snout full of gin and a head full of stories I had collected from a long night patronizing the public houses along lower Fleet Street.

"If'n you're not going to sell for me today, it'd be certain I have plenty like you who will," McNabb said. He carried a bundle of the day's edition of his broadsheet, the *London Tattler-Tribune*.

"Aw. Go easy if you please, sir," I said. My ribs where McNabb's boot struck ached, but, oh, how my head throbbed even more. February had just given way to March, and the light from the window danced with particles of dust creating a veil of sorts before my eyes. I sniffed. Oil and ink, parchment and stain. The aroma of the printing press, of literature freshly baked. And turpentine. I love the smell of turpentine in the morning.

McNabb slapped the back of his hand on the broadsheets. "Cannibalism," he cried. "Adultery and ravishing of maidens."

I love the ravishing of maidens. It sells newspapers.

The publisher was a short Scot with a gunpowder temperament, and that morning something put a spark to his britches. "'Tis death on the high seas. By God, I am good."

I asked, "Good for what?"

He aimed his next kick at my privates; I raised a knee just in time. "Don't you be insolent, y'ragged lump of gutter waste. If this story d'nnot draw a decent income today then we have no business doing business in this business."

I used the brick wall behind me as a brace for my back as I inched up—slowly, very, *very* slowly—to a standing position. War drums were beating in my noggin, and the battle for a clear head was most definitely in doubt. Too much gin last night, for certain. I took the broadsheet McNabb forced upon me and glanced over the all-important lead story beneath the *Tattler-Tribune* banner.

Spank me senseless! "Lord Thurston's shipwreck? What the bloody hell is this?" I demanded.

"A fine bit of writing, if I say so myself."

"A fine bit thievery, I say." That weasel McNabb had attached his name to the story—*my story!* I was the one who mined the details of the shipwreck over a bottle of rum from a Portuguese captain whose ship happened upon an uncharted island. The crew was taking on fresh water when they discovered what was left of a tourist yacht in the lagoon and the remains of the rich nobleman, his wife, and the others who perished with him.

"What is this dung you've printed here? What happened to what I wrote?" I wanted to rip that newspaper and wave the tatters in McNabb's ferret face. I had only turned the details over to McNabb on the promise that I could print and sell the story under my name. All I had to do was raise a couple of quid to cover the cost of printing. All the right elements of a great story were there, not the least of which was potential for profit. McNabb understood that. He held out his palm, and the way he rubbed two fingers against this thumb said it all: Show me the money.

I shook my head. "Soon."

"And what of yesterday's sales? D'ya drink it all away as usual last night?"

"'Course not," I lied. Yes, I was penniless again. Even McNabb could read that much in my bloodshot eyes.

"It is a fine story, lad, and I couldn't let it waste away a-waiting for you." That bugger, McNabb, knew a golden story when he saw one.

All they found were the bones of the good Lord Thurston and those six who were shipwrecked with him. The evidence of the extreme hedonistic life they lived and left behind created a tale so repulsive and so enchanting in one, that it was sure to shock and awe and produce profits. More important, this was a story to be told and re-told and remembered for generations. And it was mine to tell first.

"Lad, 'tis a sin to give stock to such profound pride. Be prudent," McNabb said. "You're a better man for surrendering it to me, and the story is better for it; that is my duty as editor. Now run. Run and patter. Patter and run, whichever it is that you do." He waved me off, dismissing me as one might shoo a cat from the supper table.

"Leave the wordsmithing to McNabb," he said. "You have every chance to patter your version on the street. You have a handsome face, a strong voice and straight teeth. You were made to patter, not to publish. That is your proper lot in life. Accept it."

I looked down at McNabb. He was barely as tall as my shoulder. My left hand clenched, balling up a corner of the *Tattler-Tribune* I held. I snapped at him. "This was mine. You said it was a story beneath you."

"She rose to the occasion," he said with a smirk. McNabb handed the broadsheets to me. "Do you want them or shall I find another patterer today?"

I moved to the window and bent at the waist enough to peek at the sky above the roofs of Fleet Street. The clouds were grey but not dismal. More distressing was the odor of the fish market carried on the wind. Whitefish today, and not a fresh catch apparently. Strong enough and blowing up from Billingsgate Wharf, the wind would invariably carry my voice away from the crowds I hoped to capture. Bloody hell it was, this would be a difficult day.

I turned to face McNabb, took one of the broadsheets from the bundle and waved the front page at him, not ready to back down from this duel. "You agreed I could rent your press to print my own."

He laughed, "What? You have no money and c'nnot afford it, you foul-breath alley dog. Be intelligent for once. Why should I allow you to compete with me? 'Twould be like lettin' you shag me wife and offer you me own bed for the purpose. I may be a Scot, but I'm not insane, man."

I took a step toward him, and then sharply veered right, to the large typesetting table in the pressroom. To my left, near the front door, a wall of books, pamphlets and assorted printed pages for sale stood behind the counter where McNabb serviced his customers. Everything for the literate gentleman, from pens and ink to writing paper and wax seals, sat on display across the counter itself. At the back of the pressroom, McNabb's assistants, Simon and Garfinkle, were preparing the printing press for another go and pretending to ignore our battle of wills and ink-stained egos.

Pacing back to McNabb, I considered my limited options. No respect, I say. Some day, I knew, I would have my own press and see my words, my ideas in print instead of being cast on the wind as they were now. Even on a calm day words disappeared within the moment at each street corner where I stopped. No one respects the patterer, but put your story in print? That, my friends, is a whole 'nother kettle of carp.

Change would come, of that I was certain. But until then there were meals to be purchased and rent money to be paid. Both, sadly, had been hard to acquire of late, and dodging my landlord who selfishly insisted on being paid for overdue rent had become a daily game.

"How is your head this morning?" McNabb asked, as if the matter was settled and forgotten. "And your rhyme? How will you pitch this?"

"My head? As right as ever. My rhyme? Far too splendid for the drivel you have written here," I said.

"Leeds, 'tis that attitude that makes you so difficult. If I want a bit of criticism I have only to spend more time with my wife. Show some conviction, man. And be positively positive in your expression. Be cheerful, even. Fer no mon wants to buy death from a grump."

He was right, of course. In pattering, proper disposition is nearly as important as a winning smile and the tale's details. I admitted to McNabb as much, and it placated him. So, I handed him the one copy I had waved in his face a moment earlier and stepped next to the window. I counted only those papers in my hand. "Three and twenty papers," I said. "That is two pence, half-penny short of three shilling in total."

He shook his head. "No, lad, the count is twenty-four."

"But Mr. McNabb, see for yourself."

I handed him the bundle of papers in my hand and, in return, took the single broadsheet he was holding. I rolled it cylindrical and tapped it like a baton on the palm of my left hand while McNabb counted the papers.

"I am sure I printed out exactly four over twenty," he said. He looked at the table in the center of the room. He looked to his left and to his right, clearly confused. He counted again as if he could perform the Lord's own fish-and-loaves miracle to increase it by at least one, but the stack in his hand had not changed.

Then I pointed my rolled newspaper to the printing press. McNabb's eyes followed the sweeping motion of my paper pointer. "Is it possible you left the final print on the press?" I asked. I took the bundle of broadsheets from him, and while he stumped to the press in the back of his shop I unfurled and added the sheet in my hand to the others.

"No, 'tis not here."

With a shrug I placed the newspapers in my satchel where I still had six as-yet unsold copies of *The London Gentleman's Magazine* and three books I had purchased at discount from Mr. Hawke, the bookseller six doors down. I slung the satchel's long leather strap over my head, collected my hat and turned for the door. "Well," I said, "If by chance the missing copy appears, do send it my way. I should have made three; maybe four stops by then, and will most certainly reach the Monument within three hours. I'm certain that with a story so compelling and cleverly written as this, I should be sold out in no time at all. Possibly before I reach London Bridge."

Mr. McNabb accepted that as certain fact and grinned. "Do your job, and my words will do theirs." Then he demanded payment for the twenty-three *Tattler-Tribunes* he could account for. I sheepishly shook my head.

"I c'nnot go on giving you papers on credit, lad. Why can't you pay on the front end like the other patterers? 'Tis no way to run a business."

"You tell me; you're the Scot. And don't I always make good? I am the best patterer you've had, Mr. McNabb. No one sells your trash like me."

"I'm not so very certain of that, me boy. On the soul of my sainted muther I say n'more credit. This is the last time."

"That is precisely what you said last time." I smiled. I was starting out my day with a one-paper profit. And with that extra two pence I could afford a full meal that evening. It would be my first of the week.

With a gulp of the thick London air and a sip of thin potato gin from the flask in my pocket to steady myself, I began my march across uneven cobblestones toward my first stop, a busy corner at Cheapside.

"Hummm." I drew out the sound like a monk's chant to test my vocals. I would need them proper today. The tone sounded strong enough; it carried a depth, timbre, and a bear-like resonance that comes only after a fair night of drinking. Some say London gin will put hair on your chest. I say it'll put baritone balls in your voice. At least for me, more than three nips and I sound like God on high, Himself. With what I could remember of the previous evening's rounds, I was bound to be thrice as strong that day.

I will tell you, I do not fancy the overuse of rhyme in pattering as so many of my compatriots do these days. But this was a story so full of twists, and characters uncommon in London, that it demanded just such a fine, Merriweather touch. A wretchedly wealthy, shipwrecked aristocrat, his wife and his five fellow castaways, ("fellows" being a relative description; two were lusty females—harlots, I was happy to note), left to fend for themselves on an island.

I began shouting more than twenty paces before reaching the corner. Drama on the high seas! Cannibalism! Lust on the high seas! Lusty cannibalism! Come hear me out, I have details!

A crowd formed around me like the first innocent swell of high tide when I stopped across from Cheapside. I stepped on a small platform I built there and paused. I looked over the faces before me and let tension and their expectations of entertainment build. I held up a copy of the *Tattler-Tribune* and directed their attention to first the masthead, and then the story of Lord Thurston and the plight of all those aboard his yacht the *Minnow*.

"Step right up, and come hear a tale.

"A tale of a fateful trip." My voice was strong. More passers-by paused to listen.

"It started in a distant port—aboard a tiny ship."

I told them of the first mate and the captain who was brave.

"And sure, they set sail that day for what was to be a three-hour tour."

"A three-hour tour?" a woman asked, wide-eyed.

Indeed. "A three-hour tour."

Chapter Two

The life of a patterer is not especially difficult for one with a quick wit, strong lungs, and a God-inspired talent for exaggeration, or outright disregard for the truth. Bollocks, I say. I deliver the truth in every story. I won't lie though, many a time the truth is more snooze than news so I am forced to improve upon it. Sometimes, considerably so. But, really now, isn't it simply a matter of how one goes about it? As the hangman said when he slipped the noose over the convict's neck: "If I do this right it won't hurt a bit—it's all in the execution."

Groan if you will, the pain of pun is nothing compared to the anger still building inside me as I left Cheapside that day. Cheapside, the corner south of The Royal Exchange and quick nip with the stockbrokers and jobbers inside Jonathan's Coffee-House were all profitable as I worked my way down to The Monument. But the jingle in my purse only served as a reminder of what might have been had McNabb not gone Jolly Roger on me arse.

I emerged from the deepening shadows of the canyon of coffee houses that is Change Alley, and into the open sunshine on Lombard Street. I expected to make it to one of my choice corners between The Monument and London Bridge for the late afternoon rush hour. In pausing to consider my progress, financially and geographically, I made myself an easy target.

"Oye! Mr. Merriweather!"

Aloysius Periwinkle Procter stepped from the doorway of a tailor shop and thumped the large drum he carried on a sash around his neck. Bung. Bung. Bung!

His long, dark hair was oily and tangled; it spilled from beneath a soft cap to his shoulders. His clothes were a patchwork of patches, and even on the stale London air the strong scent of horse dung told me Aloysius had spent the night sleeping on the floor of the blacksmith's stable.

"Mr. Merriweather, are you off to market?" Bung. Bung!

"I have been there already. Now I am on my way to the bridge, Ape."

"That is Ay and Pee," he said. "You must uh, uh 'nunciate."

"Ee-nunciate," I said. "A new word for you?"

A.P. nodded and grinned. Aloysius Periwinkle, being a cumbersome name to pronounce even sober, caused most of his friends to simply call him A.P.

"My enunciation is just fine, Ape. It is my humor that you can't hear."

"Humor me rightly then, Mr. Merriweather. Ay and Pee."

"Not this minute, Ape. I must get to The Monument while the

light is still good." A.P. fell into step with me. He bunged his drum as we marched. It was no better and no worse than the rest of the circus noise filling the street, but it was closer and more annoying. I snatched his mallet in mid bung and bopped him on his cap. "Now get along, I've work to do."

"I can help you draw a crowd, Mr. Merriweather. You know I can."

I tapped my chin with the handle end of the mallet. "At what cost, my friend?"

"I am a might bit parched and haven't eaten yet. It'd be a tur'ble shame if I was to keel right over, dead on the spot without being of no use to you at all. But a pence or three for a quick bite would go a long way for me health until we reach your next stop."

I turned out my empty pocket. "I can only pay you in lint, Ape."

His shoulders sagged, and A.P. lowered his eyes. I wondered how he came to pick this moment to approach me, when I actually did have coin in my purse. My story that day was fresh, my patter was perfect, and response had been gratifying. But looking at Ape I could see my day's profit shrinking by a farthing or two.

"Don't be so down, Ape." Oh, for one extra shilling at that moment to buy a harder heart. A.P. was barely seventeen, not much older than I was when I reached London half a dozen years ago. He looked up at me with his dirty face and his nose smudged as if he had kissed a horse's behind. His clothes may have been tattered and soiled, but I knew his soul was pure. Aw!

I said, "Tell you what we'll do. Go wash your face in the trough over there. Then bring your drum and help me draw a paying crowd. If we can make the day's full commission, then dinner is on me tonight."

"With beer?"

"With beer."

"Then time is a-wasting."

The afternoon was growing short, and we walked mostly in the shadows of the buildings along Gracechurch. The Monument was my last stop of the day, and a jolly good place to catch the merchant class as well as bankers and barristers as they headed home. They were precisely the sort of people who had the interest, the education and the purse to purchase a newspaper, a book or magazine, or writing accessories stashed in my satchel. Sales from a well-timed stop there could make a bad day good, a good day great. This was turning out to be a great day.

The sun broke through the clouds, and the weather was pleasant enough for the first week of March. It was all that a spring day in London could offer. Even the factory smoke seemed to take pity on us.

He asked about the top article in the *Tattler-Tribune* and the patter I used to work the crowd. I handed him the paper; he read while we walked. A.P. struggled at times, but I had been encouraging him to read, helping when I could. "Everyone will be reading soon, from the king to the lowest peasant," I told him. "I see it more every day, so you'd better learn now. It's all the rage. Reading, my boy, that is the future." A.P. was bright, and he improved much over the winter when we were stuck indoors too often.

"You must be pleased, Mr. Merriweather, sir. And handsomely paid for writing somethin' as fine as all this." And then he sighed, "If only I could put into words like you the things I sees and hears, then I could be somebody too. Then Mr. McNabb and the likes of him would pay more for what I have to offer. You are most fortunate, Mr. Merriweather."

I gave no hint at that moment what McNabb had done to steal the story from me, without even just payment. So as we approached the square I fingered the coins in my purse and prayed they might copulate in their cozy leather lair. Go forth, be fruitful and multiply. I removed three shillings and tucked them in a special compartment of my waistcoat. Emergency funds.

Ape turned heads as he bonged his drum and we merged into the flow of traffic funneling into the square. Although I still had six papers left, I wore my confidence like a mantle. I might even order meat with supper tonight, along with A.P.'s beer.

"Who is that?" Ape asked.

We shouldered past bodies at a fruit cart and slipped between several ladies admiring lace on the rack held by another costermonger. A handsome fellow held forth on the very steps where I had planned to pitch. He stood head and shoulders above the audience he held captive there. One gentleman in a wool banker's coat drifted from the crowd and passed us with his head down, his nose buried in the paper in his hand.

"Did ya see that?" A.P. asked as the man brushed past.

I swallowed and nodded. It was the *Tattler-Tribune*. That was my first sense of the troubling scene in front of me. The second was of the unusual sound in the square. For once, the air lacked what should have been a cacophony of street noise. It was as if the vendors and musicians, the beggars and the animals, every man, woman, and child all paused to give this man their attention. Even from where we stood we could hear him calling to the crowd in a clear and melodious voice.

"Gather around me, gentlemen and good gentlewomen. I have a story that is true, though it may strain your belief. Come now, I will begin and you will be amazed and delighted, confounded, and horrified. You will not walk away unfulfilled."

A rival patterer? A.P. and I moved closer. I stuffed my six *Tattler-Tribunes* into my satchel so as to be less conspicuous. He paused in the middle of the story to sell newspapers and build some tension for what remained. My heart felt as heavy as Ape's drum and thumped with a dull ache. Here was this man pitching my story of the castaways. It was my story, but it was his crowd.

"Wot d'ye think of 'im?" Publisher McNabb stood behind me. The weasel slipped up with such stealth, or I had been too engaged in my newfound rival, that I failed to notice his approach. More so, I failed to notice that McNabb's brother, Archibald, stood beside him. Archie McNabb was built like a brick shit house. A coal-hauling porter by trade, he blotted out what was left of the sun as he positioned himself behind me.

"Th'boy has something special," McNabb said. He cocked his head towards the patterer. "He's twice your talent and he pays upfront, you poxy pool of vermin vomit."

"Oh yeah? You fetid funnel of flatulence. Piss off!"

We unleashed an arsenal of alliteration upon each other, a war of insults so increasingly creative that I almost paused in order to capture them in my notebook for future use.

"Don't forget Stinky Cloud of Skunk Cabbage," A.P. called from the side. He elbowed Archie. "That's my favorite." Archie swatted him aside with the back of his hand.

McNabb made a grab for my satchel and the broadsheets inside. Thrust and parry, I whacked him thoroughly upside the head and drove him to the ground and gave him good measure with several more blows of leather on face and a fine bit of knuckle too.

Bad form. Especially when your victim's bigger brother is at your flank. Archie pulled me up with a thick forearm upon the back of my neck and a hand at my throat.

McNabb rose and dusted himself off. He straightened his clothes and then straightened his nose. Finally he said, "You can ease up, Archie, but don't let him loose until we collect on the day."

Archie relaxed just as the wind in my lungs exhausted itself. "In the nick of bloody time," I thought.

Ape slapped at Archie's back, his shoulder and even his head. Archie ignored him while McNabb came at me with a very short, but very sharp printer's knife. He reached up and tapped its point on my chin then cut through the strap of my satchel. He grabbed the bag as it slid off my shoulder and removed the copies of the *Tattler-Tribune.*

"Six left? You should have done better."

"It was a slow day at the market," I choked. I twisted. I elbowed. I surrendered.

"And what's this? *Gentleman's Monthly*. I c'not recall selling you any. How did you pay for these? For sure, no one along Fleet Street would give you credit as I have. No one is that foolish."

"You said it," I squeaked from beneath the pressure of Archie's paw.

"William over there. He sold nearly twice's many papers," Archibald said as he lowered his face near to mine. His breath was so foul I wished he would close my throat completely and leave me to die.

Publisher McNabb said, "And William'll not be a-asking for credit. Straight cash deal fer the takin'." Then he reached into my pocket and removed my purse.

Maybe it was the Scot in him, but McNabb only needed to weigh it in the palm of his hand to know the balance of coin inside. He raised a furry eyebrow and beneath it his eye twinkled with harsh delight. He was accounting for the obvious, that I had already withdrawn a portion of my share for the day.

"Always pay thyself first, just so, Leeds?"

He transferred the money to his own purse and then held two shillings before my eyes. "I'm notta thief, you see. Your snipe of an accomplice here can bear witness to that. You are hardly worth this but..." He made a grand show of dropping those coins into my purse and the purse to the ground at my feet. "For a less than stellar day's work."

McNabb held up the *Tattler-Tribune*. "Now I must get these to the audience. With good fortune and William's talent we will run out in a short time."

I struggled, but Archibald tightened his hold, once again cutting off the wind to my lungs. Like the first stars in the evening sky, I could see points of light twinkling before me.

"Your services are n'longer required." McNabb turned and backed away. "If there be questions, tell anyone who gives a farthing that you, uhm, felt it best t' explore other employment opportunities."

Flog the frog! I'd been sacked.

Chapter Three

It was my unfortunate lot in life to have grown up with education, though I don't take it as a personal affront. My parents meant well, really.

"You're a bloody fool," A.P. said, through the mug at his lips.

No, if I had been born into this life on the streets that I had taken to like a feral mouse just one fatal SNAP! away from getting caught with his nose in a bit of cheese, if I was blissfully unencumbered by knowledge, I would be comfortable in my situation. After all, what does a man care about what he could achieve when he is too busy just trying to acquire what he must have to survive? What was that, you say? My god, I'm starting to babble like A.P. Blame the ale and hear me out.

"Bugger McNabb. You don't need him," A.P. simply stated.

We sat at a table far from the hearth of the Moose and Squirrel, a small and dark public house run by a pair of small and dark Russians. From where we sat, the fire across the room was as helpful as a beer stein at a temperance revival. A.P. and I were three sheets to the wind and four mugs of the owner's "Siberian Drool" into a discussion of my future.

"But it's not just McNabb, my good little Ape. It's the bloody lot of them." I snapped my fingers with contempt. "McNabb was not the first, though, as God is my witness, he will be the last. Those publishers, they steal my ideas or maim my words with criminally negligent editing, take all the credit and profit while telling me I am too fine a patterer to be of any other use to them."

"Well, you do have fine looks, a strong voice and straight teeth. Did I mention your teeth? I'd cut off me left pinky for a smile like yours. Do you floss?"

I ignored him and thumped my mug upon the table. "Ha. But then they sack you for no better reason than they find some fresh word wanker they like better. They will respect me when I can publish myself myself someday."

"Ain't nobody in London can wank words like you, Mr. Merriweather."

I whined.

I bitched.

I bemoaned my lot in life to the point of turning self-pity into a higher form of art.

A.P. rolled his eyes and endured. I knew he would never abandon his friend and mentor—at least as long as his mug was full.

I couldn't see how things could get any worse, so naturally they did. The door to the Moose and Squirrel burst open like a trumpet blast announcing the triumphant arrival of a hearty party of half-dozen men or so. They paraded in behind my better dressed, stipend-baby, remarkably-undistinguished-member-of-Parliament brother Deuce. Just my bleeding luck.

The group chortled and raised the roof, certainly raising the volume inside the tavern, with boisterous laughter as they stumbled all over themselves to a reserved table across from us. It was really quite festive—a dagger to my heart. Deuce stopped long enough to acknowledge us. He brushed the brim of his hat with a finger, gave me a measured squint with a hint of amusement and a subtle shake of his head.

"Looks like 'e don't need your company tonight, Mr. Merriweather."

"Judging from what I can see of that motley crew, impeccably dressed though they may be, my friend, joining those tossers would be the last item on my wish list on any night. Especially tonight. They make me sick."

"They make me sick, too," A.P. responded. His face was mostly white with shades of green. "Really sick. Or maybe it's the beer." He jumped up from the table and disappeared out the side door. It was a commendable effort; he almost made it. A.P. painted the door with something vile just before he darted out.

"You'll grow out of it, lad," I said to the empty bench where Ape had been sitting. I sniffed the remnants of his mug and then poured it into mine.

My brother Lancaster was six years older. Father gave him the nickname Deuce because he was son number two. Coming in at number four, I had no special designation. I didn't see much of

Lancaster in London; we lived at the extreme opposite ends of society. I had my social circle, and he had…well, it was more of a trapezoid of friends. But the one thing we had in common, along with the Merriweather surname and good looks, was that our oldest brother London pressured both of us out of our family estate, Wittyglib Manor. Yes, stay with me. London is my brother as well as the town. Lancaster and I are more or less in exile, though for entirely different reasons. Deuce got a seat in the House of Commons that our brother bought for him, as well as a monthly stipend and townhouse. All I got was a friggin' shirt. Oh, and fifteen lashes. And the toe of my brother's boot up me rump.

A.P. is as thin as you'd expect from a regularly undernourished teenager of the streets, but he dropped onto his bench like a fifty-pound sack of tired grain. He pushed away what was left of the mystery stew we had for dinner with a retch and buried his face in his hands.

"If I had known Lancaster was going to bring his little social club here tonight I would have gladly endured the swill over at Bashful Bull instead," I said.

"Lancaster?"

I nodded toward my brother, "Yeah. Deuce."

"And your other brother?"

"London. And then, naturally, there's Lincoln. He's after Lancaster, but before me."

"You're daft, Mr. Merriweather."

I admit it was a bit odd. The truth is, and I am to this day uncertain of how much truth there is to this, but as the story goes my father traveled frequently on business and, as was his habit, would impregnate my mother upon his return from some corner of the land. The offspring of that encounter was given the name of the most recent stop on my father's travels. We are five children in all, the first four boys and my sister. In order, we are London, Lancaster, Lincoln, Leeds, and Hereford.

Pity the girl, my sister Hereford, and the unfortunate timing of her birth. I suppose it could have been worse. My father was aging by then and sometimes confused the itinerary of his travels. There was apparently much discussion about whether Her, as we had taken to calling her, should be named after that city, or named from what my father suspected was truly the final town of call. How dreadful it would be if she had been christened Snout-upon-Avon.

Though I confess, Snout-upon-Avon Merriweather is a name that rolls from the tongue with gentleness reminiscent of the hills surrounding Wittyglib Manor. Snout. Possibly a fine name, come to think of it, for a bold, handsome, and full-bodied woman. However my younger sister was a nervous wisp, a mousey sort built for a name like Islip or Peepenshire.

A.P. caught me studying my brother across the room. "You'll be your old self soon enough," he said. "You always buck up. And b'sides, it ain't as bad as all that. You've done well for yourself so far, Mr. Merriweather. It's a right life enough, I'd wager."

To a lad who thinks a single pound sterling is a King's ransom I couldn't really argue poverty. I was always broke, but I wasn't starving.

A.P. stood and wiped his chin with the sleeve of his blouse. He picked up his coat and thanked me for the meal that he cheerfully assumed was my duty to pay.

"I wish I could be you, Mr. Merriweather. Really I do. But I ain't got your talent for the words." He paused and looked my brother's direction. Then he said, "You know where you could go to do what you would do if only you don't stop yourself from doing what you should do by going there, I say."

Somewhere in A.P.'s tangled net of mangled syntax was a bit of logic, a bit that I really didn't want to consider.

"That would be like going straight to hell." I attempted a laugh, but the thought was a stinging one.

"Your brothers got money. They could lend ya wot ya need, so whose hell is it, Mr. Merriweather?" A.P. shrugged as he left.

Christ on a crumpet. I hate it when he chirps like my bloody conscience. But hell is where your home is. And that is exactly what A.P. had proposed.

I watched my brother Lancaster and his friends raise their glasses and toast someone or something. Three cheers! Whether my family would feast and welcome the prodigal son, or transport me directly to the pillory was a gamble at best, a flip of a coin.

My brother London became patriarch of the family after my father's death. If I returned to Wittyglib, London might actually call for a public punishment, just on principle. I suppose I could endure being locked down head and hands in the village stocks to be pelted with mud and sludge, dead cats and road excrement. Dead cats are particularly plentiful and useful projectiles for the citizens who turn out for such public displays. Once one has been pummeled by a dead cat, any other shame would be, I suspect, shallow and short-lived. But it wasn't that easy.

First, London always felt unappreciated by my father and blamed me. Father placed great expectations on him with a very business-like and rather arms length approach while I, with no inheritance at stake, was much closer to my father's heart. It seemed everything I did to please father vexed, annoyed, and otherwise ruined London's disposition towards me.

And then, of course, there was that other tiny matter, the one with London's wife Emily. Ah, sweet Emily. She was a much older woman at twenty-one while I was merely fifteen the year I was schooled in that most significant Bible lesson I somehow missed in Sunday school about the Eleventh Commandment: Thou shalt not shag thy brother's wife.

That alone would be enough for London to be the pisser in the pot of life.

At that moment, so exclusive was my attention to the tale of two Londons, one being the city that was increasingly hostile to my existence and the other a sibling who was hostile to it from the moment of my birth, that I failed to notice the shadow that settled upon the table top. However the knife from nowhere that jammed its blade into the wood a mere inch from my hand was an unmistakable call to attention. Its hilt quivered, punctuating the force with which the knife was planted in the table.

And it came with a message, or rather a messenger who looked down upon me with a sneer that would make a pirate whimper. His curled lip ruined what would have been an otherwise pretty, boyish face. He was a few years older than me, maybe thirty years of age, and freckled. He wore a fine silk coat and an air of conscience-free menace.

"Your brother. He wants a word with you, Merriweather."

I wondered. How is it that a man can go his entire life without being significantly accosted, and it was my misfortune to wind up on the pointed end of a blade twice in the same day?

I rose with a weariness in my bones that was more emotional than physical and followed him across the Moose and Squirrel, scuffling up sawdust as we went. Lancaster looked at me from the front of the table. His face was noncommittal; this was not his idea.

The others ignored my arrival. As my knife-wielding escort rejoined the group I could not help but notice the effeminate stroke he gave the nape of my brother's neck as he reclaimed the seat to Lancaster's right.

A round stranger in the center seat stood and reached out a hand to me, bumping the table in the process with enough force that the others rushed to protect their glasses from spilling wine. Only one bottle was lost, and it appeared to be one mostly empty and useless by that time anyway.

"You must be Merriweather the younger," he said in a voice rich and pleasing yet lacking well-rounded vowels so that I could not place his accent.

"Leeds Merriweather, sir. At your service." I bowed slightly. Well, it was truly no more than a nod. Any company my brother kept expected more civility than they often deserved; I was not about to give him reason to feel superior despite whatever class he might have been born to. Take that, you graying pudgy wanker.

The stranger said, "Your brother has spoken highly of you this evening." Then he winked at Lancaster. "Although begrudgingly, I suspect. And we have much in common, I believe, so I am pleasured to make your acquaintance. I am Franklin, Mr. Merriweather. Benjamin Franklin from the Pennsylvania Colony.

Chapter Four

You could have flattened me from behind with a sack of horse manure and not shocked me more. "*Doctor* Franklin? The inimitable *Doctor* friggin' Franklin?"

"I've been called worse," he chuckled.

I apologized for my crude outburst and for mucking up our introduction. I bowed again with the proper amount of respect this time and said, "I heard that you had returned to London. It is a pleasure to make your acquaintance."

He nodded in response. Then Doctor Franklin turned to the club members on his left and then to his right with arms out and palms up pleading, "Gentlemen? Shall we let our potty-mouth new friend Merriweather here be the impartial voice to put this argument to rest for the evening?" He placed his fists on his hips, daring them to vote no. I considered him and thought he had the look of a wise old monarch with a noble face and a perpetual twinkle in his eye. Yes, it was a face you might imagine engraved on a coin or a bank note. Rubbish, I know. What country would be insane to the point of putting a commoner on its currency? The natural laws of class and society will have to be turned upon their heads before that would ever happen! Rubbish, I say. Rubbish.

Those members of my brother Lancaster's entourage with whom I was acquainted grumbled, though not loud enough to offend their guest. Those I did not know grumbled a bit softer in support of the grumblers.

"Good."

"That settles it then," my brother Lancaster said.

So I asked, "And what debate is it that I should judge?"

"Let me recite a scenario for you," said Doctor Franklin.

"Strictly hypothetical," added someone in the group to much laughter.

Doctor Franklin explained that some in this group felt that the experiments in electricity he had conducted had led to the death of someone who tried to emulate those studies.

"Now, I never published a definitive outline of my methods so as to warn of the risks, no matter how slight, so the question before us is: am I to be held accountable for the outcome?"

"Guilty!" the shout went up from two or three in the group.

"Should I be held morally responsible in some fashion for the death by lightning of some subsequent practitioner of the experiment?"

"Guilty!" the jury cried again.

I wiggled uncomfortably both inside my skin and probably noticeably on the outside as well as he watched me with a smile, benign and professorial. It was as if I had been dragged to stand before Doctor Franklin—he the master and I his pupil—and this was some examination to be passed. "You are no doubt referring to that most unfortunate professor in St. Petersburg. I do know of that."

"Bloody Rooskie," someone said.

"German," another countered.

"German? Russian? Still no great loss," said the young, freckled man who appeared to be my brother Lancaster's companion du jour. "Better had he been French, but we can't have it all," he added with a laugh that was nasal, high-pitched and totally irritating.

Doctor Franklin ignored the chatter of the others as they debated the greater value of eliminating a Russian, a German, or a Frenchman. Spaniards never entered the discussion. They get no respect. "Don't be so modest, Mr. Merriweather. Your brother insists you know quite a bit about the story as it happens. He provided us with this, and it sounds as if you are quite the expert in this matter."

Doctor Franklin took from the table in front of my brother a news broadsheet, one I had not seen in years—not since the days I was fresh to London.

"Let me read," he said. He peered at it through thin glasses that balanced perfectly on the end of his nose. He cleared his throat and then lubricated it with a generous swallow of wine. "It was an exercise in scientific experimentation not unlike the now famous test of electricity performed by an American, Mr. Benjamin Franklin,

recently given fellowship in the prestigious Royal Society of Arts."
He peered at me over his reading glasses. "That is I, no doubt?"
Rhetorical sarcasm favors Franklin's face like the latest fashion on
a beautiful woman.

How could I forget that story; it was among the first of mine
that found its way into print when I arrived in London. I was
eighteen and the *Westminster Herald* was my introduction to the
workings of publishers. Seeing that story in print seduced me into
what became my love affair with the news business. Watching the
printer claim credit for it as was his right by owning the press that
produced it with no regard for true authorship slapped me like a
jilted lover.

"Your brother suggests you had a hand in this. And this has
been the centerpiece of a lively debate this evening."

Lancaster had shown no particular interest in the newspaper
when I gave him a copy after it was published. That he would
have preserved his little brother's work amazed me. That is just not
Merriweather.

"I'm glad I could provide your evening's entertainment," I said.

Lancaster said, "Well yes. In publishing, as in Parliament, the
devil is in the details. And it is the details of this story that has kept
us nailed to our seats." It was sarcasm oozing mockery, seeping
disdain like pus from a lanced...well, best not go there; you get
the picture. Lancaster placed spectacles on his nose much in the
fashion Doctor Franklin wore his. "Let's see...shoes scorched and
smoldering with rising smoke, found next to the unrecognizably
blackened body dropped upon a red spot."

Lancaster passed the broadsheet across the table while I con-templated the most direct line to the nearest exit.

"...the stench which would make even the odor of London's sewage gutters as pleasant as a lily pond," recited the next reader in this performance.

The *Herald* passed from hand to hand, and it seemed every member of that club wanted to quote a portion of the post.

Doctor Franklin leaned on the table and placed his chin upon his palm. He raised his wine glass in my direction with the other hand. "I believe my favorite to be ...the world has not seen such an horrific burning death since Joan of Arc."

That was a sentence I was particularly proud of. "Gentlemen, you give me too much credit."

"Pity," Doctor Franklin replied. "For this story has everything that makes a newspaper worth the reader's effort. An horrific death with grizzly, exaggerated details, a beautiful, charismatic virgin in your allusion to Joan of Arc, and, ho, if you include the reference I see here to '...his skin resembling that of a chicken long forgotten on the spit,' well, by golly, you could make a case that you've covered the issue of pets as well," Franklin said. Oh, the laugh that received.

"Death, bosoms and pets. Leeds, isn't that what you and your sort feast upon?" Lancaster's smile was nearly as broad as my own.

"No fucking, though. And definitely no buggering," someone quipped. They all found this hilarious. Lancaster, his companion, and three others in the group raised their glasses in some private toast. They tossed down their wine and poured more. An empty glass is wasted space at times like that.

"It hasn't any sex in it, now does it? No lust. No intercourse. No copulation," one of the toasters said. "Not even a suggestion of depravity that might give us something to imagine in our heads. I'd say that's a major disappointment."

"Well, three out of four is not bad," Doctor Franklin returned. "My good fellow Merriweather," he said to me, "Your brother tells me you have a mind to publish. There can never be enough of us. Sharing your company and another bottle of wine would certainly make dealing with these politicians and rogues more palatable."

His insult was taken with good humor by the others but I don't for a minute believe the invitation was as well received.

"I am probably overstepping my authority; I am only a guest of this group, but join us, won't you?" In short order someone produced a chair. The personal invitation from the incomparable Doctor Franklin was not lost on the group. A death-eye stare from some members at the table confirmed how distasteful the idea was to them. Despite my family connection with Lancaster, I was as much an outsider as the man in the moon is to a stable of donkeys. They were far superior to my current station in life, but butter my bum and call me a biscuit if any of that mattered to me that night. That is not to say I could join them with no reservations at all.

You see, I was ill at ease with the whispers of an unspoken secret that swirled around Lancaster's social club among those who knew just enough to be credible. They confirmed to me, delicately put, that several of the friends had a strong physical attraction to one another. Very strong. Less delicately, I will suggest to you that, well, they were homosexually bent raging mollies. But then I had known that of my brother since age eleven when I happened upon Lancaster and a stable boy in the throes of whatever mollies feel when they are reclined to such behavior. We never spoke of that encounter to anyone, not even each other through the years. Part bond, part wall, it was always there between us.

Still, on this evening I found them of good cheer, and eventually I was asked again to settle the matter of Doctor Franklin's accountability for experimentation gone wrong. I suggested that Doctor Franklin should not be held culpable. "The professor should have been wary enough to take proper precaution knowing that..." I paused in true patterer form for dramatic effect, "...that a ounce of prevention is worth a pound of cure."

Not guilty.

That brought more table thumping and walking stick applause. I had appeased more than half the group. Doctor Franklin, himself, honored me. "Well said."

"Well, those are not my words this time. I give credit to Poor Richard and the wisdom of his Almanack." I smiled at Doctor Franklin and he acknowledged the compliment with a wink.

My brother's youngish companion, named Ian as it turns out, raised his head from where it had been resting on his chest and rejoined the conversation. "Poor Richard? That dolt. Useless dolt."

Dolt? For half the club members, shock and annoyance circulated through them as fast as the lightning that scorched the esteemed Russian professor. The other half proved equally ignorant that Poor Richard himself sat among us. Lancaster was among the enlightened and elbowed his companion. Ian Jasper took that as encouragement to continue.

"Wasn't it Poor Richard who said 'Early to bed and early to rise makes a man healthy wealthy and wise?' Well, my friends, not only am I handsome..."

"And modest," someone slipped in.

"It is now well past midnight; I might not rise until noon tomorrow, and yet I sit before you extremely healthy, quite wealthy, and," here Ian leaned forward as if sharing a secret, "and very wise."

His observation delighted the crowd. Naturally they nodded in agreement since they were all indistinguishable in class and character. From there the discussion fragmented into many different topics. Doctor Franklin finished his drink and rose slowly. He wobbled under the effects of wine that, frankly, I shared through my own unsteady vision.

"Gentlemen, I am not as youthful as you. And as such it is best that I take Poor Richard's advice. So it is time for me to take leave."

Ian the freckled sot, reinvigorated by the attention given his observation on the famed author whose identity he still did not understand, also rose. You, sir, are from the colonies. Do you know this American, this Poor Richard fellow, per chance?"

The smile never left Doctor Franklin's face. "Aye. I would say I know him as well as one can know oneself."

Ian was surprised at this. He said, "Well, then. When you return to your colonies you tell him Ian Jasper believes he is a dolt. I stand by my words." But he dropped into his chair.

Franklin laughed heartily and reached for Ian Jasper's hand. "Shake on it, sir. Consider your message delivered as if you had said those words to Poor Richard's face yourself."

Then Doctor Franklin straightened up and looked at me with his eyes twinkling above flushed cheeks and a ruddy nose.

"Mr. Merriweather the younger, would you be so kind as to escort me on the walk back Craven Street. My legs are weary, my mind is dull, and I'm not entirely certain I could make the trip without help."

As I said, butter my bum. I put a hand on Doctor Franklin's arm to steady him as much as to steady myself. The events of the evening wreaked havoc with my equilibrium. I led him to the door. Then, sensing the sharp stares of my brother and his colleagues as we departed, I crossed my hands behind me and let them know what I thought with a single raised finger. If envy were a dagger they would most certainly have made me another bloody victim whose sordid death spilled out on the front page of the *Tattler-Tribune*.

Chapter Five

It was an angry bird. That explains what you need to know how in the name of Saint Bacchus I tumbled into this life in London so far away from the family estate Wittyglib Manor, hearth and home and all that. Blame the bird.

Oh, maybe it was fate. Perhaps it was God having a go at me. You see I was just born to patter. Mother tells me I exited the womb screaming and never stopped talking since. From my earliest days I loved reading and writing, but even alone in the library with *Aesop's Fables* or *Gulliver's Travels*, or my own pen, paper and imagination, the words always found their way out of my head and escaped through my mouth. I read aloud. I wrote aloud.

"Literary vomit," my brother London called it.

My mother encouraged my reading and writing. She introduced me to the likes of Jonathan Swift and Oliver Goldsmith. I loved the many classic books in our library. Who could not be moved at age seven or eight by the tale of Goody Two-Shoes? Where is your heart, man?

My father had other ideas but tolerated this in an effort to advance my overall education. "Reading is fine enough," he told me. "But it is making you soft. You are given to flights of fancy and daydreaming that serve no purpose at all." So that year he took it upon himself to balance my love of reading with my destiny as he proposed to shape it. He began mapping out for me a career in the military.

"I will not leave this earth without leaving at least one son to serve His Majesty. There are fights to be had in the colonies, India and the Americas. The French and the Spaniards are always good for a thwacking whether they deserve it or not. Nothing would make me more proud than to have you go off and die for God and the King."

My father was tall with square shoulders and a block chin. His eyes were as grey as the sea and just as susceptible to changing passion with the tide. He could reach for you with a twinkle of joy there, but cross him and you would see the fury of lightning, the kind of which could turn the seat of your britches brown in a flash.

His most interesting feature, one he seldom failed to call attention to whenever he could, was what remained of his left ear.

"Sliced off by a Spaniard's saber in the heat of battle," he would say. "Just before I dispatched the brute with my own." Then he would pinch the air in front of my nose, his fingers separated only the width of a blade. "I was this close to dying a hero, my boy. This close."

"I'm not interested in dying, Father. Not for the King or anybody."

"That's because you're still a boy," he replied. "Your mind will change when you are a man and wear the uniform."

So it was out of his desire for a military legacy, and in no small part to counter the influence of my mother who encouraged reading and enlightenment, that my father felt it was his duty to have me master hunting, marksmanship and swordplay. I would carry on his legacy, one cut short by a Spaniard's blade, near death and early retirement, with a military pension to our family's business concerns near Coventry.

"That's not cold. I know cold," he shouted to me as the icy water of the winter stream nearly froze the life out of me long before any Frenchman could take his best shot. That was one of the first regimens Father instituted as part of my preparation for a military life. Father believed the torture of baths at dawn regardless of the season was fine training for a future military officer. "You want to hear about cold?" he asked.

No, I said with what little breath I had left.

"Let me tell you about the time we defended the King's empire in Iceland against marauding Scandahoovians in the winter of '09."

My history lessons never mentioned the Great War against Scandahoovians in '09. But it must have happened. Father was there.

"That's not heavy. I know heavy," he shouted as I strained under the weight of an oak limb that he forced me to lift fifty times each day after calisthenics. "Bloody hell. Try moving tons of stone on your back to build a fortress to rival the desert pyramids. That was a smashing campaign in the summer of '18 and we routed a full brigade of Iraqaranians when they paused to admire our out-post as one of the tourist sites. Fooled them completely, but my, *that* was heavy lifting, my son."

Growing up at Wittyglib I was a foot soldier in the battle of wills between my parents. Mother wanted her son to spend his days with Plato, Shakespeare, or at the very least, lowbrow novel serials of literature. The writers my mother encouraged me to read were, in effect, my nannies in the afternoon after I engineered a tactical retreat from training for the career my father had chosen for me.

"You love your father, don't you, Leeds?" My mother posed the question after I questioned her about father's commitment to my future.

"Of course I do, Mother."

"Then you must do as he says. He is, after all, your father. And father knows best." She studied me for a moment and smiled in a way that left no doubt my fate was sealed. Still, she promised to have a word with father and appeal my case.

"Now take this and read to me."

She handed me her Bible. It was open to the book of Job, naturally. Toss that at me, there is always someone like Job deeper in shit, I suppose. But knowing that was as useful as a doorknob on a badger.

Soldier up, boy. I accepted my fate.

But all my father's personal attention chapped my brother London's backside like nobody's business. Father had left him in the capable hands of tutors and associates who would school him in ledgers and contracts that oiled the family business interests.

For my fourteenth birthday father presented me with the pistol he carried during his years of military service. It had a fine balance with a handle of deep brown walnut and an engraved brass barrel. It was an officer's weapon, a manly sort of gift given to men by men because they are, well, manly men, I suppose. It was a gift that did not go unnoticed and was deeply resented by my brother London. That was a debit about as big as they come on the dark side of my life's ledger with him.

Papers were drafted. Bribes were paid. Father set into motion everything necessary for my acceptance to the military college in Woolwich upon my sixteenth birthday. And a spiteful fowl stepped in and left bird droppings all over his master plan.

Don't get me wrong, I grieve my father's death many a day, and I miss him greatly. He died three months after he sealed my reluctant but dutiful agreement to join the military by giving me that pistol.

Father's heart gave out whilst he was on the run from an angry pheasant he had failed to shoot down during a hunt. The bird, not being at all pleased at father's attempt to make a meal out of him, turned on poor father and chased him half a mile before he collapsed and the pheasant crowed triumphant. When father died so did his dream of turning me into a soldier. So if not for that killer pheasant, I might very well be Colonel Merriweather today instead of patterer and scribe. And I say Huzzah. I may be nothing more than a wandering street performer broke and in a drunken state more often than I would confess, but I daresay I am better for the angry bird.

Chapter Six

I would like to say Doctor Franklin and I beat a steady path to his home the night we left my brother and his social club at the Moose and Squirrel. In truth, it was a spectacularly unsteady march. We leaned on one another for support; our journey was one of many stops and starts. The road may have been straight, but our path was decidedly less so.

We had only gone a block when Dr. Franklin paused beneath a street lamp and said, "They are a strange collection of fellows, are they not?"

"Aye." I wondered if he meant what I believed.

"In some ways, not too unlike our Royal Society of Arts. Fine fellows those. And yet there was something this evening..."

"The R.S.A. is, no doubt, respected beyond any other club in London. It certainly gets my vote. Dare I say there is not a man who is a man who wouldn't want to be a part of the group." I wondered if groveling might gain me an invitation to join, or at least attend a meeting. Apparently not.

Doctor Franklin laid a finger alongside his nose and continued. "Ah, yes. While the camaraderie tonight seemed normal on its surface, the thread of their jests, and sometimes their mannerisms, suggested an intimate bond of, shall we say, unhealthy nature." He studied me in the lamplight. "Am I right?"

It was a moment that called for discretion. So naturally I had none whatsoever.

"You are very perceptive. Rumors, of course. Only rumors." I paused long enough to make clear I wanted to be delicate in this matter, resisting every pattering instinct from the base of my soul that screamed out: "tell him. Tell him in exquisitely sordid detail the revolting stories of man-love that goes on when the club goes private. Doctor Franklin is a man of the world and understands such things. Impress the man, you git!"

Crush the thought. I said simply, "The club has a special status of humor among those who know of such things, so they have quietly acquired a, ehr, descriptive appellation."

Doctor Franklin scratched his chin and began moving again out of the reach of the street lamp. In the dark I imagined him grinning. "And this group's name?"

"Misbehaving Roosters."

"Naturally."

Sometimes less is more. The label said it all.

We traveled several blocks tacking to and fro like a pair of ships in a gale. One such maneuver blew us into the Tamed Shrew, a tavern at the west end of Fleet Street, one of modest quality and minimal traffic.

"This seems like a quiet place to catch our breath," Doctor Franklin said.

The street had become tolerably quiet with the late hour, though we had passed a reasonable number of souls headed home for the night, their weary boots slapping heavily against the cobblestone and echoing off the brick walls of the narrow street. Inside the Tamed Shrew fewer than half a dozen customers sat scattered across the tavern sharing their loneliness. Compared to the rowdy collection of free spirits gathered at the Moose and Squirrel, it appeared people were avoiding the Tamed Shrew like the plague.

In fact, they were. "Her proprietor died of the pox less than a year ago; it has been this way since," I told Doctor Franklin.

"Then let us inoculate ourselves with a spot of wine, shall we?"

"Preventive medicine?"

"Exactly."

We took two comfortable chairs near the fire, and I motioned to the tavern's owner. "Doctor Franklin, let me introduce you to the widow Anastasia Fullbright. She is the proprietress responsible for all of this."

I continued, "Did I mention that not only is Mrs. Fullbright the owner by way of her husband Percy's unfortunate death, but it is she for whom the Tamed Shrew was named?"

Anna swished the back of her hand at me as if swatting away a fly. I stopped her and took her hand gently in mine. She leaned forward as if to kiss my cheek but whispered instead, "For that, there'll be no nookie tonight, love."

Now that was dire punishment, a dagger to the heart, indeed. In my mind the jest didn't warrant being banned from her bed, especially since my fallout with McNabb left me few choices to lay my head that evening, nookie or naught.

Franklin sent her to fetch wine, and I watched him take measure of her retreating backside the way an artist might consider a classic painting by one of those Flemish masters who like fat-bottomed girls. Anna had an ample derriere that a connoisseur like Franklin could appreciate.

"I don't believe I am making any headway with my mission here in London." Doctor Franklin turned his attention back to me.

"How so?"

"This entire trip has been fruitless. I came as an agent of the Colonies to convince our Parliament to reject that odious Stamp Act it is about to pass. I've wasted too much time lobbying members like your brother. But it was quite apparent tonight that he and Jasper and those like them have no appetite to challenge our prime minister on this one."

Anna returned with the wine. She placed the bottle on the table just as Franklin finished his thoughts on the matter. "No disrespect to your brother, but I don't know if those Misbehaving Roosters in Parliament are more interested in buggering America or buggering each other."

Anna gave Doctor Franklin a wide-eyed look, then covered her mouth and snorted like a plow horse.

"What a lovely laugh you have, my dear," Doctor Franklin said. "Charmed."

Once that passed, Anna stood in silence waiting for us to pour, and, more importantly, to pay. Whether Franklin felt the uncomfortable weight of the silence I never knew. Anna seemed not bothered by it, for she had nothing better to do than wait and collect. It wasn't until I reached into my pocket and put those precious three shillings I had hidden from McNabb into her hand that Doctor Franklin offered to pay for the wine he had ordered.

"Nonsense." I shook my head with more conviction than I felt in my heart. "You are a guest here. It would be my honor to buy this now."

"Well then, I accept your offer," Franklin said. "And should we require yet another bottle I would accept it again, for you are a gracious host."

Even though I was drunk, I was aware enough to understand that I had been disadvantaged. But yet, and I might add a wistful sigh even to this day, I was decidedly satisfied. I knew there must be only a few on earth so privileged as to be skillfully beguiled by Benjamin Franklin. It was well worth the price. At any price. And at that moment it seemed well worth a possible trip to debtor's prison—should we overstay my finances—just to count myself among the Franklin hoodwinked.

He turned the discussion to the news article that drew us together that evening. "Serendipitous, no? I am happy we have had this opportunity to get to know one another. You have a gift of great imagination, Mr. Merriweather, which will serve you well in your publishing endeavors. Though I would strongly suggest that, where news is concerned, you try to shade your stories with just a touch more fact and less fiction."

He said that with no rancor and even slapped my knee in good humor. Then he asked me about my publishing prospects.

"The prospects suffered quite a blow today, I'm afraid." I told him of my sudden unemployment at the hands of McNabb. I shared my frustration of being stifled, cast in the role of patterer and good for nothing else.

"Well, you do have a fine face. A strong voice. Straight teeth as well."

I hear that a lot.

He said, "I have found that whenever I encounter a barrier to any goal the quickest way to a successful resolution is to eliminate the barrier."

I considered for a brief moment about putting a knife to McNabb's throat. It might be a bit extreme, but it would undoubtedly be quite satisfying. I reached into my satchel for my pipe. I still had a bit of tobacco left and offered my pouch to Franklin, but he refused. From inside his coat he produced a thin silver container.

"Cigar, sir," he laughed. "From the Americas. This quality is quite impossible to find here in London."

Doctor Franklin rose, stiffly and with great care. He lit a cedar wick at the fireplace and held its flame at the tip of his tobacco for what seemed a long period. Good God! Parliament could have acted more swiftly. He returned to smoke his cigar and offered me the wick. I lit my pipe. It was as if he organized his thoughts in his trip to the fireplace and back. I watched awareness in bloom. Satisfied with the conclusion he had reached, Doctor Franklin slumped into his chair with a relaxed, almost arrogant air reserved for undisciplined noblemen or fraternal schoolmates.

"Unemployment notwithstanding, Mr. Merriweather, your problem is not what you believe it to be."

"No?"

"Not in the least," he poshed. "You are an imaginative lad; think. What is it that you are offering for sale? Your commodity. What is it that people will pay for?"

I told him I wished to produce newspapers, journals and books, literature written and distributed by my own hand.

He snorted.

Wrong answer, I assumed.

He thumped his cane on the floor. "Oh, you might print newspapers, even volumes of books, but that is merely the wagon, my boy. Never forget, what the people value, what they want, what they will pay for is the product up here." He tapped his temple.

"It's the stories you create to enlighten and entertain the public with. Information, my boy. It is information that you sell; the rest is just technology."

"But how can I accomplish that if I have no way to deliver? I have no press with which to publish this," I said as I tapped a finger to my temple just as he had.

"I am a captain without a ship. A horseman without a horse. I am tobacco without a pipe, light without a candle. I am...."

"You are a geyser of metaphors with no cap," he frowned. Franklin held up his hand, his cigar wedged between thumb and two fingers and pointed it at me as one might measure the throw of a dart. "And a negative one at that."

I parried with the stem of my pipe. Back at you, sir. "That does not alter the fact that I am sorely lacking the wagon, as you say."

"I know that all too well. I was once there myself." He shifted in his chair and studied the tip of his cigar again. He blew gently on the tip and made it glow red. "Maybe that is why I have taken such an instant liking to you. I see myself in you, myself twenty, uh thir…mumble-mumble cough… years ago."

Franklin drained his glass and then rose in need of some relief. I watched him shuffle across the tavern as one watches a prince at court. He tipped his hat to Mrs. Fullbright and engaged her in a brief, animated conversation. Doctor Franklin gave her a friendly embrace, and his hand slipped to rest upon her beautiful bottom. She, with practiced politeness, removed it and pointed him to a door near the kitchen that would lead him to the tavern's outbuilding.

"He is a friendly sort for one so esteemed," I said to Anna when she came to the table and replaced the bottle I had just emptied into Franklin's glass. "What did he want of you?"

She did not look at me, but her cheeks were as rosy as the flowers in a Hyde Park garden.

"Oh." It was the best response I could muster. "Oh," I repeated, more strongly after her meaning took root. Had it been any normal man I should have challenged him for making a play at the woman whose bed I hoped to snuggle in that night. Then again, how could he know? The fact that he favored Anastasia Fullbright was, in no small way, a validation of my own ability as a wooing, winning, womanizer. And should Anna decide to favor Franklin in return, well then, wouldn't that elevate my status to be Franklin's equal in, shall we say, the art of diplomatic debauchery? My head throbbed, puzzling the notion.

Franklin stopped to plead his case with her on his return. They shared a good laugh and she was smiling as she escorted him back to his chair.

"A fine woman," he said when she left. "If only she were French, you might not have my company for the remainder of this evening. Ah, we are better for it, though. Drink. Drink up, my boy."

And we did.

"I have been considering your current status in regards your relationship with this publisher McNabb," Franklin said.

"Piss on him."

"I would have, had he been within my reach only minutes ago."

Franklin then leaned toward me with the elbow of his cigar hand planted on the armrest of his chair. With the other, he motioned me closer with his sloshing wine glass. Nose to nose we were.

"I am drunk. Are my eyes as bloodshot as your own?"

"I can't see my own. But I don't believe the devil himself could scare me more than what I see in yours."

Franklin reeled back in his chair and roared, he spread his arms and sent half a glass of wine to the floor. His face was flushed well beyond the bald crown of his head. "Excellent. We are beyond reason tonight. And at crucial times like this reason would only constrict our ingenuity. We must think boldly. We must not box ourselves in. We must think outside of that."

"Outside the box?" I reached for my journal, a quill and my traveling inkpot to capture that thought on paper. Most certainly it would mean something some day, if I could only figure out what. I think.

"You see, my boy, we agree, and the actions of the publishers like Mr. McNabb confirm that you have a gift for storytelling with the additional talent of voice and appearance. Have you considered the stage?"

"Not at all. It is the events of today that intrigue me the most. I have no desire to play someone's character, nor create my own. It's news I wish to deliver."

"Just as you might on a printed page. So you only have to find a way to induce an audience to pay for that privilege of hearing you speak it. To be all you can be, this not as a job, it's an adventure."

Adventure. I scribbled that in my notebook while I argued against it. The tiny inkpot I balanced on my knee slipped, and I caught it halfway to the floor. The spilled ink painted my hands and made further note taking futile. I explained that from experience I knew passing the hat and pattering for tips on the street was not a road to success. I had been there and done that. "What man would pay a patterer for his story when for the same amount of coin he can purchase a newspaper and own it. And so many more people, common men, and women too, are learning the art of reading. I fear pattering is doomed to die before I do."

Doctor Franklin leaned forward again, moving his frame to the edge of his chair. Once again he beckoned me as if preparing to share a secret.

"I will advise you in this matter, and if you take my words to heart you will succeed, potentially much more so than you might imagine. In fact, it is incredibly simple."

Now I leaned into him, my senses awakened, sharpened by his manner and the conviction in his voice. Then as Franklin was about to reveal his solution I stopped him. I repositioned my journal on my lap, scraped ink that had puddled in my palm with the tip of my quill, and nodded. The page was badly smudged, but I was determined to record his insight word-for-word.

"This is how you shall be successful," he began. And then from the depths of his intellect and the vast wisdom of his experience he charted my future in three words. Three words and no more.

Chapter Seven

"Just do what? What the blazes does 'e mean by that?"

I had spent a sleepless night examining that question posed by A.P. from every direction and still didn't know the answer.

"Just do it." I repeated the words Doctor Franklin left with me. A.P. and I squatted like a pair of gargoyles on a step of a tailor shop on Drury Lane across from one of my favorite corners, not far from the Theatre Royal. "That is what Doctor Franklin believes. He said it, I believe it, and that settles it." Though I had pressed him to elaborate on our journey home from the Tamed Shrew, Doctor Franklin would only say I alone would know what "it" was when "it" bit.

A.P. scratched his cap. "Well, he ought to know I s'pose, him being a genius and all. Tho', Mr. Merriweather, if it was *me* that said 'Just do it' instead of him, people would claim I was right barmy."

"Ah, that is the benefit of genius, Ape. Doctor Franklin is a genius and what he has to say is profound, whether we understand it or not. You, my friend, are a wastrel. Admired by some, but a wastrel nonetheless."

So it was that my good friend Doctor Franklin planted a seed. Unfortunately he expected me to nurture the bastard. Bother.

"Bother," A.P. said as if he read my mind.

The day was grey as usual and mild enough to be pleasant. The number of folks passing by settled into its afternoon lull before the end of the day's wave of humanity washed through on its way home for supper.

I watched the scene, hoping to spot "it" playing hide-and-seek with my intellect among the bodies and the fruit carts with their noisy venders, or possibly peeking out from one of the alleyways. I sat still as a statue in the square hoping that "it" would drop from the sky like inspired pigeon poop upon my head. "It" was a master of disappointment. So I mused about how, on any normal day, I would have been across the street preparing for my afternoon patter at that hour. The closest thing resembling, while not at all resembling, patter in the air was the vulgar pitch of costermongers. An apple vendor here. Lace and handkerchiefs there. A perfumist to my right. Some, like the tobacconist, said nothing at all. He was only loitering, perhaps simply waiting for customers to approach him, and confident that they would approach without any effort on his part to draw them aside.

"No sign of your lovely little flower wench, yet, eh, Ape?"

"No, she ain't nowhere abouts, Mr. Merriweather." If A.P. harbored any disappointment, you wouldn't see it in his face. His eyes were afire with young love. "But, you wait. Liza will be here when there's a crowd. Count on it, Cap'n."

And so we could. It was not long before the lad jumped up and pointed to a girl on the edge of a very small parade making its way down from The Strand. With a horn announcing his arrival, William the too good-looking wunder-face patterer that the rat McNabb sacked me for, led this merry little group. He set up a pitch directly across from us.

"Liza!" A.P. shouted.

Liza smiled with crooked teeth and sooted cheeks; her dark hair was like a waterfall flowing behind her from her bonnet to her waist. She twirled with the grace of a dancer for Ape, her basket of flowers circling the young woman like the earth around the sun. Then Liza skipped off to a spot on the corner, positioning herself between the audience that was now building in front of the patterer and their escape route west to anonymous little homes on anonymous little streets in Westminster. It was a strategic location, a good one, where she could sell her violets and daffodils.

Pedestrians and costermongers with their carts slowed to listen as the patterer began. Some stopped and formed a respectable, if not large, audience. I had done better. I had also done less. The baker and candlestick maker, the fruit vendor and other cart merchants closed into a semi-circle just behind the crowd.

William stood on his pitch a full head and shoulders above the crowd sporting a new jacket and all-too-perfectly barbered wig. His voice carried across the street so that I had both a clear view and sound hearing. That is, I was in perfect position to observe him until a cutlery grinder pulled his cart to within a few feet of us and stopped directly in our line of sight.

"Care for a go, sire?" he asked. "Sharpen your blade? Do the lot of your house tableware for three shilling ana 'alf." He held up a stone block and a knife with outstretched arms, using them to beckon me to his cart.

I waved him aside. "Sir, if you would move along, you are in our way." To which he spit in response, twice, once on his stone and once at us. Then he stroked us off, dismissing us with a swipe of his blade against the stone in our direction.

"The devil," Ape said. "Shall I dispatch 'm for you?" He stood and took a small step forward.

"Not worth the trouble." I stood and stayed him with a hand on his arm. I nudged him along. We passed behind a lamp oil seller and, next to him, a pie cart before slipping through to the edge of the audience between the lace maker and a troupe of juggling mimes. One of them dropped his imaginary ball, to which Ape kindly bent down and retrieved it for him. The mime tipped his imaginary hat, but it was blown off his head by an imaginary gust of wind.

I paced along the edge of the audience, studying their faces and gauging their level of interest in the story William-the-wonderful teased them with. His assistant worked through the crowd offering up copies of the *Tattler-Tribune* and an assortment of pamphlets for sale. There were some buyers but this crowd was more inter-ested in whatever information they could get for free.

I thought it interesting to see the effect of the patterer from this vantage point. I had always been on the pitch and too attentive to my story to really examine the ebb and flow of bodies around me. I could only look out and judge its size and potential for profit. It was if for the first time I was watching myself through a window.

"I'll be with Liza," A.P. said. He pointed to where a nice looking gentleman seemed a bit too engaged in negotiating with Ape's pretty little flower girl.

William paused his story to sell his wares. "More in a moment," he promised. Many in the audience trickled off, drawn to the merchants who had surrounded them. Some lingered over the items on a table William set up next to his pitch while his assistant chased after first one and then another gentleman, taking coin from them in exchange for a copy of the *Tattler-Tribune*. I recognized many a face. They had been my own reliable customers from my days on the pitch.

But it seemed the real money was changing hands into those of the costermongers who had attached themselves to the patterer like leeches on a hippo's heinie. The patterer did well enough, but with ten times as many merchants competing for the available silver of the audience I could easily observe how many a passer-by might flirt with the patterer but go home with the baker's sweet bread.

"Sup with me tonight, Mr. Merriweather?" Ape held up two pieces of silver. He said, "Liza has done fine today and if you'd join us, 'twould be a grand time, I swear."

Ape rattled off items he intended to make as part of the meal:

stew, cheese, bread that was less than two days old and, of course, pudding. He listed the possible venues for our meal and judged the competing value of different taverns' menus. I barely noticed.

A ten-year-old pickpocket known to most of us on the street captured my attention. He drifted like a piece of debris in a river of pedestrians, conspicuously inconspicuous, looking for a victim. The costermongers began barking up their merchandise when William finished pattering. There were two at the tobacconist, and the candle maker was similarly engaged. Several people lined up at the pie cart buying dessert before heading home to their evening meal.

I'd like a piece of that, I thought. And then "it" happened.

"Ape, how did you know Liza would be here this afternoon?"

He shrugged. "It's where the people are." He looked at me as if I were as thick as a rump roast with twice the gristle.

It was where the people were. Well flog the frog, and call me toad. In the past I myself had mapped my route, timed my performance and set up my pitch at locations I could count on for steady traffic. Often as not, there was an established attraction or amusement nearby that created a pool of potential customers already in place. A market, a theater, or tavern would do quite nicely on days of fair weather. One particularly productive location was amidst the better brothels of Covent Garden late in the day. Not only were their customers plentiful, recurring and dependably steady, but also I have found many an educated man who is well versed in reading and writing is naturally drawn to dipping his quill. And it is quite likely that some of his most profound expressions are laid out not on the paper but between the sheets, if you gather my drift.

"A.P., if you were not a snot-oozing, dog-smelling, sewage-swilling bed of lice, I might very well kiss you right now."

Taken aback, he replied, "I think very highly of you, too, Mr. Merriweather."

I snatched the silver from his hand and tugged him toward the nearest inn. "You see, Doctor Franklin had it right. And so terribly wrong," I said.

"Just do it?" Ape said as he vainly tried to take back the coins I now waved before his eyes.

"Supper is on me," I said as I placed the coins in my pocket and patted them with delight.

If Doctor Franklin had been more illuminative, perhaps sketched a diagram from his most noble mind of how one might *sell* the news without a printing press, I might never have conceived what I dare say is a most brilliant form of commercializing my gift for patter.

And I say that with all modesty; it may one day rival the contribution to society made by the man who discovered electricity. Yes, Doctor Franklin planted the seed, but I, Leeds Merriweather, nurtured it into one beautiful, money making flower.

Chapter Eight

The mother's face was tired and creased, ravaged with the pain of recent loss. A tear trickled down her cheek. The light of the small oil lamps A.P. and I had assembled on the leading edge of a stage in the corner of the Tamed Shrew ravaged her appearance even more. The soft black smoke rising from the lamps must have been like looking through a veil for those in the audience leaning heavily on tables, watching.

That was the beginning of my grand invention: News Performance. Live accounts of current events, only at the Tamed Shrew. Arguably the world's first, organized News Performance. Simple as ABC.

I pulled the woman closer to me and said, "Mrs. Martha P. Brown, of number six Devonshire Place, when you at last reached the edge of the quarry and were able to identify the body of your lovely sixteen-year-old daughter for yourself, a daughter violated by a fiend and disposed of like that, I ask you Mrs. Brown—how did you feel?"

The words were barely out of my mouth when I wondered exactly of myself: how would *you* feel, you twit? But the audience wanted desperately to know, and that was all that mattered.

Mrs. Brown looked down, her chin lowered to her chest. The silence in the tavern, the crowd holding its collective breath, told me that at that moment her answer was of critical importance to them.

"Sir, I can't describe it," she mumbled too softly for the audience.

Canes rapped the floor. Men thumped their fists on the tables. "Speak up."

I stretched to my full height, flexed my shoulders back and said, "Yes, I see, Mrs. Martha P. Brown of number six Devonshire Place. You felt a pain that seared your heart like the fury of hell unleashed upon your soul. The sight of your daughter there was a knife to your eyes. Madness was at your shoulder with so strong a temptation to jump from that ledge and join your daughter in death that it would have come as a relief to oblige."

Right. Was that a bit much? I wondered. Metaphorically speaking, it was, how shall I describe it? Overly accurate?

Mrs. Brown of number six Devonshire Place wept openly now. And then she nodded, confirming my interpretation of her misery.

The audience finally exhaled, nay, gasped. I heard a sniffle. It was Charley Cartwright in the front row far to my left. Mr. Cartwright was a butcher with a shop on Grosvenor Street. A barrel-chested man as big as a building and with a reputation of being harder than the brick it was made of, Mr. Cartwright fought bravely that night to keep from bawling. And I heard angry murmurs. One man openly suggested marching to Newgate Prison where the perpetrator was being held. Others agreed they should mete out a mob's justice upon the man who would break this poor woman's heart with his crime.

I put an arm around the shoulders of Mrs. Martha P. Brown of number six Devonshire Place and escorted her from the platform to where A.P. was waiting to assist. I paused and pulled two shillings from a pocket. Coin was still hard to come by those days, but I placed them in her hand just the same.

"For the burial," I said softly.

"No, sir, I can't" she replied. Her grateful eyes told me it was lie.

A.P.'s glare told me I was a fool; she had asked for no compensation, and Ape had offered none when he convinced her to bear witness that evening.

I returned to the stage. There was not much left to say of that story except two details that I had borrowed from that morning's *London Chronicle*. First, a fair trial was to be held tomorrow. Secondly, the hanging had already been scheduled for Saturday. The Lord Mayor had declared it a holiday.

A murmur of approval rolled through the tavern; you could almost see in their faces the mental preparations beginning with what to wear, what to eat and how early to rise to guarantee a good view at the event. Nothing rouses the London middling class like a good picnic of wine, bread, cheese and a limp body dangling at the end of the executioner's rope.

"Good sirs and ladies, I have so much more to tell you this evening." I teased them with what lay ahead in our news performance. "I have new and shocking information on what has become of Mr. Kevin Siderham who, this very evening, is running from justice after surviving a duel in Hyde Park. His aggrieved rival was not so fortunate. For that you must stay with us. We'll be right back."

Tankards of ale rattled and thumped on the tabletops, and the tavern took on the gentle buzz of a beehive. The crowd numbered better than the tired old Tamed Shrew had seen in many a day. Working men, mostly, and a few women quaffed the remnants of the previous ale service to prepare for the next round. Proprietor and hostess Anastasia Fullbright and her daughter Andrea rushed forward with pitchers for the customers. This was no ordinary intermission. No, it was payday. Something took root in my head in the middle of the night after my epiphany on Drury Lane. News performance? Why not visual advertisement? No one had done anything quite like it before, I knew.

I yielded the stage to Mr. Andrew Dunlop, a purveyor of fine pipes and delicious tobacco. Mr. Dunlop was an old rogue who had been the premier tobacconist on Willow Street since Jesus was just a toddler learning to walk on puddles in the street. Still getting his feet wet, so to speak.

"There is no substitute for encountering the customer eye-to-eye, hand-to-hand, and pipe-to-pipe," he once told me. So it was natural that Andrew Dunlop became my second sponsor to this adventure in news performing. The tavern, the Tamed Shrew, was itself my first.

Dunlop had the two most important ingredients necessary for the position. The first was an ego large enough to pitch his product directly to the crowd. The second, and critically important, was his willingness to pay me for the privilege. For it had come to me in the public square that day of my epiphany that my customers were not my customers at all. Uncle Ben (Doctor Franklin) was wrong when he suggested that information was my product. No, my product was the audience it attracted.

I daresay London's largest newspapers contain an occasional advertisement to help expense the news they sold. Am I right, or am I right? If I could provide honey to attract bears, hunters of said bears would pay for the privilege of shooting fish in a barrel, so to speak.

"That went well, wouldn't you say?" I asked Anna as she rushed past with pitcher in hand. She swept past me.

"It'll do, ducky."

I retook the stage after Mr. Dunlop finished, just long enough to engage the crowd with one more promise of things to come.

"Death in Hyde Park, all for the sake of honor. But honor is no excuse for Lady Justice, and she is hunting the survivor tonight." Oh how I was beginning to love the art of teasing the audience. Few words, impactful words that kept them in their seats. That was critical, so I crooned, "More on that in a moment. It will be worth the wait. But first, a word from a sponsor of tonight's performance."

My cobbler took the stage. He was a squat fellow with a mop of matted dark hair and a walrus mustache. His left thumb was in a perpetual state of bruise from the many miss hits of his hammer. He pledged a full month of paid sponsorship for the news performance as long as we were able to maintain a decent audience, and that thought warmed the pocket of my trousers now lightened of silver by my impulsive act of charity toward Mrs. Martha P. Brown of number six Devonshire Place. The cobbler was a push-over. The deal with Mrs. Fullbright was of a more difficult, and more delicate nature.

"A right good crowd tonight, Mrs. Fullbright," I said when she paused between servings.

"Lucky for you, 'tis, Leeds."

In our negotiations, I was in favor of sharing the profit of the evening's sale of drink and a place to lay my head at the end of the evening. She held fast to bartering only her bed for the night whilst keeping the receipts of the night for her bank. Hardly cricket, that. In the end we reached a compromise that was both monetarily and physically satisfactory to both parties.

"Leeds, that was quite the story there that Mrs. Brown had. Touched, I was."

I read the account in that morning's *London Chronicle*, and I knew I had to do something. Something that would work on the stage and rip your heart out like the greatest Shakespearean tragedy. Except that this was fresh information, and not some fictional sorrow. Then it struck me. I sent A.P. to sniff her out like the mongrel his is. I said, "it took a bit of charm and consolation but we convinced her to unburden her grief for us."

"You don't feel even a wee bit shamed by putting her up there, taking 'dvantage of her distress and what?"

"You saw the reaction," I replied. "It is exactly the kind of real emotion that will keep them coming back for more. It is quite something they'll never get from the printed newspaper account."

"It still seems a bit smarmy. It doesn't seem…right."

"And yet you were touched. You said it yourself. Are you going to kill the messenger when you are so receptive to the message?" She couldn't argue that, so she fled to the safety of a table of drunken sailors who groped her as she poured another round of gin.

Restlessness seeped and then swelled in the audience. The cobbler was stretching their patience. I had an apothecary, a barber and a hat maker waiting to pitch their services to the crowd so I reclaimed the stage. I launched into the curious story of Kevin Siderham. Siderham was a rising member of the social community in Ipswich. Vanished. Gone like the smoke of Dunlop's pipe.

"It was at a social gathering that, alas, Mr. Siderham, with too much brandy and too little discretion, made the mistake of critically, and somewhat caustically, criticizing a woman who was badly performing an aria in the parlor to entertain guests," I told them. It turned out the woman was the wife of Mr. Siderham's host, a Mr. Casper J. Boatwright.

Words were exchanged. The gauntlet was tossed. A duel was arranged. On the following morning, Mr. Siderham dispatched his former host with one shot, more deadly than the words he used the previous evening to eviscerate the talent of Mrs. Boatwright, now widowed.

"And what had become of Mr. Siderham?" I asked the audience.

As if answering that question, the door to the Tamed Shrew blew open. A gust of wind forced itself into the room like a drunken ruffian, and I could see rain was falling heavily outside. Distant thunder faded as two figures hurried into the shelter of the tavern. My barber was sitting near the door. He helped push it back into place against the wind and secure its latch.

One figure was fully cloaked in a fine dark traveling robe. The other was a maid and companion. I could tell from the cut of the mistress' cloth and the strength of the lady's posture that she was of good standing. It also helped my observations that Anna Fullbright attended to them immediately and with more eagerness than a fox-hound on the hunt.

But those observations ruined my concentration and muddled my patter.

"So what happened to the bloke?" a sailor in the audience shouted. Others knocked on the tables, demanding an answer. So I called up a porter to lay witness to Siderham's escape.

"He sailed for France last week," the porter said.

Like the murder victim-mother, Mrs. Brown, we located a party to the story with a testimonial to offer. This time it was a porter mentioned in the *Daily Advertiser* account, and who helped Mr. Siderham avoid what would certainly be several years of prison. I had no fear of his involvement being considered old news by virtue of its coverage in the *Advertiser*. No, I judged these good working class people were too busy earning their pay or lacking strong reading skills to pay attention to a newspaper account. The porter continued, "I heard that bloke say he was in no mood to risk prison after he ducked the duel with nary a scratch upon him."

Not as heinous as the aforementioned murder, but dueling was still a crime. It was a juicy bit of news if told with proper embellishment, whether or not you had to create some of the details on your own. Siderham was now on the run for the slip of a tongue.

No charges would be sought against the unfortunate Mr. Boatwright. The justice of the peace found Mr. Boatwright's death to be a hindrance to prosecution.

I know that I dismissed the porter and restated the key elements of the duel and Siderham's subsequent flight from justice. Words escaped my mouth faster than Siderham could run from the law because my eye and my curiosity were on the lady in the rear of the tavern.

When she tossed back the hood of her cloak and leaned forward, fixing upon me her total attention, I lost the last shred of coherence. Her face was soft, yet full, with high cheeks and a lush mouth. She eschewed a wig in favor of natural golden hair that dripped in ringlets over her left shoulder. The light from the fire behind danced off the beads of rain that had shaken free when she dropped her hood, and it created a halo that made her no less angelic than a imp in one of Raphael's paintings.

I surrendered the stage to the apothecary for a sponsor's break and dashed to the bar where A.P. told me that, had I been speaking French, it would have made just as much sense.

"I hope the storm stays over our heads for a while," he added after a moment's thought. "The longer it rains and these fellows do not venture out, the more they drink. The more they drink, the more jingle we make."

"Maybe when I return to the platform I should tell them this storm has no intent on moving on for another hour and they should eat and drink up."

"And if you are wrong?" he asked.

"But Ape, if I am right?" I countered.

"That'll be something well worth their interest, worth another shilling, I'd say, Mr. Merriweather."

"Ape, do you know of the lady this storm brought us?"

"Aye. Don't you?"

"No idea whatsoever."

"Tits you can't forget. She's Lady Jasper, she is, Mr. Merri-weather. Hitched to that fellow you know, Sir Ian Jasper the fourth. You know, Moose and Squirrel?"

Ah, the night I met the good Doctor Franklin in the company of my molly brother and his "companion du jour," that youngish sneering, effeminate knife-wielding tosser who dared call the good doctor a dolt to his face.

"Jasper? Misbehaving Rooster-Jasper? Jasper the mild-faced molly?"

"Aye. Though it would do you well not to announce it so boldly in public." A.P. held a dirty finger to his lips.

I suppose my disappointment was clear enough. I watched the Lady Jasper until she looked up at me. I quickly turned. I dipped the tip of my forefinger in my beer and raised it to my tongue. And then, with that finger pressing my lips, I smiled.

"Well it seems my brother and the good Lady Jasper have the same taste in men."

A.P. Looked from me to the lady and back. "And it seems to me, Mr. Merriweather, that Sir Jasper and yourself have the same taste in women."

Chapter Nine

Married?

Of course the comely Lady Jasper would be married. Bloody hell, that is. It's always a married woman, isn't it? That will be the death of me, either by a broken heart or at the hand of the husband. Most likely both. It was at the hand, and other more pleasurable parts of a married woman after all, that forced me to leave the family estate Wittyglib for a life pitching bits of news on London's streets for pennies.

God really had *His* hand in it, I was certain. One day He was just sitting around on his cloud, hanging out with all the angels who were too pure to do something interesting like get snockered on cheap Irish whiskey, run around and sneak up on one another from behind, tug upward on the hem of their robes giving each other a holy wedgie. Never would the idea of such an act occur to even the most devilish of them. God must have been bored with the bloody lot. Wouldn't you? So in his infinite boredom He decided to have some sport at my expense. And here I am.

No, it was a woman. A married woman. Married to my brother London. Well, there you have it. Mrs. London Merriweather, my brother's wife.

Emily was a worldly, much older woman, more than twice my age, when I fell in love with her. I was seven. She was almost fifteen.

"Hello, my Leedsy Weedsy," she would say when I encountered her at times her family visited Wittyglib. I loved her at age eight. And nine, ten and, well, perhaps still a bit of my heart belongs to her to this day.

Emily was kind but spirited. Very spirited. She was as beautiful as a meadow buttercup and fresh as the morning dew upon its petals. She laughed easily and was given to tousling my hair or stroking my cheek and looking for ways to make me blush.

She would ask, "Have you found a sweetheart yet, Little Leedsy Weedsy? No? Pity that. You need a girl. Perhaps I shall find you one." And then she would ask in a whisper tasting of conspiracy, "Would you know what to do with one if she caught you, Weedsy?"

Play a game of tag? Perhaps Blindman's Buff? Of course I knew what I would do, a little. I didn't know why the question she whispered made me uncomfortable.

Emily and I had a great deal in common, not the least was our devotion to reading. The newspapers in particular. While Emily would be comfortable sharing the doings of the gentlefolk described in the society pages with mother and women friends who visited, she and I reveled in the mayhem, political news and court follies that jumped from the first page.

And her taste in music? She played passably at the harpsichord and the lute, but the instrument that captivated her, and for which she gained considerable attention, was the Scottish bagpipes.

Oh, the sweet honking she coaxed from it with those lips I would only later know enough to describe as sensual. Many found it odd that Emily could perform so well; we knew of only men who played the bagpipes. It was considered to be a pursuit by and for men. By the time she married my brother, Emily brought a reputation all across the British Midlands as excelling in the act of blowing a man's instrument. Or so I had heard.

The year I turned fourteen was the year my father died. It was also the year my voice went south, approaching the deep richness you hear today.

"You sound different today, Leeds," Emily noted one afternoon. She was the first to announce it. Until then I had been only vaguely aware of that change, concentrating instead on other physical bits.

"Must be a cold."

"No, I like it. It sounds, ho? It sounds manly in a Weedsy sort of way. I like it very much."

Well. Fine enough.

But on a glorious, lazy Saturday afternoon I meandered to the library at Wittyglib Manor. I was intent on taking a copy of Robinson Crusoe to join me for an hour or two of reading under my favorite oak tree by the stream. I stopped at the door.

Emily and my brother London had been married two years by then. That day she lounged on the sofa, so engrossed in reading that she took no notice of me at first. Ringlets of walnut hair draped over the back of the sofa. Her head tracked back and forth so slightly as she followed the words on the page. I stood a few feet inside the doorway and admired her with every fiber of my fifteen-year-old's body.

When at last she felt my presence and turned, her head popped up like a rabbit from its burrow and then, with a twitch of her nose, it disappeared just as quickly.

Thump. She landed on the floor out of sight.

"Oh bollocks!"

Then Emily stood and collected herself. "You should not creep into a room to catch someone unaware."

"Let me help you." As I moved in that direction I asked, "What is that you're reading?"

"Reading? I was not. It was mere daydreaming." She hurriedly arranged the pillows upon the sofa and attempted to hide the book that owned her attention until I committed literary interruptus. I got there first.

"Ho. What is this?"

"None of your concern. Give that to me," she demanded.

I fingered the book with its simple brown cloth cover and no title. Dismissive and demanding at once, Emily held out her palm for it. I stood my ground, opened to a random page and began reading.

"...I saw myself stretched nak'd, my shift being turned up to my neck whilst I had no sense to oppose..." I looked up from the page. I cannot say how wide my eyes must have been, though they would have rivaled any good-sized serving platter. Emily stared back, her eyes bright. Her lips slid upward and to one corner. They formed a sly smile. I flipped to the title leaf. *Fanny Hill* — *Memoirs of a Woman of Pleasure*.

Emily said, "I hear it is all the rage in certain... well, certain social circles of the city. They say everyone at court has read it." She flicked a dismissive wrist toward unseen royals. "They will say they've never heard of it let alone admit reading it, but prigs lie."

I read another passage, this time to myself and felt a flush in my face and, quite frankly, a flush in other regions. So much so, that I lowered the book to below my belt, a shield against Emily's measuring eyes.

"Oh, don't be such a... a boy!" she snapped. "You are old enough to have a man's voice now. A very pleasing one at that. You are growing up quickly, you little Leedsy-Weedsy."

"Yes, mum." Emily hated when I called her mum. It defined her as head of the house, a much older woman, though she was only twenty-one.

"Well, then. You'll see it's harmless. Read to me."

"This?" My eyes raced across the tall shelves and even up to the dust-covered titles on the top shelves. Gulliver, Robinson Crusoe, come save me. Flog the frog. So desperate at that moment, I would have even accepted help from a Frenchman, but I hadn't yet met Voltaire. Parlay vous, "Just say no?"

I stammered. "It seems so, so descriptive. Not really proper reading. Not aloud. Not for you." I knew from my brief introduction to *Fanny Hill* that I needed to investigate her story further.

Alone. In my bedchamber.

"Proper?" Emily asked. "This is a love story. And what is really *proper* in love these days? That is something of a grey area, now isn't it? I might even argue there are at least, uhm, fifty shades of grey in telling a story like this."

We went back and forth, but eventually Emily's persistence won out, though I negotiated a bit of distance, a sex-free zone between the window where I could stand in the safety of light, and the sofa in the shadows on the opposite side where Emily would sit with her back to me.

I read of a young woman in the company of others at supper. That was innocent enough. They all seemed proper and enjoying themselves. Emily stopped me long enough to explain that Fanny was a girl about my age, orphaned and turned over to a community of women in London where she was to be groomed for adulthood and marriage. All very decent, I thought, until I reached this particularly strong passage when a man enters Fanny's bedchamber after supper.

Fanny described it thus: "He seemed transported of my naked person and covered me with a profusion of kisses, sparing no part of me."

I nearly dropped the book. I coughed. "I think that is enough for now, don't you?"

Emily was relaxed on the sofa, her head back as if inspecting the patterns on the ceiling. "Don't."

"Don't?"

"Stop."

"Stop?"

"Don't. Stop," Emily said.

I continued cautiously. The prose creating a buzz in my head that seemed to drown out the thread of a narrative that was filled with words like "nipples" and phrases like "sweaty thighs," "pleasurable passion" and, good God! "Stiff, staring truncheon." My mouth went dry. All I could see was the back of Emily's head. I watched it roll lazily from side to side as if my voice and the prose before my eyes were nothing vulgar at all, but rather light and soothing chamber music.

She sang, "Truncheons and man-poles and thrusts. Oh my!"

"Truncheons and man-poles and thrusts. Oh my!"

Emily paused and turned an ear to me.

"I know. Don't stop," I said. And in truth the story fascinated me and left me wondering how this scene would end.

Badly, I'm afraid.

As I continued Fanny's description of her "passionate pleasure," Emily's humming became louder, more full of increasingly labored breath, until she let out such an audible gasp I dropped *Fanny Hill* on the floor. Emily had swooned upon the couch.

Panicked, I was. I snatched a vase from the table beside me and ditched the flowers. Rushing to the sofa I splashed its water upon poor Emily's face. The water streamed down her throat and skin above her neckline that were splotched and flushed in all manner of red.

"What in blazes are you doing, boy?" she coughed and sputtered.

Emily was not at all faint as I imagined. I stammered but had no answer. She reached for the vase and I stepped back, bumping awkwardly against the tea table, which only served to jostle me, and I splashed upon Emily again, this time at the waist. It was then I became fully aware she had pulled the hem of her skirt above her hips, exposing her undergarment, silky, white, and full of thighs and legs and all. What's more, the water had soaked her shift, and it now clung to her skin to reveal things I had only dreamed of.

I heard her giggle. Fixated as I was on her body beneath that soaked veil of unmentionables, I never saw her hand as it latched on to my shirt above my breeches. She tugged and I flopped on to the sofa with her. She laughed all the more merrily as I struggled to rise. When I slipped again, my head did a nosedive, quite literally nose first into her lap. She threw her skirt over my head making me a prisoner against her thighs.

"Let me up, please," I said as nonchalantly as I could, as if we were sitting properly in our chairs and I asked her only to pass the sugar.

"Not yet."

"I insist." I wanted to exude some worldliness as if it was common for a man to find himself in such a position beneath a woman's skirt on most days of the week. Then I became aware of her perfume. The fragrance she wore on her neck, she must have dabbed down below as well. I knew that scent as well as I knew my heart.

Ah, sweet Emily. But in such a confined space as this it served only to bring me to the edge of a sneeze. Lord, not now. In order to stifle the bugger I pressed my nose into Emily's thigh inches above her knee and wiggled it to and fro.

"What in blazes are you doing?"

"By dose ishes," I replied from beneath Emily's skirt.

"Well, that is one bloody hell of a way to scratch it."

I froze. The voice. When Emily slowly and sheepishly lifted her dress and released me from under the fabric, I found myself staring up at my brother London. He wore a look I had only seen in the illustrations of Dante's Inferno.

My hell began that afternoon, dragged and tied to a post in the stable where London used his cane to lash out punishment and rant about the embarrassment, the dishonor and the evil I had personally inflicted upon poor Emily and everyone connected to Wittyglib.

"You have no concept of how degrading this is for me," he said as he whacked my back.

"You should view it from my perspective," I grimaced. "Much more degrading to be whipped than to do the whipping, I imagine."

The sting of the next blow emphasized that London didn't care for that observation. He began talking of options. He spoke of alternative deaths I could suffer, almost as if he already had a dozen or so neatly arranged on a shelf in his mind. Each was equally horrid and so inventive that I actually gave London high marks for imagination I never expected from him. Well, I suppose necessity is indeed the mother of invention.

He left me there through the afternoon and evening while he decided which was to be my fate.

Long after Wittyglib bedded for the night a faint glow of light and rustling at the entrance to the stable pulled me from a fitful nightmare of having my privates mounted on the tip of London's fork at the dinner table. Emily stole into the stable. She was barefoot and covered her nightgown with a cloak. She carried a large, sturdy cloth bag on a sling, and she pulled a large kitchen knife from it. She commenced to cut the rope that bound my hands to the post.

"You must run and not come back until I send for you," she said. "By that time London will have forgiven you."

"Forgive me? I did nothing."

"Let's not debate that now." And then she handed me a letter and instructed me to go to her sister's home in Coventry. The letter would explain all to her sister. "She will take you in until we can be sure London is no longer hunting you."

"And then?"

The lantern fired a glint of light off her white teeth as she smiled. "We'll write that part of the story when we get to it."

London had stripped me to the waist and he left me half naked after tiring of whipping his cane against my back. Emily fetched the shirt London had tossed carelessly to the side. She paused, teasing me, pulling back when I reached for it. I felt as if more than just half of me was naked. I started to rise but Emily placed a hand on my shoulder.

"I am so very sorry for causing trouble," she said. "I hope some day you will find a way to forgive me."

"I won't hold this against you, Emily."

"No?"

I shook my head glumly, not really certain.

"But here you are whipped and punished for a mere misunderstanding."

I moped at the ground with one arm across my chest supporting the elbow of the other and my chin buried in the palm of a hand. I mumbled a despondent apology of my own. Then she placed her bare foot against my shoulder and pressured me to lie back in the hay. God, how that stung the flesh that was now raw from London's beating. I bit my tongue.

"It seems a shame that you have been punished without having committed a crime. Logically, don't you think one should never be punished unless they deserve it?"

Placing her feet to each side of me and straddling my waist, she said, "Conversely, once punished I would think one might want to do something to deserve it. Don't you agree? I mean, really now, if the horse has already left the barn."

Emily gathered the folds of her gown, inching its hem toward her hips. She murmured with a musical lilt, "Truncheons and man-poles and thrusts."

Oh my!

I do not know which torturous end to my life London settled on as the moon rose over Wittyglib Manor that night; I really could not have cared less. Still, I left before sunrise with a smile, hoping never to find out.

Chapter Ten

"Good God, Ape. You have fish all over the news!" I said, pinching my nose with one hand and holding the *Daily Advertiser* up to the light in the other.

Dawn had long come and gone, though you'd never be quite sure at this early hour in London. Fog was giving way to the cloudy skies that I hoped would give way to sunshine. Eventually.

A.P. grumbled. "If I had a couple pence for a fresh copy I would have invested in one, I would." He held out his palm as if he actually expected the coins to land there. His eyes were hopeful as ever; reality dashed his prospects as usual.

Mrs. Fullbright's daughter Andrea wandered over with a steaming pot of tea, placed it on the table between us and removed the remnants of breakfast. The Tamed Shrew was empty of customers as we sat near the Fleet Street window. We had designated that table as our office in the two weeks since we introduced the tales of Mrs. Martha P. Brown and Mr. Siderham to the world at our first news performance. A.P. and I met each morning to harvest items from the daily newspapers.

"Where are all the killers? Not so much as a decent mugging," A.P. said. He turned to the reverse side of the *Tattler-Tribune*. "What's a panoply?"

"Read it to me."

A.P. read the article in McNabb's broadsheet about a "dazzling panoply of a costumed procession by the Duke of Earl and his entourage at the most lively social event of the season."

"I believe it means they wore armor, or military costumes, or some rot like that. Special outfits?" I said after some thought. A.P. read aloud the entire article and confirmed my opinion as the event reported had distinct military overtones.

"A fine bit of reading, Ape. You are improving each day. Keep at it and you'll be a right solid patterer yourself some day," I promised him. A.P. beamed and picked up another newspaper.

"Hello, what is this?" I leaned in to a story that caught my eye, then immediately backed away again. The lingering moisture and residual stink from its most resent resident, a fish that had to be a day or two past its sell by date, were enough to blind a man, let alone leave him with a clear eye to read the words there.

"There is a story here, of a man in France who has been exonerated of the murder of his son."

"Is that a good thing?" A.P. asked.

"Indeed. And it may be just what we need for the performance."

Ape leaned to the windowsill and looked up at the clouds. "Do you think it will rain today?"

"No." I answered without much thought.

"I think it's going to rain."

"The innocent man, one fifty-three-years-old Gaspar Per-quoit, was found to be not guilty of killing his son, as so decreed by a court in Paris. But a bit late, I'm afraid."

"Late?"

"The court exonerated him two weeks after he was put under the executioner's blade. Sliced at the neck. Dead. Nasty way to go, I imagine."

A.P. said, "Well, yes, that is a bit too late to do much about it, now isn't it?"

"Ah, my grimy little rascal, the story gets better. It seems the man's son was upset with the father for being disinherited. He staged an elaborate scene that gave evidence of murder with signs pointing to Monsieur Perquoit as the culprit. It was all a hoax."

"What a bastard!"

"No, he was a legitimate son. But no matter. The younger Perquoit was taken to court himself when officials found out about his ruse. He was tried and convicted of deliberately causing his father's death."

"Can they do that?"

"Indeed, they can. And they have. And now they have gone off and executed the son as well. For murder."

"Dead?"

"Quite dead. The executioner probably used the same axe blade as with the old man I suppose."

A.P. sighed. "Well, you know what they say. Like father, like son. Two pence says 'tis go'n to rain today, Mr. Merriweather."

I slapped the damp newsprint on the table. "Ape, pirates are running amok on the trade routes, the colonists in America have their knickers in a bunch again, and frog-flogging French are executing innocent men and your only concern is the weather?"

A.P.'s face fell. "Everybody talks about the weather."

"Right. Well no one does a bloody thing about it, now do they?"

A.P. spent only a moment in the doldrums and then brightened considerably. In fact, he was in generally good color and reasonably hygienic these days. He rose and stretched. In the grey, flat light from the window he looked positively healthy for the first time I can remember. We were inching away from poverty since the beginning of our news presentations. We had eight advertisers now. That steady income allowed us to eat better and replace our tired and patched attire. Ape had taken a room above the tavern and advantaged his residency with the use of the kitchen sink at least once a week to wash.

"I need you to find someone for me, Ape." I must have cocked my head to the left, as I noticed A.P. mimicked that tilt of the noggin. I drew his attention to the story about the poor, late, Monsieur Perquoit and of the French apologists who did too little too late to save his life. Maybe they could yet resurrect, like Lazarus, his reputation. Not bloody likely, though.

"I need you to find someone who has experienced an execution by beheading. Can you do that?"

"Not likely. Though if I could, what use they would be to you is beyond my thinkin'. Them being dead and all."

"Not someone executed, you nitwit. Someone who's seen one and can describe for us the scene, the woeful cries of repentance, the blood gushing, the head dropping into the basket. Or better yet, the head missing the basket and rolling across the executioner's platform. I want a live witness account of a beheading, any behead-ing, so we can better inform our audience of French justice."

"How they execute the execution, you say?"

"Exactly, my friend."

"Hang me if I know of one such fellow."

"Then find him for me and bring him in."

"But what words of repentance will we share with the folks, Mr. Merriweather. I don't see any account in this here report."

"Invent something, Ape. You've seen enough executions here to know the lyrics of a dying man when he changes his tune at the foot of the gallows." Oh, that was good. I paused to capture it in my notebook.

"I musn't drag, then," A.P. replied. "I want to return before it begins to rain."

"It's not going to rain. Trust me." I folded the *Daily Advertiser* and was about to tuck it under my arm when I thought better of it. Two-day-old fish cologne is never appropriate this time of year. It occurred to me in reading about the poor, unjustly accused, tried and executed Mr. Perquoit (bad luck that, Oui? Je suis désolé! Sorry, old boy) that the one great question that every compelling news report should address was left unanswered. "Could it happen here?"

I need only find one father, mother, sister, brother, lover, or significant other with a personal experience of losing an innocent loved one to the hangman's noose. One story would suffice to plant the slightest little seed of fear in the minds of the audience that would draw them into the tavern to hear my story. Well, by God, yes, indeed, it could happen here. And if it could happen here, it could happen to you. So drink up, friends. Order another round, for it may be your last. Beware! You could fall prey to the fickle finger of injustice running rampant on the streets of London between the tavern and your bed. That is my news story for the day. That is how news is made.

I left the Tamed Shrew and headed toward Old Bailey where a veteran court bailiff I knew might point me in a proper direction for the assignment I had given myself. And I mused, how might I weave sex into this story as well? Blood and lust, I say.

As I attempted a shortcut through Dilly Alley I found my path blocked by a monstrosity on wheels. An enclosed cart with a roof and walls of misshaped bits of wood and shingles that swayed over rusty iron wheels like a drunken sailor halted all movement in both directions. A plough horse the size of a navy frigate pulling it had gotten it into his horse brain to rest at the corner. That created a commotion as people tried to squeeze through the slim opening between the horse's head and the rump of the cart he was no longer moving. A queue formed both coming and going around the obstacle, and folks stuck in the traffic jam pelted the horse's owner with angry shouts.

"Oy! Move your blooming ass!"

A tall and slender gentleman struggled with the petulant horse and tugged on its bridle. He responded, "He is not an ass, sir, he is a Flemish Draft." He grunted and struggled without success. "A very fine horse on most mornings, though today I confess I am considering turning him over to a butcher.

"Do you hear that, Wilbur? I have not the patience for your dawdling this morning."

Wilbur responded with an outburst of flatulence, thick and odorous enough that one longed for a deep breath of sewage scented London air on its most putrid, smothering summer day.

A springer spaniel added to the confusion. The dog circled the wagon and darted back and forth beneath it, and then between its master's legs, barking furiously. Then the spaniel came up behind the horse and nipped at its hind legs, ducking away from a kick that the horse aimed at him. I took hold of the bridle opposite the gentleman, and between the two of us tugging and the dog nipping we were able to coax the mammoth nag to the main street.

I looked over the cart for some indication of the man's occupation but found no hint there. I assumed this was his wagon home. Dangling pots, ladles and other implements of household nature clanged as they rocked with the carriage. Odd-looking rods of metal and tubes of glass sat on wooden blocks that formed shelves, and rope held them fast against the walls.

"Thank you, sir, that was most kind of you."

I turned to accept the man's gratitude only to find he was talking not to me at all, but to Wilbur, the cranky horse. He was stroking the animal's nose and feeding him a carrot. "You are such a fine fellow, really you are."

It was a tender moment and I was reluctant to disrupt that bit of equine bonding. I coughed and was about to take my leave when the gentleman turned to me. "And you, sir. Your help with Wilbur here is most appreciated." He held out his hand with what was left of Wilbur's carrot wedged between his fingers like one of Dr. Franklin's cigars.

"William Nye is my name. Professor emeritus. Until a recent most unfortunate turn of events, employed at Manchester School for the academically gifted."

We shook and I found myself holding the carrot.

"I taught science and the laws of nature." He looked down at his shoes and shook his head sadly. "Damned combustibles." Then he lifted his head and his spirits. "Fortunately, the lad only lost his eyebrows in that experiment. And his hearing has probably returned by now. Ah, but the roof of the science building, well, that was a whole 'nother story, that was."

The professor pulled an umbrella, slightly heavier than a gentle lady's parasol, from a quiver attached to the driver's seat of his cart. There was precious little sun still and no need to cover from rain, but he handed it to me. Then Professor Nye disappeared. After considerable clatter and rattle, he showed up on the roof of his shelter. I backed a few steps in order to watch him. He had paper in hand and scribbled some observations of a weather vane that stood up against the sky at the front of his wagon house. It was spinning at a moderate but not frantic pace in the breeze.

"It's a southerly wind," he called down to me as if I would understand. Nye took a watch from his pocket, timing the spin of the weathervane.

"May I inquire, sir," I began. But the professor paused me in mid-question with a raised finger. Then he returned to earth, at least physically, I thought. He was quite nimble and animated for a man of such height. Taller than me, or possibly it was the thin frame he worked from that only seemed to make him a vertical specimen. The cuffs of his coat stopped well above his wrists, for his arms were long. Mr. Nye had high cheeks and face so angular that it could have been whittled from wood.

"Help me with this, won't you sir?"

He pointed to the side of the cabin, and together we lowered the shutter that formed most of one wall. He propped it open with a leg of lumber so that it formed a hinged table. Professor Nye made more notations in a book, moving his lips as he did so. A kindred spirit, though I had overcome that habit on most days. He reached around the corner of window we had created in the cabin wall, fumbled for a second, and then carefully withdrew a long, thin wooden box.

It stood about three feet high with a long, glass tube secured to one side. Along the tube's edge a brass plate with many measuring notches. He called it a barometer and noted in his book whatever the instrument was telling him at that moment.

"Ah, yes. Just as it should be." Then he said to me, "Good job, Johnson. You've been quite a help."

"Excuse me, sir. Not Johnson. My name is Merriweather. Leeds Merriweather."

"Merriweather? Good name. Well, that hardly changes a thing at all, now, does it?"

I couldn't agree more, although I had not a snot's worth of inkling what he was going on about.

He said, "One last measurement and I will be gone. I must get to St. James Park by one on the clock this afternoon to take my next reading."

"If I might, sir, what is all this?"

"I will tell you Mr. Johnson..."

"Merriweather, sir."

"Yes, well, it's the weather, my good man. The storm and the drought, the coming winds and rain, and unbearable stretch of summer heat."

"And these instruments will tell you the weather? Can't you just look at the sky or the clouds?"

He shook his head. "That is only good for the moment. I am measuring changes that will determine the weather tonight and, perhaps, tomorrow as well. You know, everyone talks about the weather..."

"I know. But nobody does a thing about it."

"Except me. I can predict it."

Nonsense, of course. "What shall I do with this?" I held up the umbrella.

"Ah, my last observation. Place it on the ground and step away, if you will, Johnson."

"My name is..." Oh, well, forget it.

Nye pointed at his dog, the forgotten spaniel, retired beneath the wagon for a nap. Chasing Wilbur out of the alley had taken its toll on him. "This is Doppler," Nye said. He introduced us with a bow. At the sound of his name, Doppler rose to two legs and yawned at us. "Doppler, the weather hound."

The professor emeritus, exploder of school buildings and scorcher of school children, was as barmy as a parade of gits. In fact, I would suggest to you, he would be among the gittiest, perhaps the grand marshal of that parade.

"Of course," I nodded. I extended my palm, face to the heavens, and shrugged as if I thought there was nothing suspect about Doppler's abilities, although it did occur to me that if one could actually predict the weather that would be—well, that would be news. Rubbish, I say!

Professor Nye stroked his chin as if reading my mind. He then turned his back to the dog, looked at the clouds, and said in a loud voice, "I wonder what the weather will be like today. Do you think it will rain, Johnson?"

Doppler jumped to his feet and began barking. He ran around in a furious circle and then fetched the umbrella. He brought it to me, plopping down at my feet, cocking his head as if to say, "take this." When I refused, he growled. "Take this, you dolt. You're going to need it," he seemed to say.

"A fine bit of training. Quite a trick," I said as I picked up the umbrella and wiped the dog slobber on my breeches.

"Not training. Doppler is a natural. You see I am attempting to calibrate my instruments with Doppler, here. He is quite accurate for predicting storms."

Professor Nye climbed on to the driver's bench after lifting the dog into position as passenger. Taking Wilbur's reins, he looked down at me and said, "Good day, Johnson Merriweather.

As they rolled forward I ran to catch up. "Here, sir. Your umbrella."

"Keep it by your side, and avoid the rain if you can, sir."

"Rain? Today?" I looked at the sky. The air was thick and the clouds gray and shapeless, but the wind gave no scent of storm. "I see no rain in our future."

"Not presently, but I suggest that if you are safely indoors in a few hours, you will thank Doppler."

With that he rolled away, and I started off again for Old Bailey. Three blocks along I sold the umbrella for three shillings to a street vendor.

I looked at the sky again and chuckled as I slipped the coins into my pocket. Doppler the weather hound be damned.

Chapter Eleven

And damn that dog to hell!

That was my thought on my return trip as I ducked into a shop to get out of the rain that was coming down in torrents by then. And damn him I would have, too, if not for the fact that I was beginning to see a use for Doppler and the science professor. I suppose I should not be angry. After all, the dog had warned me sufficiently. Who's the mutt now? It was the dumber animal that sold his umbrella to a costermonger on the street just before his hour of need. Someone, indeed, got a three shilling bargain.

I assigned myself the task to track down Professor Nye and convince him to join our live news performance. Really now, if everyone is going to talk about the bleeding weather, then this should really give them something to talk about. News Performance—live accounts of the most interesting current events along with William Nye the weather guy and his most accurate climate forecasts.

Just inside the door I removed my hat, and the rain that collected around the brim dribbled down the back of my neck and under the collar of my jacket. I nudged the door closed with an elbow while brushing water from my shoulders. The tiny bell that announced my arrival tinkled again. The air in the front of the shop was of fresh, rain-washed lavender. Voices drifted from the far side, but racks of women's hats made it impossible to identify the two people involved in a discussion there.

One was obviously female. "And could you spice this with, perhaps, a feather. Peacock? Oh, how lovely."

The other voice could only belong to the shop owner, Mr. Richard Draper. It was low and as rough as dragging a rake across cobblestone. "Most certainly, madam. My skill at improvisation is only exceeded by your good taste."

I knew the owner of that voice well enough. Half of London knew Mr. Draper well enough. He was a premier hatter to those successful in business, society and, well, those successful in all senses. That weasel publisher McNabb shopped at Draper's, and I had, on occasion, accompanied him there. I purchased my very best hat from Mr. Draper with a loan from McNabb.

"A hat makes the man," both Mr. Draper and McNabb insisted, telling me I needed to look a cut above the rabble in order to patter properly and attract a higher level of clientele that would part with shillings for a broadsheet, or a book, or a magazine.

"If you look like riffraff, you'll only attract riffraff," McNabb said. Then he loaned me money to purchase the topper and joyously deducted it from my sales. With interest.

"Hell-oh?" Draper sung out. He stepped from behind a rack of bonnets. "Oh, it's Mr. Merriweather. How lovely, sir. How lovely." I smiled at him and said nothing, noting his preoccupation with the customer. I merely waved my hand to acknowledge him and shoo him back to business. I only ducked into the shop to escape the rain, thankful that Mr. Draper was still open as the afternoon closed around us.

"I shall not be long, sir," he said waggling an index finger as if he were scolding the ceiling.

There was more talk of feathers and adjustments and a price that the woman I could not see negotiated from Draper. She had a voice that was both firm and thick with honey. She drove the hatter mad haggling with him. In the end, when everything was agreed to and a delivery date set, Draper escorted the woman to the door. My heart nearly stopped as they walked past me. I would love to say our eyes met, she melted into my arms and fireworks ensued. But, in truth, it wasn't until she reached the door that she even glanced in my direction. I must have looked like a ghost, for surely the blood had drained from my face. She was *that* lovely. She was the good Lady Jasper.

All the countrified breeding at the hands of my parents that I so conveniently abandoned when I took to a life on the streets of London rushed back and tied my tongue tighter than the drawstring on a Scotsman's purse. Despite every inclination to do otherwise, I was about to allow her to pass for the second time in my life without a single word. Lacking a proper introduction and all, I had no recourse but a faint acknowledgement with a cordial nod while my heart was screaming, "Please fall in love with me. If you do not I shall run off to join a colony of love-sick Madagascar lemurs and die a lonely, flea-ridden bit of human fluff."

Not so original, I admit. Probably nothing she hasn't heard from some mad suitor before. Fortunately I kept it to myself. Then, as if reading something from my pleading eyes, she stopped. Her sideways glace became a full frontal inspection, and her brown eyes did indeed latch on to mine. She was a woman with little regard for social convention. Thank you, God. I owe you one.

"Oh. You are the news patterer."

I gave her a minimal bow, considering the narrow space that had us confined between the shop counter and a rack of bonnets.

"An honor, madam. And gratifying, too, that you would know of me and my, for lack of better description, humble profession."

We stood eye-to-eye silently waiting for what seemed like an eternity until Mr. Draper finally realized his duty and made proper introductions. "Mr. Merriweather, this is Lady Jasper. Her husband, you must know, is the Baronet Sir Ian Jasper, the third Baronet."

"Fourth," she corrected him.

"Fourth. Lady Jasper, may I introduce Mr. Leeds Merriweather."

"I have been hoping I would have a chance to meet you one day," I said.

"How so?" Kate Jasper asked as if it was the most natural thing that anyone who was anyone would dream of just such a chance encounter.

"I am familiar with my Lady, introduced to her by fate at our inn weeks back. It was a dark and stormy night; you arrived on the wind in the middle of our news performance, and your entrance immediately took the chill out of an otherwise bone-chilling night."

"I am flattered that you would take notice with such detail."

"I must admit, my lady, in that audience there was no other woman of such stature and radiance, let alone one who would stand out like a dove in a herd of zebras." Herd of zebras? Now where in the world had that come from? I made a note to cut out my tongue when I returned home.

She said, "My. You do indeed have a gift for words."

I attempted a laugh. "A professional hazard, I'm afraid." Ah, self-deprecation. That was better.

"Merriweather. Where have I heard that name before? Do you have kin here in town, Mr. Merriweather?"

Indeed. I explained my brother's involvement in his social club minus any hint of the reported buggering among some of those Misbehaving Roosters. "My brother Lancaster is an associate of your husband and, of course, the House of Commons."

"Of course. *That* Merriweather. He is a frequent," she stopped to search for a word. "...visitor at our home. I didn't realize your brother had a brother in London."

"Yes, indeed. The London brother but not the brother London. He is the eldest son in our family." I grinned, a little more at ease. I enjoyed my little joke. Her eyes narrowed in puzzlement. Pity to annihilate the moment with what should have been a clever comeback only to have it land with a thud in some distant heap of comic cowplop. So I rushed to explain with excessive detail how my siblings and I were each named after a city, starting with

London. Still no laugh. Why couldn't I shut my gob? No corner pitch, no stage in London had made me this anxious for the approval of my audience. And I feared my excessive effort had only the opposite effect.

Her long lashes flicked but her eyes registered nothing. Lady Jasper said only, "How odd. It would never have occurred to me. Lancaster, Leeds, London? Of course. Then you must know my husband Sir Ian, as well." Her full-lipped smile dropped ever so slightly, and I swear I could detect a shadow of disappointment there.

"I have only made his acquaintance once," I replied. I did not tell her Ian and I were formally introduced at the pointed end of his dagger. Rather, I provided a colorful and mercifully quick sketch of my encounter with his group and their special guest of the evening, Doctor Benjamin Franklin.

"Dr. Franklin? How wonderful."

"Yes," I said. "We have spent quite a bit of time together." Truthful if you measure it in minutes or, better still, seconds. "In fact, he is quite a fan of our news performance, practically inspired it himself."

The tinkle of the bell at the door stopped us at that point. A large fellow in a soggy tri-corn hat, straw wig and heavy coachman's coat stood in a narrow opening he had created between the door and its frame, blocking the storm from entering the shop with broad shoulders and ample waist. "The rain is letting up a bit ma'am. I was wondering if you are ready to take your leave now before she kicks up worse." He eyed me with great suspicion.

"Thank you, Charles. That might be for the best."

Mr. Draper scurried to the door holding Lady Jasper's rain cape open for her. She moved with no sense of urgency, squeezing every bit of attention she could from the men as she slipped on her gloves and into the wrap. She was two steps to the door when she asked, "Mr. Merriweather, are you heading back to your establishment now?"

I told her that was so.

"Then why don't we provide you shelter from this nasty weather? We can part at your doorstep. I would love to hear of what I shall miss with this evening's news performance. If you'll allow me the liberty of being so bold and offer you a ride."

Slap me silly with a flounder, I vote for boldness. Anything to spend a few more minutes with the lady. "Of course, madam. It would be my pleasure."

As I followed her from the shop I pledged to stop soon at the butcher for a bone, an offering to my patron saint of inclement weather. Praise the mutt Doppler; he's all right by me.

Chapter Twelve

The Lady's carriage was not so regal as one might expect. Driven roughly and replaced infrequently, it showed signs of wear though it was still notches above any cab I had experienced. The family coat of arms was fading on the door. Gold and red paint had long lost its luster. It featured a bounty of Irish Dog Rose above the shield with an image of a vicious looking hamster waving a sword in one paw, an acorn in the other.

He menaced as much as a hamster could menace, I suppose. My rusty Latin left me a bit hazy, but I believe the motto on the crest written there translated to "Family Honor-One Nut At A Time."

The rain slackened to a light, late spring shower. Even the skies lightened. Charles protected his mistress with an umbrella not too unlike the one I had foolishly abandoned. He supported her with a gentle hand as she stepped up and into the coach. For me? No umbrella and his help at the door was a hearty heave-ho on my bum that put me nose to wall with the opposite side.

"So what news do you have for us today, Mr. Patterer?" She asked when we were underway.

Against the clacking of the horse hooves and rattle of the coach's iron wheels on the cobblestone, I began to tell her the sad tale of Mr. Perquoit's premature conviction and execution in Paris.

"Been there," Lady Jasper said with a voice that dripped with utter boredom. She stared out the window.

Changing direction I tried to interest her with an item from the society section. "It seems a member of parliament was found in a rather unnatural and compromising position with Siamese twins from a passing circus troupe.

"Done that."

Really? Figuratively or literally, I couldn't help but wonder. Shame on me.

She perked up a bit with that story but was unimpressed just the same. "Have you no fresh news?"

When in doubt there is always a new report of pirates a-plundering.

"Yes, I know," she replied.

"Well," I said. "I'm sure you have not yet heard of the unusual being from a distant planet who fathered a love child with the King's fifth cousin Mariette."

"The child was a male, I believe," she replied with a straight face. "We don't really know for sure yet about the being who impregnated her. Though I'm sure inquiring minds would like to know." She said it with a tone so bored I might just as well have been informing her that mud, on most days, is brown.

Then as if a fairy whacked us both over the noggin with a wand full of magic dust we laughed in unison.

"That was imaginative, Mr. Merriweather."

"Only slightly less truthful than much of what we are given to believe is news these days."

"Are you indicting yourself among those who provide it for us?"

I shook my head. "That, I will not answer."

Lady Jasper's laugh was pure honey.

I said, "At any measure, Madam, I can see staying ahead of you with news of the day would be an Herculean task. You are well informed."

She leaned towards me, tugging apart the opening of her cloak at her shoulders to make that easier. With her hair and gown misty with rain and her perfume so close, I might close my eyes and believe I was sitting amongst dew-kissed roses. The strain it took to keep my eyes from wandering below the lace that framed her bodice so full of flesh was enough to herniate a man.

"I have spies," she whispered.

"Spies?"

"Oh yes. Yes, indeed. Ask anyone inside the court or out, around Whitehall or Vauxhall Gardens, and they will tell you that Kate Jasper is a busybody of great repute. So they naturally queue up to share their rumors and gossip to return in kind." She paused and lowered her chin. She looked at me through hooded lids. "Shameful, isn't that?"

"Lady Jasper, you are talking to a man whose stock-in-trade

is gossip." I brazenly placed my fingertips upon the back of her gloved hand and found not a hint of objection. "You are obviously a candidate for what I like to refer to as 'The Industry of Dispensable Information Distribution'." When she laughed at that I suggested, "It doesn't seem to bother you. We are kindred spirits."

"My, such a regal name. Much better than gossipmonger. I think I shall adopt it for myself."

"Then take it, my lady. As a member in good standing of that profession I am so passionate about, I can bestow it upon you in your amateur status. Though I can see you are by no means an amateur."

Lady Jasper cocked her head and turned her eyes toward the window. "And what does your wife think of this?"

I told her I was unmarried and unattached, Mrs. Fullbright's benefits notwithstanding.

"Hmm. Would you like me to find for you a wealthy widow to woo? I'm sure that could be arranged."

Where had I heard that before? Oh, yes, the last woman who offered to find me a mate took matters into her own hands and got me banished from Wittyglib. I declined gracefully.

"Imagine what fun you could have with access to society by marrying well. The wealth of information you would find there for your news performance. Tremendous, I should think."

"Ah but then married to money and saddled with the worries of the gentry, I'd no need to go on pattering, now would I?"

She thought about this for a moment and then spoke sadly, "Yes, you are where you belong. Aren't we all?"

"But you? You might be my eyes and ears in and around court, could you not?"

"I have already admitted to spying on them. My sister married a ninny with no money and more titles than toes, but he has a direct entrée into society even I haven't been able to breech. Thankfully, my sister is quick to share every hint of scandal she finds among the naughty nobles."

There was disappointment in her voice, so I offered as a way to console her, "Sir Ian is a member of parliament. Not just your average, run-of-the-mill MP, but titled." The words seemed to affect her, but what I really wanted was to pull her close and let Lady Jasper bury her disappointment in my chest. Better still; let me bury mine in hers.

She dismissed me with a wave of one hand while turning the palm of the other, which I had laid fingers to and squeezed. "Ian is a mere baronet. Not much better than being knighted with no title at all, only much more expensive. I suspect even my brother-in-law, he's an earl, you know, the earl looks down on us. If not for my sister Jillian and her husband Sir Earl, we'd have no entrance to the peers at all."

Sir Earl the Earl? How amusing.

"Well, we are almost to your tavern. Let us part with a bit of news for you," she said. She slapped her hands upon her thighs, rejuvenated in spirit and sitting up proper now. Her smile was as mischievous as the devil collecting the signature for your soul. "Remember the story you were telling the day we first came to this establishment?"

"I must confess your arrival distracted me. My memory is hazy." In fact, her arrival obliterated any memory but that of her face from that night.

"It was Mr. Siderham and the duel. Well, I know where Mr. Siderham is this day."

"As do I, madam. He is hiding safely in France by all accounts."

She shook her head. "Not so. And you call yourself a newsman. Per-shaaa!"

"Then I implore you, relieve this ignorant soul of his faulty observations. I have, as I mentioned previously, a reputation for truth, justice and the British way."

"Yes I was quite intrigued on that night. You see, I happen to know Mr. Siderham's relations quite well."

"Don't tell me you've been in communication with him?"

"Not directly. But as I said, I have my spies. Mr. Siderham never traveled to or intended to travel to France. It was all a ruse while he prepared for another trip."

She explained she had a close confidant with a cousin in Wheaton who had an employee with family in Ipswich, whose son was visiting on a short holiday from his position in Oxford where he had rented out his room for the fortnight to a man who, it turns out, is Mr. Kevin Siderham. The line of connections was dizzying. Bacon on a biscuit! There must have been at least six degrees of separation, a crooked road to useful intelligence.

"Isn't that glorious?" She asked as we arrived at the Tamed Shrew. "Mr. Merriweather, it is so very...heartening to know that I could turn the tables on you, sir, and provide you with information you did not know."

"You would be a fine news patterer," I said with a tip of my hat. And I meant it.

I took her hand and was about to take my leave. She would not let go. "There is more," she said. "You should know that Mr. Siderham has now returned to London and plans to set sail on the morning tide. But you must not reveal where you came by this information."

"Some anonymous source?" I suggested.

"Definitely anonymous."

"And where is our elusive Mr. Siderham headed this time?"

America, she told me. "But he won't make it because he will be boarding the ship this afternoon where a pair of thief-takers are waiting to arrest him. How is that for fresh news?"

"Madam Jasper, you are an octopus," I said. "Oh, but I mean that only in the most delicate and complimentary way. Your tentacles of information are astounding. From the King's Court to the dregs of my world, down to and including the bounty hunters of Bow Street.

"And you should sample their suction," she replied in turn. And then she looked away; I am sure for that moment she blushed. Flirtation or invitation? Awash that moment in a sea of sexual tension, if she was the octopus, I was, well, I suppose I was an eel. At least I was beginning to feel that way in my breeches.

Lady Jasper rapped on the side of the coach, and Charles was there immediately to help with my exit.

"Mr. Merriweather, if I have learned nothing else from traveling in the social circles I am familiar with, it is that gossip, and I suspect its twin, what you call news, is like currency. The more you spend the more you receive."

From the doorway I once again tipped my hat.

"I do hope we meet again, Mr. Merriweather. I have enjoyed your company. And I believe I shall have more stories with which to relieve your pitiful ignorance."

The rain was still falling lightly as I stepped back and Lady Kate Jasper's coach rambled away. A.P. was leaning against the brick in the shelter of the doorway to the Tamed Shrew.

"A very nice ride, Mr. Merriweather."

I shrugged. "It will do in a pinch, Ape." Then I told him to search and find Constable Marley either at his station with the justice of the peace or near the wharf. "It is the most urgent matter. An arrest is going down on our dueling Mr. Siderham this very afternoon." I gave him the gist of Lady Jasper's report without revealing her name.

"Truly?"

"As God is my witness," I said as I clapped him on the shoulder. "Stay close to the constable. I want you to witness the arrest and bring back a full accounting. Convince Constable Marley to return with you and provide details as well for this evening's news performance. We will feast on this story tonight. Let the morning papers settle for leftovers for a change."

"I will stick to the constable tighter than my underwear after one of Mrs. Fullbright's dinners of bad beef and beans."

I quickly withdrew my hand from his shoulder. Some images, no matter how vivid, are best left unsaid. "This is information no one else has. Do not share it with anyone. Not until tonight."

A.P. asked where I had acquired the information. After a moment I slapped him on the back. "No matter, time is a-wasting. Run, Ape. Run."

A.P. headed off in the same direction Kate Jasper's coach had taken. I stood for a moment more in the rain looking down Fleet Street after her. I whistled softly to myself. Of all the taverns in all the towns in all the world, she had blown into ours.

Chapter Thirteen

The summer I was banished and sent on the lam from our family estate at Wittyglib Manor was the summer of the great outbreak of illiteracy amongst widows, spinsters and the matrimonially challenged women around Warwickshire and stretching from Coventry to Birmingham. I never found out what Emily had written in that letter of introduction she wrote to her older sister before sending me off with a sweaty farewell that might one day make for reading as lurid as the *Revenge of Fanny Hill,* but her sister Jane seemed quite amused by it. And that summer she was not alone.

Jane Puckstopper was twenty-seven and widowed. Her husband, Austin Puckstopper, died a hero for His Majesty in the seven years war near a town called Montreal over in the Americas. Felled by an arrow from one of the savage natives attached to a French regiment, I hear. Had my father still been alive, he would rue the fact that Jane's husband had beaten me to that honor.

"Young, handsome and literate. We don't find much in the way of that around Coventry these days. Are you really perfect, Master Merriweather?" Jane peered at me over thin reading spectacles, barely visible above Emily's letter she held before her at a table in the kitchen.

"Not *that* young," I replied. Not anymore, I thought. I was, after all, fifteen years of age by then.

It took me two days of dispirited walking to get to Coventry. Emily packed a change of clothes and enough provisions for the trip in the bag she left with me, along with the address I needed to find. It turned out that her sister Jane had a large home in the watchmaker district. With Emily's letter of endorsement to my good character, Jane made quite a fuss to take me in and provide me with a bed in the attic. The room was dusty but spacious, formerly a workshop of sorts with an enormous skylight window that let the day wake me at first light and allowed me to ponder the night sky as I lay on my bed in the evenings.

"It will be comforting to have a young man about the house," she said, smiling as she tucked away Emily's letter on the night I arrived. Jane's hair was darker than Emily's, and she was more rounded in figure. She wore her spectacles even when she wasn't reading. But the glasses, from my point of view, served to magnify a familiar gleam of the imp in her eyes. She lacked a little of Emily's spunk, but I attributed that to the weight of widowhood. All in all, I found her quite pleasing.

My first full day in Coventry she made a trip to the apothecary shop for ointment to treat the welts London's cane had left on my back.

"You have fine shoulders," she remarked when she applied the ointment to my back. I was a bit shy about my body. Naked above the waist, I straddled a chair in the kitchen while she worked the ointment into my skin. Though I admit I was much less bashful than I would have been before my roll in the hay between Emily's thighs.

I spent many a day scouting for employment in the week that followed, returning to Jane's in the evening, bone tired and sore in the feet. Jobs were few and far between for a learned man in Coventry those days. Certainly limited for someone caught between the age of youth and the age of adult reason such as myself.

Jane and I spent the evenings together, reading in the parlor. I frequently would purchase a newspaper or the latest broadsheet with money she supplied. I protested but Jane would have none of that. "Emily tells me it is a passion of yours. I want you to feel at home here. Besides, I would like to know what is the news myself." She said this, but I never noticed her nose buried in the paper.

Jane's attention favored romantic poetry; stories of love and a new, particularly passionate form of novel that had bindings the color of a pale rose. Sneaking a look when Jane had already retired for the evening, I flipped through a stack of them. The stories seemed quite interchangeable as the hero woos and wins over the heroine and vice versa. It seemed after breathlessly recounting their surging romance each book ended when love conquered all. They had titles like *Two Quarts and a Galleon of Love* (about pirates), *The Crown Jewels* (about a well funded prince), and *The Farmer Sheeps*

Alone (about how the love of a milkmaid saves a herder after he loses a certain appendage in a nasty shearing accident).

One evening she removed her spectacles and rubbed her weary eyes.

"Are you alright?" I asked. I sat across from her in a corner of the room.

"The strain to read is making my head ache tonight." She held up her book about the milkmaid and the farmer. She wrinkled her nose and shrugged. "I'd like to finish this story, but I simply can't with these eyes tonight." And then struck with inspiration, she said, "Perhaps you can read for me. Emily says you're quite good at that."

"Perhaps not," I replied. I was thinking how badly things ended at my last reading session with Emily. But Jane very much wanted to finish the story before bed.

"Sincerely. She says you are quite the entertaining reader. I should like to experience you for myself. Experience that, I should say."

Owing to the fact that she had taken me in, and that each day I availed of her kindness my debt grew, I relented. I sampled a few pages silently at first. *The Farmer Sheeps Alone* was titillating but left much more to the imagination than Emily's *Fanny Hill.* It seemed safe enough.

The story climaxed for the milkmaid in a fit of passion with her shepherd amid fiery kisses and wildly beating hearts beneath alabaster breasts and moist regions of bodies swept up in a torrent of love. I admit I became a bit caught up in the drama myself, reading with reckless animation and amusing myself with my performance in the process. I reached a climax in the middle of that scene, still six pages from the end of the book when Jane stood abruptly, bid me good night, and rushed to her bedroom. At least by then I knew enough not to rush in and rescue her from a swoon when I detected heavy breaths not too unlike those of the milkmaid I had been reading about escaped from the not-quite-closed door of Jane's bedchamber. They culminated in a short, high-pitched squeak that seemed worthy of a mouse in rapture, for all I supposed.

She was quite content the next morning and apologized for her sudden withdrawal. She said she needed relief from her ache.

"My head," she quickly added after reading the look on my face.

"Of course. What else could it be?"

A few days later I returned around teatime from a half-hearted attempt to find work that wouldn't soil my hands badly. Jane Puckstopper and three lady friends were in the parlor chatting away with a great deal of gay commotion.

"Oh. You're home a bit early."

Jane introduced them as her book club. The club consisted of Jane, twin spinsters, and a cousin whose age split the difference between Jane and myself. She said two or three others were absent that day.

"A book club? How swell," I said before attempting to recuse myself from the room.

"Oh Leeds, would you do us a small favor?" Jane asked. I stopped at the doorway.

"I've been telling them all about your fine voice and ability to add life to these dreary scenes." She held one of her pink books. The women tittered and blushed. "We only have this one copy of the story among us and I simply can't do it justice. Would you indulge us in a short reading? Please? I'd like them to see my brag upon you is true."

"Ma'am you underestimate yourself."

"Come now, Leeds. Please?"

The other women added their voices to encourage me. I was clearly needed and badly outnumbered. Jane handed me the book and showed me the page where she last left her heroine.

"Dunes of Desire," I read the title. It was a sultan-teasing, bodice-ripping tale of an Arabian prince and his harem. The women fanned themselves and mocked swoons during certain passages of lust and desire that seemed to come up time and again within a precise number of pages like clockwork. The fact that the book club took it none too seriously, even making jokes of their own about the characters and the plot, made it comfortable for us all. I inserted my own sense of drama or playfulness as dictated by the pages. I became more animated with both.

"You were right," the cousin told Jane. "It does sound more…" she searched for the proper word, "provocative this way."

The book club decided to call it a day after my performance of the second chapter. I admitted I had enjoyed my time with them and agreed to do so again. Some day.

As she was leaving, the cousin admitted she was not schooled enough to read comfortably on her own, and thus her need for the book club. Jane suggested that I would be happy to service her. As a reader, mind you. After some awkward hesitation we agreed upon a time for my visit. Then the spinster sisters, arguing over which of them would get to finish the novel first, decided that if I should read for them they would be able to simultaneously enjoy the story. And that was agreed to.

Summarizing. I never did find employment that year leading up to and just beyond my sixteenth birthday. Nearly all of the members of Jane's book club and two similar clubs of women apparently were in need of my talents. At first my compensation was tea and biscuits, perhaps supper with wine. Then it was a shilling here or a shilling there to buy a newspaper on the way home. And then the shillings changed hands with no mention of the newspaper at all.

"Jane," I asked one day. "Do you think it's proper for me to be paid just for reading to the ladies?"

"Oh, Leeds. You are much more than a reader of stories. If you don't understand that fully now, well, you will. So consider it as the price of entertainment. Actors are paid. So should you be."

"Does your sister Emily know?"

"Sworn to secrecy, yes. And she seems quite pleased by it."

That made me happy and longing to return to Wittyglib, but I knew that was impossible. I tried to counter so many hours spent in the company of women by returning to the calisthenics and cold river baths of my military training days with father. Manly things. I added several inches of height in one quick spurt that summer, and the unintentional benefit of my routine was that I cut a fine figure for the ladies. If anything, it made me more in demand.

Not all the books were devoted to stories of leather against lace in an intoxicating race to the depths of passion. The pink books made up only a portion of the material I read for them. Sometimes I would read works about true crimes or fairy tales, adventure, or even the occasional political treatise. Sometimes I would read to small groups. Sometimes a woman would have a companion or maid sitting quietly nearby. But a small circle of women of means, usually friends of Jane Puckstopper, proved to have an insatiable appetite for literature and my services. They were the devotees of the pink novels. On more than one occasion when I was reading for an audience of only one, even more provocative titles made their appearance.

"I found this in my husband's library," one older but handsome lady told me. She wanted to know what had captivated him so but dared not take up the book to read the words as if she could avoid those words tainting her reputation by merely listening to someone else read them. She said she found it quite "educational."

"Is that what a man wants?"

I gulped. "I'll let you know if I'm ever fortunate enough to find out."

I learned a great deal from the women. I read with a practiced eye and developed a keen sense of their bosoms and how they would swell with the peaks of plots and rested as crises ebbed for the heroines. In a short time I could apply that to reading nearly anything. My confidence as a reader grew, and I came to believe

I could cause a swoon with a proper inflection reading even the most mundane topics. Cake recipes I described had moist layers of indulgence, while political debates might include the rigid, unbending members of Parliament, and news from America might involve exploring virgin valleys with reckless abandon. I had the entire Regency Street Ladies Club melting like butter beneath their fine petticoats with that one.

One morning Jane greeted me at the breakfast table dressed for travel. "I am going stay a few days with a dear old friend in Birmingham. Would you like to come along? I'm sure she would be pleased to meet you, and I fear you shall be, oh, so bored here alone."

We made the trip in a day, arriving just after supper. Martha Middleton turned out to be anything but an "old" friend. She lived in a fine home just inside the township that had been in her father's family for generations. Martha was tall and lithe with curls black as printer's ink and full, sensuous lips painted red by wine from the glass that seemed permanently attached to her hand and never empty that night. She could easily have been a character from one of my recent readings: *Tales from a Bordeaux Boudoir, a Grape Stomper's Guide to Passion.*

The hour being late, Jane announced our travel had taxed her and she would retire for the night.

"And you, Master Merriweather? Would you share with me one final glass of wine for the evening?" Martha asked. She had that flirtatious look in her eye that I now could recognize. I may be slow to catch on sometimes, but I am not stupid. I could not have

resisted her if I had wanted, and there was precious little of me that
wanted to resist.

Over the first glass of wine she probed me. I told her of my
upbringing at Wittyglib, leaving out the reasons for my sudden
departure.

I probed her over the second glass. Martha was only three years
older than I and had a privileged childhood spent primarily in
efforts to outwit and escape her nannies in order to "discover life,"
as she put it.

"So you are that handsome young fellow with the gift."

"Gift?"

"Storytelling. I've heard you have unsurpassed oral talents."

I must have blushed for she smiled and wagged her finger at me
as if I was attempting some charade.

"Well, someone once told me I could read the London Directory and make it sound like a rip-roaring good time is had by all,"
I admitted.

"Did they? Well, we shall see about that. I will judge."

She just happened to own a copy of the directory, and the
thick volume was sitting next to a lamp on a writing desk in a
corner. Martha told me to stand in the middle of the room, and
then dropped the book like a heavy stone into my hands.

I will be honest. Nothing in those pages could be construed
as the least bit entertaining, much less provocative. I attempted
farce and exaggerated gravity by intentionally distorting names
of people, businesses, or streets as they popped into my brain
while I swayed and turned and paced a few feet to the left and

then to the right. Martha reclined on the sofa and sipped her wine.

When I reached the entry concerning Mr. Van Lingo Mungo, Martha's wineglass shattered on the floor. I whirled and bumped into her in the process. She was only inches away. The book fell, and Martha rose to feast her lips upon mine. Tuck in, old girl. She was a hungry lioness devouring her first bite in some time, and I was supper.

Hours later I was in her bed naked and well spent after two appetizers and the main entree. I worried about having the stamina for the dessert she hinted at. With our legs intertwined she gently stroked her finger up and down my chest in the soft light of the bedside oil lamp. I lay there dreamily existing in only that moment. Then she bolted upright.

"Did you hear that?"

I tried to concentrate. Yes, there were noises downstairs. "Jane is probably rummaging a late meal," I said. "She does that sometimes."

"Shhh. Listen."

The clattering was more prominent now, and the sound of heavy boots unmistakable.

"My husband!" she whispered hoarsely.

"Husband? You never mentioned a husband."

Martha returned my amazement with schoolgirl innocence. "Oh, dear. Did I fail to mention that? Oh, dear. I hope he doesn't want to kill you like he did the last bloke."

"He killed a man? Here?" The light from along the bottom of

the bedroom door was glowing brighter and closer with each step that thudded on the stairs.

She shook her head. "I'm just teasing so you don't freeze up on me now. Quick. Quick. You must be off."

She pushed me from the bed. I gathered my clothes and flung them out the second floor window. A trellis of ivy reached from the ground to the roof to my right and I swung out the window and onto it burying my privates uncomfortably deep among the leaves. I navigated with caution about half the distance to the ground before falling the final few feet. When I looked up, the window was closed and the curtains drawn.

Plucking my clothes from the ground as quickly as possible, I held them tightly to my chest as I scampered to the shadow of the house on the far side.

Struggling into my breeches I cursed my fate. I thought of Emily, the first, and now Martha Middleton, the latest, and I could do nothing but swear. "Married women. They'll be the death of me someday."

Chapter Fourteen

It was a pretty good crowd for a Saturday and Mrs. Fullbright gave me a smile. She knew it was me they were coming to see, and they wanted nothing better than to forget about their lives, if only for a while.

That was the evening following my carriage ride with Lady Kate Jasper. We had our exclusive news item about the arrest of duelist Mr. Kevin Siderham. A constable with the help of his bounty hunters, the Bow Street Runners, shackled Siderham and dragged his sorry carcass down the gangplank from the *Boundless,* a four-masted carrack hightailing it for America on the next tide. A.P., who had done his job well, was on hand to give witness to the fugitive's arrest and stood ready with the ticket agent who arranged passage to America for Siderham.

"Shocked. I'm shocked to find that there is illicit travel booked upon our ships," he told me. The ticket agent was a small, portly fellow with greasy dark hair and a thin moustache. He said, "He seemed like such a normal gentleman. Not at all the sort who would kill a man and try to get away with it. Shocked, that's what I am."

The facts: this ticket agent was well-known to provide passage to anyone with the coin to pay for it—as long as they also paid a premium commission for his personal discretion about the identity and destination of the traveler. But I say never let the facts get in the way of a good interview.

"We shall do well tonight," Mrs. Fullbright said as I leaned over the oil lamps that lined the front of the pitch earlier, prior to our performance that night.

"A good thing," I replied without looking up. The Tamed Shrew was busy enough to earn a smile.

"Yes. The rent is due."

I was well aware of that. Mrs. Fullbright, bless her bean-counting, business acumenative heart, decided that she was no longer satisfied with revenue from increased business for the spot in her bed, the roof over my head and the meals she supplied. Although the rent she now charged me for room and board was below market value, and had the added benefit that the bed came with Mrs. Fullbright's warm and willing body, it did bite into my cash flow.

"Broadcasting. That's what I think, Love," she said.

"What was that?" I asked. Anna followed me as I moved from the last lamp to a table where I sat down, took a pencil and my notebook, jotted notes for my story and committed them to memory. I could not give Mrs. Fullbright the attention she deserved.

"Broadcasting," she repeated. "When my father scattered seed on the farm in Southwickhamshire he called it—broadcasting. Tossing seeds about willy-nilly and they'd be landing everywhere. Wasted a lot, I think. But he said the more seeds he cast, the better opportunity for some to take root and deliver crops. He called that broadcasting. And that is what you are doing with your news, Love. From your mouth to their ears."

"Ah, yes. Then, for the sake of this discussion, you would suggest that the fields I am cultivating are the hearts and minds of those who might hear my stories?"

Anna Fullbright patted me on the head as if I were one of her children. "You are a fine man with a fine willy, which, nilly I may add, has been neglected recently. We ought to remedy that soon, Love. But no, I'm just saying you don't give a king's snout about their hearts and minds. It is their eyes and ears you are after."

"And so are you, my dear. So are you. And let us not forget that it ultimately is the content of their purses we're after."

"Ha! Their purses and your promises are all that have kept me from turning you out these past weeks."

Yes, the rent was due, but there were other expenses to consider. A new coat for the stage and boots for the rounds I made to gather information and promote the news performance. Pen and ink and notebooks for note assembling and record keeping. Bribes for information and drinks to lubricate witnesses. Oil for the stage lamps. And compensation for my news staff, A.P. Yes, indeed, news performance was not cheap. Packaging blood and lust came at a price, and it was bleeding me dry.

"To continue our metaphor, Mrs. Fullbright, this seed we are sowing appears to be taking root this evening. And the seed you referred to, which I am about to spread, is today's news. Right. So wouldn't that make this endeavor, oh, news-casting?"

"There is truth to that, I suppose."

I pulled my watch from my waistcoat pocket. Half-past six and the tavern was as full as we could hope. Ready to begin?

Newscaster. News-caster. Perhaps, News Caster? I tested several versions of the title softly, testing them on my ear. Like barrister or tailor. Certainly there was a first "Barrister" to be so named in that occupation, as well as "Tailor" and many other first in lines of industry who created an identity for others to follow. I could go into history as the original newscaster. Would anyone follow in my steps?

News-caster? Would I care to call myself that? Rubbish. No, that is surely a title destined for the trash pile of history.

Mrs. Fullbright tapped my shoulder. "If you could, perhaps, mention the fine quality of our Badger Spit Ale tonight I would love to get that swill off my inventory."

"I've had me a taste of donkey piss with better flavor." A.P. had come up behind Mrs. Fullbright. He made a face and shuddered. I retched at the thought of asking how that experience came about but, as with most of Ape's stories, feared the answer.

"Better wait until they've already tipped enough of the good stuff," I said.

That evening's receipts notwithstanding, our news performance was running at only a modest profit after expenses. Nights when the news was bad (for Siderham), good for us. Nights when the news was good (a new hospital for the poor in Westminster), bad for us. Blood? Good. Politics without scandal? Bad. Lust? Extremely good. Celebrity lust? Even better. And so it went. Some days the empty tables left me massaging the tension from both sides of my jaw and wondering what blockhead of a jester could have possibly believed this scheme would be financially rewarding in the long run?

"Doctor Franklin!"

Anna Fullbright hailed the esteemed American with fists full of tankards she had just lifted from a table near the center of the tavern. Some patrons cheered and raised their mugs in salute before leaning over to a fellow on one side or the other of himself to ask, "Who is that?"

"I recognize this tavern," Dr. Franklin said. "And I recognize this fine lady." He sailed into the tavern and stopped at the head of a sizable table with a half dozen companions riding his wake. Just like that, Doctor Franklin filled the room to its capacity. He waved to me.

"Mr. Merriweather, it such an honor to see you again."

"Doctor Franklin, I believe the greater honor must be mine." I went to him and pumped his hand.

He introduced me to the others in his group. I must admit it was quite a heady feeling to be not only drawn into the circle of Franklin's friends, but to be introduced as one who deserved their attention.

He said, "I am here to find out for myself what you have made of yourself since our last conversation. I have been hearing things. Good things, Mr. Merriweather."

If the buttons on my waistcoat had not contained my chest, if my hat had not contained the swelling of my head, well, who would blame them? I was about to burst.

"Well, we shall see. We shall drink and eat, and I expect that we shall enjoy your news performance this evening."

And so they did.

Our description of Kevin Siderham's arrest and the testimony of Constable Marley, and our aforementioned ticket agent, returned a rousing applause from the audience. And when I explained we learned of the fugitive's whereabouts "by person or persons known to me but shall remain anonymous," well, that was a smashing success with the crowd. They were particularly drawn to that mention of a secret, anonymous source.

"More to come. We'll be right back." Then I turned my valuable real estate on the platform over to Mr. Howard to sell his cutlery, to be followed by a sales pitch from the tailor.

"Quite ingenious. You are making something of their time up on the platform, no doubt?" Doctor Franklin winked at me when I joined them for a break and a quick brew.

"Live advertising."

"That could be lucrative." He nodded approvingly. "Let us chat when you have time."

With Doctor Franklin, as well as his followers and hangers-on that he attracted, we had a standing room only crowd that night. Mrs. Fullbright, as well as our sponsors, did a brisk business and all was right with the world.

"Except that your brother London would like to see you

covered in honey and set out as bait for bears." Doctor Franklin laughed as we loitered after the news performance ended. Our conversation had been rambling quite splendidly to that point.

"Still mad, is he?"

"I was at a gathering during my most recent lecture tour around Birmingham and Coventry. I made the acquaintance of your brother London and his wife, and even dined with them one night at Wittyglib after I mentioned that I had met both you and Lancaster here in town. Your brother is not shy about mentioning how vile you are."

I started to explain, but Franklin held up his hand and stopped me. "This is none of my business. Passionate men tend to speak above their heads. You are my friend so whatever your trespass, real or imagined, I am on your side."

I thanked him. I should have been more enthusiastic that he would call me friend. But any stroke of the ego that may have provided was tempered. I was disappointed, though not at all surprised, to find that London still had such strong feelings nearly ten years after that unfortunate misunderstanding with his wife Emily.

"Emily?" Doctor Franklin asked.

It took me a moment to realize the question was an introduction and not accusation. I had spoken her name aloud.

"Mrs. Merriweather appeared genuinely interested in how you are managing your life these days. Maybe she will soften the old boy's heart some day."

"I doubt that."

"Well, I certainly have no sway. Perhaps I can direct them to take in a news performance when they visit London next."

London in London? He hates the city.

"Having them experience your success might mitigate a bit of those ill feelings, whatever their source."

More than likely London would find some reason to hold this against me. I might consider escaping town for the week. On the other hand, if my oldest brother did attend a performance, I would scour the streets and purchase the posteriors necessary to fill every seat in the tavern and perform with my thumb at my nose in his direction. Sweet.

Franklin surveyed the tavern and nodded. "I am quite impressed with the business you have made here. And all this from our little chat?"

"If only we could have this kind of audience every performance night. Your presence this evening has been quite a help."

He promised to recommend it heartily to any and all who would find the news performance enlightening. "And I know many who would." Then he asked, "And what of your future, Mr. Merriweather? Have you found yourself in this news performance, or is this still only a temporary stop toward your destiny?"

"I still hope to own a press, maybe two, if that is what you mean."

I reached for the pipe in my satchel nearby. Doctor Franklin stopped me. He withdrew a case from inside his coat and took out two cigars, offering one to me. Although I had only attempted rolled tobacco a time or two, I followed his lead. We savored the act of lighting them, puffing deliberately and leisurely. Then we sat back.

"I admire your spirit and your dedication to the craft of information," Franklin said.

"And I, yours."

"Alas, I have no hand, no juice in the publishing landscape of England. My contacts from my youth here are long passed. But if I could, I would consider you a worthy partner."

"You say that with such sincerity, I am tempted to believe you," I laughed. "If I might be so bold to suggest, an offer with no means of backing it up is not much of an offer at all."

His eyes twinkled. "Well said. Still, the compliment is genuine."

Doctor Franklin asked if I had ever considered emigrating. "Should you be tempted by the vast opportunities in the Americas, now *there* I have some considerable influence, in a modest way. I could provide a letter of introduction that would get you started."

I thanked him again, but told him I felt more comfortable closer to home. "In fact, if I establish my own press, probably in Coventry, I could be successful in the shadow of Wittyglib Manor and bedevil the bejeezus out of my brother London."

Doctor Franklin puffed up his cheeks and grunted with amusement. "So that's what this is all about."

No, in truth, like many a patter of mine, I was making up my life as it occurred to me.

"Let us just say the thought of living out my days as a boil on my brother's backside holds such delicious appeal." I mused that I would bottle that feeling if I could. Then every day I would take it out and place one drop on my tongue. One drop a day to set your attitude, akin to having your own personal happy drug. Better than Laudanum, I thought. All the opiate without the drooling.

Franklin rose and bid adieu. "If you change your mind about the Americas, I do hope you'll keep me informed."

"If the colonies become a serious option, then I assure you, Doctor Franklin, you will be the second to know. Certainly in the top ten."

"Yes, I know how word gets out." He took the tankard of beer that had been sitting on the table in front of him and finished it off. He stood for a moment, wistful and contemplating the empty mug. With a satisfied crook in the corner of his mouth he made a show of setting it back on the table. "That, my friend, is proof that God loves us and wants us to be happy."

Chapter Fifteen

"Well, that was certainly interesting," I said as I shifted all of my weight on to the back of the carriage seat in order to pull up my breeches.

It was the Thursday following my news performance for Doctor Franklin and his entourage. Kate Jasper sat opposite me and leaned dreamily against the blind that covered the window. She dabbed a kerchief at the still moist corner of her mouth. She had a smile on her lips and a look in her eyes as far away as the moon, most likely reliving each pleasurable moment of the past half hour.

Dash everything she had just given me in that confined space. I would have given all I had to make the contentment her face revealed at that moment a part of our lives every day, to wake up to that smile each morning and to watch her lovely face upon its pillow as she drifted off to sleep at night. In a word, I was quite taken with the lovely Lady Kate—Mrs. Ian Jasper. Yes, well, right. There was still that "Missus" part of it, now wasn't there? Curdling cockroaches.

We were returning to town after a glorious early picnic at a quiet site I knew of along Corkinhole Creek on the road north out of London. Kate's handmaid and companions were in a separate carriage on the road behind us. Or before us, I cared to know neither. I did know that Katherine Jasper was quite a woman, knowledgeable of so many things in arts and politics as well as literature and philosophy. And now I discovered just how proficient she was in pleasing a man.

The picnic, itself, was gloriously pleasant. We relaxed with the others beside a babbling stream that provided a musical underscore as she and I traded rumors, innuendo, lies and other bits of news. On that return trip our exchange of intimate information veered for the first time down a road of a different intimacy.

I do not recall exactly how it happened. One moment we were discussing Captain John Galt's recent plundering of a small Spanish fleet off the coast of Jamaica and the next moment Lady Jasper was plundering me. Not that I put up much resistance, mind you. I dropped my flag and surrendered faster than an unarmed schooner under the gun of pirate Jolly Roger. In this battle I was not a fighting man-o-war. I would describe myself as more a love boat.

"My, but you are fresh, Mr. Merriweather," she said now that order had been restored in our private cabin.

I apologized, with no conviction whatsoever for taking advantage of her in such a manner as her eyes sparkled. "It was only a matter of time, I am certain," she said.

"That is what you believe?"

"Mr. Merriweather, you most certainly knew that I could resist your obvious charms for only so long."

I did?

"And I am only a weak, vulnerable woman," she continued.

Vulnerable? Lady Kate Jasper? "I don't quite know how to respond to that," I said.

"Then tell me simply that you are in love with me."

"But that is all too true. It is my blessing and, you being married, my curse."

Kate nodded. "Just knowing that I have your love washes me of any ill feeling for my weakness and my behavior just now." As she said this she leaned forward and stroked my knee, she stroked my thigh, and I closed my eyes as she stroked more.

And then she leaned back against her seat again. "You are so fortunate to have not married. It is only a wall to happiness."

My turn. I placed my hand upon her knee. "It seems not to hinder you, thankfully, my lady."

"No. Thank *you*, Mr. Merriweather. My husband has too often ignored me. He has other interests where that is concerned, or haven't you heard?"

I told her I only knew that Ian Jasper associated with certain individuals. "Things have been whispered, but I take no stock in them," I lied.

"He is a homosexual," she said with no emotion. "He hides it well and as his wife I provide the proper appearance for him. Lord, do I have any choice in the matter?" She said this while concentrating on the floor of the coach.

"No need to explain, my love."

"Ian has made it clear that there is not enough room in his bed for a wife." He voice was rising now. She fanned herself, but that did little to contain her growing anger. The rumbling of the carriage sounded like thunder inside the cabin. I feared a storm was brewing in the mind of Lady Jasper. But then she closed her eyes and took several slow deliberate breaths. She pulled a tiny-jeweled snuff tin from beneath her sleeve, placed a small amount in one nostril, sneezed, and smiled.

"Better now," she said merrily as she replaced the tin to its hiding place.

"You could leave him. The grounds for annulment are indisputable. Even the king would recognize that," I nearly pleaded.

But she shook her head. It was a marriage built on financial and social convenience. "My father arranged it, thinking it was a path to peerage," she said. Sir Ian Jasper, what a poor joke that turned out to be. "Ian paid nearly everything his family had for a title, and all he received was a mere baronet. Baronet? White trash nobility. That's what that is." The happy effects of the medication she sniffed moments earlier were either wearing off quickly or couldn't mollify the lady.

"Now Ian is donating heavily to the crown to advance again. If it fails, I fear we shall be ruined. Ian has been wearing out the road to the palace traveling there quite often trying to make his case for a true noble title."

"You would think those frequent traveler miles would be good enough for an upgrade," I joked.

She brightened and her rapid change in mood had the effect of a whiplash on my brain. "But if he is successful, why he might be elevated to earl or even a duke. Oh, I would make an exquisite duchess, don't you think, Mr. Merriweather?"

"Fairest in the land." I shifted uncomfortably. Was there room in the Jasper Duchy for a poor patterer like me? She seemed to catch my thoughts like so much dandelion on the wind.

"Oh, the fun we could have. With Ian's elevation to the House of Lords and the connections of the title and business opportunities, why you could give up the news business."

I told her I wasn't interested in being a kept man, if that was what she referred to.

"Nonsense. We all need to be kept," she said. Then with a husky whisper she added, "And loved." Lady Kate Jasper leaned over and laid her lips upon mine in a slow, wet, grinding kiss guaranteed to perk up a man's pants. Then she leaned back and raised the shade.

"Cheapside," she said. "Nearly there. We shall have to let you off here, Leeds. Can't have too many tongues wagging."

"I would hate to be the subject of my own scandalous news report. That just wouldn't do." I was light-headed and muddled from all that had happened that afternoon. Perhaps the walk to the Tamed Shrew would clear things up for me. Lady Jasper promised to send someone around the following Thursday afternoon with information of a time and location where we could meet discreetly.

"We must be careful now," she said in a soft voice as I disembarked into the late May sunlight. "Discretion. I trust you."

It seemed to me that cat had already slipped out of the bag. Shagging a lady in her carriage with her entourage in tow was anything but discreet, but that's the nobles for you. That's why bringing them down one scandal at a time makes for a lively news performance. Lust in the King's Court. At least those of us living on the streets make no apologies for our lack of morals. In fact, we're bloody proud of them. This discretion thing? Never really tried it before. It could be a fascinating sort of ride. Well, mount up.

Chapter Sixteen

Thursday. Then Thursday again. And again. No dipping the toe there. I plunged into an affair with Lady Kate Jasper like a rudderless skiff over a waterfall. Each week Lady Kate's passion was constant and never far away even in those moments when we surfaced for air. In those moments, our talk turned to news from her social scene and the opinion its members held of the King and his doings. Unlike the ladies of the Warwickshire book clubs, Lady Kate needed no help from little salacious novels to inspire her. Together we wrote our own chapters that featured everything lovers could experience between the pink-tipped mounds struggling to contain a pounding heart and the volcanic eruptions of desire that consumed us. The book club ladies would wither with delight to read about them. So I tried to recreate those afternoons in my notebook, lingering in the little flat near the docks that Lady Kate acquired for us. Who knows? I might need pink material once I had my printer's shop.

"That is sooooo yesterday's news," she would say dismissively when I tried to entertain her with the latest information I had about some happening or other.

"Let me tell you what *really* happened." Her natural ability to out-gossip the gossip created within her circle of friends and mere acquaintances was so pronounced that she became a funnel of information from all points north, south, east and west. And the best of the gossip found its way from her lips to my audience.

"I may only be the lady of a baronet, but let me tell you what I heard all the peers have their knickers in a knot about today," she would say as she undressed. It was hard for me to discern at times which gave her the biggest thrill, getting naked or getting even with those who might look down upon her.

Since Thursday was a day free from the news performance, I could spend it rooting out news stories. I spent two hours of that rooting around with Lady Jasper in the bed of a musty second floor flat overlooking the ships out in the Pool of London on the river. On one afternoon when I returned from my weekly news "consultation" with Lady J., I had a notebook full of ideas for the newscast performance. I stepped out of the heat of the summer sun and into the dim, cool comfort of Mrs. Fullbright's tavern.

"Leeds!" several voices greeted my arrival in unison.

I loved walking into a tavern where everyone knows your name.

A.P. looked up from the *London Chronicle*. "What've y' been up to Mr. Merriweather?"

"My neck in possum piss. And I just realized I can't swim," I replied as I hustled to the bar for an ale.

One quick one. I drowned my thirst and then carried the refilled tankard to the table where A.P. laid aside his newspaper.

"News today?" I asked.

A.P. shrugged. "Same old unenlightened intelligence as yesterday." He studied me with his chin down and narrow eyes timing my response.

"Unenlightened intelligence? Where did you come up with that?"

"Mrs. Fullbright gave me them words. Yesterday's words to use."

"Anna, I do believe we have created a verbose little monster here."

She delivered a small plate of bread and cheese with an apple on the side. "Today's word is vacate. As in it is time to vacate the premises." Mrs. Fullbright the landlady, not Mrs. Fullbright the lover, frowned upon me. She had only a hint of the details, but a mere hint of my affair with Lady Jasper was enough for that bed to go as cold as a penguin's arse on Artic ice. I was no longer a favored tenant with benefits: the sooner I found other lodgings, the better for us both. Can't say as I blame the old gal. I was working on that one.

"So how is your anonymous source of news today? It is today, is it not Leeds? Did she reveal anything? Anything news worthy, that is?" Anna's tone dripped sarcasm like poison in a witch's brew.

"Why do you believe she is a she?"

Mrs. Fullbright snatched the bread I was reaching for at that moment and handed it to Ape. They exchanged a look that screamed skepticism and conspiracy.

I suffered it in good stead, I think. I could worry about the verbal knife wound later. "Well, I learned the Earl of Darnitall still hasn't produced an heir. And now the Lady Darnitall is telling everyone it's because he's afflicted with venereal disease."

Anna said something to the effect that I should be so lucky as she turned away and headed to the kitchen.

A.P. tapped his copy of the *Chronicle*. "The Lord Sheriff arrested a thief who has been robbing parishes across London. The devil walked off with several poor boxes, the whole bloody box and all, sometimes right in the middle of services. Even those big iron and lead ones. He must be awfully strong, that boy."

Another Jasper-ism. "The Lord Mayor of Falmouth initiated a lottery to pay for city improvements. Raised a significant sum."

Not impressed?

"Guess who bought the winning lottery ticket."

"The mayor?"

"He said he had never purchased a lottery ticket ever in his life but felt it was his duty to lead by example. Amazing that his first and only attempt rewarded him with a small fortune when he plucked the winning numbers from the lottery drum himself."

We exchanged a few more items of interest, but it seemed each potential news story reeked of doldrums. A.P. reached into his pocket and withdrew half a dozen shillings. The boy was learning to accumulate coins almost as fast as he built his vocabulary. He stacked them with care and precision on the table in front of him.

"We're doing quite well, are we not, Mr. Merriweather?" His face was as clean as I had ever seen. The new coat I had purchased for him no longer hung like an oversized sack. He filled it admirably those days. Regular meals will do that for a growing boy.

"Yes, Ape, we are doing well."

It was the third time that day that I could recall he counted his money. Perhaps it was to make sure not a single piece of silver had disappeared since his last inventory. "I've never been so rich," he said. "Have you, Mr. Merriweather?"

The question begged of innocence and awe. "No Ape," I replied. "Not in a very long time at least."

A.P. took one coin and tried to bend it between his teeth. It was as solid a shilling as they come and more valuable to him than anything it could buy. "You and me and all this silver. You're the real deal in my book, Mr. Merriweather. And I can barely read." He looked up at me with soft eyes that belied his rough upbringing on the filthy streets. They were not the eyes of the sixteen-year-old rascal I had known only a few months previous. Fear grabbed my throat from within, so convinced was I that A.P. was about to floor me with a sentimental comment. I braced for its blow, and A.P. paused, sensing that no words were needed. The moment said it all, so he winked and his countenance returned to its impish old self. My god, he will make a great patterer some day.

"Anything else before I go?" I asked, looking toward the door. Lady Jasper had been particularly enthusiastic that afternoon and I was whipped. Not literally. Not this week anyway. I needed to rest and think.

A.P. scooped up his treasure and stuffed it into the pocket of his coat. He had a glass of Mrs. Fullbright's weak gin on the table.

There was barely a sip left but he swallowed that before answering. "We have a wolf looking to steal our sheep," he said. "But you will outfox him, I'm sure, Mr. Merriweather."

I asked him what he meant.

"Why, the Firkin crowd is plotting against us. Thievery, that's what I call it," A.P. said. "Mrs. Fullbright says there is nothing we can do. That any public house has just as much right to perform the news as we do, she says."

"The Firkin Inn? Newscasting?" So. Now our success is giving rise to mimics. Flog the frog! I gave my collar a slight tug, straightening it at my neck. And I laughed. Modesty prevented me from pointing out my superior pattering abilities, but I assured Ape that they could never match our performance at the Tamed Shrew. "First. Better. Best." I liked the sound of that.

Ape gave me the look he reserves for times of exasperation. Never call the boss a dolt, at least not to his face. But it seems that the innkeeper at the Firkin, if gossip be true, hired the same bold and beautiful fellow that McNabb had sacked me for as his news actor.

Competition. I must admit in my one life to live I never took for granted that, as the world turns, we would be alone in this new form of news performance all the days of our lives. A guiding light? Maybe. Perhaps I should have given more attention to our chance of success, or that we would be something to imitate by these Johnnys-come-lately so soon after setting down this road.

How would that affect us? I needed to find out.

Chapter Seventeen

"I swear now there's a balcony big enough y' could rezite Shakespeare off of." A fellow with a bushy beard and sallow face to my right planted his elbow in my ribs. The hair on his face parted enough to form a thin break in the middle. I could just make a smile of rotting teeth buried under there. Open graves half filled with paupers couldn't match his foul breath as he wheezed and leaned into me. He pointed to the news performer at the front of the Firkin.

A.P. had been misinformed. Our competition was not William the Wunderkind Patterer, last seen shoveling worthless bits of McNabb's business on my watch. Not that it bothered me any longer, I'm just saying. No, this was worse. He was a she. And she was quite fetching. The Firkin had hired a woman to present the news, and the crowd licked up each word. She lacked style and substance, but who cared? She more than made up for it with an innocent face full of expression and a figure that her low cut blouse struggled to contain.

"Much better than t'other news performance over there," the sharp-elbowed stranger on my right said. He raised a tumbler of gin with one hand and jerked his thumb in the general direction of France or Spain or the moon. I couldn't tell which.

I shook my head. "I think they do a fine performance at the Tamed Shrew."

"Nah. Not there," he said. "That other pub. Say Ernie, whaz the name of that spot we'z at t'other day? The one with the newser show."

Ernie was a tall fellow with an enormous head under a small sailor's cap standing just off the wheezer's shoulder. "The Rusty Scupper, for sure."

"The Scupper has a news performance?"

Ernie and his friend nodded.

"You damned fools!" That came from my left. A third man jostled me and joined the discussion. "'Tis the Cheshire Cheese wots got the news thing a-goin'. I've been there. But you're right on the spot, Harry. This here is something for the eyes."

Harry scratched his beard with enough vigor to chase the lice away. I leaned back just in case they made a break for it. He said, "I believe you're right. I would say it's both of 'em. Tho' the Cheese is a bit pricey for me, mate."

Ernie nodded and rubbed his thumb and fingers together.

What a bleeding idiot. What rock had I been living under? So wrapped up in reporting the news I was, that I missed the most important news of all. London was teeming with rival newscasting performances and I had missed it. My heart sank; I deserved a flogging for that one. I stood with my hands behind my back. I stared at the floor and raised my eyes to the roof. Mostly I watched the crowd with dismay, knowing there were at least half a dozen performances like this going on in other taverns when they should be at the Tamed Shrew. Then I took a breath to consider the situation.

"What did you say your name was?" I asked Harry. He introduced me to his mates. Without casting any personal judgment against their utterly worthless lives, I weighed the value of their patronage against that of having someone like Doctor Franklin in my audience. I couldn't spend even a full second on that one, so obvious the answer. I felt better.

"And then there was, like, this terrible feeling that the fellow had and he…" the news presenter tried to shout over the crowd. They weren't there for the news, I would have told the wench. Beer and boobies, that's all. Feeling better all the time. Nothing to fear but fear itself.

"And what of the Tamed Shrew?" I asked. "I hear they got a slap-up decent news thing going over there."

In unison all three replied, "The Tamed Shrew has news?"

It was news to them. Now that was a spot of trouble. Then Harry asked, "But do they have theyselfs a tart as fine as that Heather Louise up there?" Again he jerked his thumb in all directions.

"Nah," I growled with a bit of Cockney. With no intent to mock my new knuckle-dragging companions I tossed my shoulders back and affected a swagger I learned through dealing with this sort of chap so many years on the streets. I thought it best to blend in and become one of them. "But pop 'round and get your gander on. Y'll see there's more to a dish of news than the pretty face serving it."

"Well, of course, there is." All three nodded in agreement with sober faces and thumbs tucked behind the labels of their jackets. Then they broke out in such a hearty laughter at me that I had no alternative other than to retreat.

I grabbed a spot of real estate at a table in the back. The Firkin Inn was smaller than the Tamed Shrew. The audience suffered in comparison to ours, but the intimate setting helped it fill most of the space. In no time at all I was able to establish a few salient points to explain the evening by observation and interrogation of the barmaid.

First, the young woman on the stage was the proprietor's niece and would not have been in that position without the obvious connection to the owner. (The barmaid assured me the fix was in for she, the server, had much more talent) Second, what the News Niece had to offer was nothing more than regurgitating items from the London newspapers. Third, the inn had established what it called the "Happy News Hour." For the length of the news performance the price of a beer was discounted, and if they cut the cost of their cheap gin any lower, the owner would be paying you to drink it. I drank the gin.

Considering those three selling points and evaluating the quality of the clientele, only the drink specials concerned me as a potential problem. They chose to make a mockery of what we had established, and I refused to take that personally. Let them have this crowd. But learning that news performances were sprouting up across the city faster than I could have dreamed was more unsettling. Apparently news had become a fertilizer for blooming bloomin' copycats. And where in blazes did I have my nose buried while this was happening around me? Lady Kate Jasper. No doubt that distraction on top of the work involved in producing a live news performance slapped blinders on me.

"Bollocks!"

The threat of competition from this one public house seemed only a minor irritation until Heather the News Niece stepped down and gave way to that evening's advertiser. The man who took up the pitch was none other than my Willow Street tobacconist Mr. Andrew Dunlop, our first patron of the news performance. The same Mr. Dunlop who two weeks earlier had told me he no longer wished to pay for time.

"I do believe my welcome has been worn out and perhaps a fortnight is in order to give customers around the district relief from my chatter," he had said at the time.

"Patter," I replied.

Dunlop sucked Sperm Whale.

That was the source of ivory from which he fashioned the pipe in his hand that night. I watched him tout its benefits to the crowd at the Firkin Inn. No doubt he paid for the privilege of performing there and I felt like a jilted lover. When he finished and moved off to a table not too far from me, I didn't hesitate to join him.

"I see you have found renewed value in the advertising pitch. I must say, Dunlop, old fellow, you have improved considerably under my guidance and the experience you gained at the Tamed Shrew."

Mr. Dunlop then tapped me on the chest with the pipe's stem. "Hah, quite right. A reasonable investment of time, it has been. Perhaps we shall resume it at a later date."

Give Mr. Dunlop his due; he looked me directly in the eye. His twinkled with the certainty of a man holding superior cards and the largest stake at the gaming table. I knew the audience well by now; I didn't have to look. Decent though not overwhelming, more male than normal due to the attraction of the woman news actress, but each one in that crowd was bathed in a cloud of his own tobacco smoke.

"Ours is bigger and a better quality audience."

"But them in your crowd can't measure up to this crowd for smoke," he replied. "These fellows here buy tobacco like there will be none tomorrow. And the price of the pitch is better at this place."

How much better? I swallowed my gin, and it landed hard in my stomach when he told me. So that was it. At least in this instance my competition was not the live performance itself, but the price that stole Mr. Dunlop from me. We debated the finer points of audience size and quality of the customer. He was not pig-headed but not moved either.

"How many of these men do you recognize as your customers?"

He only shrugged. None was the number I guessed.

"And don't you think they are no better than you, looking to buy at a bargain rate from some shop near the wharf. I would wager they've never been within spitting distance of Willow Street."

We bandied that about without any definitive result. I would have pressed him further, but my tailor caught my attention. He had promised to join our performance, but that was before my Firkin competition began its live news. Now there he was in someone else's tavern. Keeping a tally? That raised the score of advertising theft up two for the competition to zero for the Tamed Shrew. My tailor obviously felt the folks at this Firkin tavern were clearly a better fit. Bugger that.

The three jokers who set my evening on its downward spiral had suggested that this was not the only spot in London now offering live news performances. I had my work cut out for me to investigate the others. So I strolled to another location for a spot of gin and information. I weaved to another after that. Later I stumbled and eventually found myself nearly crawling as I made my way from tavern to inn to alehouse that night. I stopped in every establishment to Covent Garden and back rumored to have interest in copying our success.

By the time I returned to the Tamed Shrew I was desperately drunk and the tavern was shuttered for the evening. Locked out, I sunk to the ground, curled up and laid my head against the stoop. Everything around me was spinning, but my calculations were firm. I counted no fewer than six more public houses in the district that offered live news or had plans to do so, including my good Russian friend, Boris, at the Moose and Squirrel.

Hardly Cricket, I say. Well, if that was the game we're playing I vowed to the stars above me I would out report, out perform, out wit them all. If only my head did not hurt so much as to block any reasonable attempt to design a plan.

Chapter Eighteen

"News Performance Cancelled Tonight."

The sign next to the door of the Tamed Shrew was only a headline scribbled on the back of a playbill from our Wednesday performance. The story that night, if it were to be written, would probably include descriptions such as "day-long heaving bile fluids of excessive gin" and "head squeezing tourniquet of pain." I think I would like to have written, "News actor Merriweather was found in the gutter before the Tamed Shrew Tavern, curled into a fetal position after he succumbed to a fatal cocktail of depression and alcohol." At least that spot of news would have put me out of my bleeding misery. Sadly, putting it in print would not make it the truth. Never does.

Hair of the dog?

Kick a poodle and pass the bottle. Don't mind if I do. It was late afternoon when I eased my way downstairs for a medicinal snort.

"It must have been something you ate," Mrs. Fullbright suggested with an executioner's smile.

I nodded weakly. "No need to be so snide about it, dear."

It was Anna who rescued me from the cold stone stoop of her establishment as the skies turned rosy with first light that morning, and I slept deeply through the day except for the periodic interruptions when I bounded to the window to divest myself of the poison in my body. Pity anyone in the alley below.

I transferred a kiss to the cancellation poster with the tips of my fingers as I paused on my way out of the Tamed Shrew. Thank God I wouldn't need my faculties that evening. Friday is normally quiet as the working class geared up for the weekly payday that followed. I wandered west along Fleet Street with no real purpose in mind. As I meandered into the Westminster borough, the ill effects of my "research" from the previous night slowly departed.

"Have a go at a play, sir?" A ragged girl with the promise of sprouting into a beauty one day stepped out of an alley.

"Not tonight, child." I was in no mood to shag a prostitute, or even haggling for a low enough price to make her palatable for that matter.

"G'wan. You'll enjoy it." She stepped closer and waved tickets in front of my nose. That was certainly a new approach. I couldn't help but wonder how many tickets a ride of lust required these days. It was only then that I realized I had wandered down Drury Lane and stood in front of the Theatre Royal.

"The play has already started, but you ain't missed much. Still good laughs left."

Raindrops tapped gently on my hat, the air was thick and warning of worse to come. I wondered what Doppler the weather hound would have predicted just then as I purchased a ticket from the girl. I took up a seat on the last bench of the pit. A gentleman with a pipe clenched between his teeth and a quill in his hand sat at a narrow table between my seat and the back wall. He scribbled notes by the light of a small candle. I was just settling in when he leaned forward and tapped my shoulder.

"Mr. Merriweather, right?" he nodded with no prompting from me. "I'll get to you some day."

I asked him to explain but he made it clear the answer would have to wait when a woman large enough to cover three seats on the bench to my left told us politely to shut our bleeding gobs. "I can't hear the friggin' actors," she complained in a voice loud enough to draw the verbal condemnation of the patron in front of her. That led to more discontent in the entire section, causing the actors on stage to pause until the wave finally died.

The play was the latest episode in an ongoing comedy written and performed by the master himself, David Garrick. He had stretched the storyline across more than a dozen separate plays so that patrons returned with each new performance to see what comic situations their characters had gotten into this time around. And it was always about—well, essentially about nothing. A group of friends seemed to exist solely to annoy each other with their antics and to provide entertainment for us in the audience. No plot? No problem here. Save Shakespeare for the highbrow audience; this was a workingman's performance.

"Needs a bit of polish and maybe pluck. Some spark." The man with the pipe told me at the intermission. "Not one of Garrick's best, I say." His wig was ill fitting and one eye permanently sealed. His cheeks were prominent bubbles on each side of his red and vein-mapped nose. He didn't laugh; he cackled.

"Spunk," I nodded. "It definitely needs some spunkification in my estimation. Have we been introduced? You seem to know me, but I can't recall you."

He shook his head and said he wrote stories to critique theatre performances for the weekly magazine *Westminster Standard* and *The Grub-Street Journal* as well as a number of other papers. "But I have seen you at the Tamed Shrew. I will write up a report of you some day. Interesting show of news patter you got going there."

"Well, it appears we're not alone in our performance these days."

"That makes it all the more interesting. I think you've hit upon something, though I believe you have much to improve," He said through clenched teeth relaxed only enough to let his pipe waggle up and down as he spoke. Then he handed me his card. "Roland J. Penny is my name. Writer, consultant, and entertainer's best friend."

"Ah, so you are the Mr. Penny I have read. I am quite familiar with your byline."

Penny nodded. "I can help you, Mr. Merriweather."

"Is that so?"

His head remained still, but his pipe nodded. "I am meeting with some friends after this performance tonight. I think you'll find kindred spirit there, and we can chat. Join us, won't you?"

Mr. Penny dissected the flaws in Garrick's latest effort after the play as we strolled to a coffee house closer to The Strand.

"This is Mr. Anderson Wallace," Mr. Penny said when we arrived and found his two colleagues in the middle of a chess match.

"Andy, old boy. I haven't seen you in ages," I smiled.

"Leeds Merriweather, you stale codpiece. I see you are still alive."

"You obviously know each other," Penny said. He dislodged his wig as he slapped his forehead. "Of course."

"Anderson and I bunked up at a rooming house with two dozen other starving souls, writers mostly, in the Grub Street Slums," I explained.

Andy was medium height, average weight; passably good looking, dressed in inexpensive but tidy clothes. In other words, Anderson Wallace was most ordinary. Yet I knew he had a quick and devious mind that simply would not be held back by his hack writing.

I clapped him on the shoulder. "Everybody knows Anderson Wallace, or at least *of* him. Your pamphlet last month was a fine example of literary excrement. And I mean that as a compliment, of course. The segment on the Lord Mayor of Ripplekin? Did he really have his mistress tattooed *there*?"

Andy shrugged. "I believe so, but the truth is a small matter. You should have seen what he paid me for the things I held back." Then he reached below the collar of his shirt and withdrew a ruby ring on a chain. He tilted it to catch the light before dropping it back into its hiding place. He said, "And Leeds, I hear you are thieving my stories every time you open your mouth these days."

"It's a living."

"This is Monsieur Jean-Baptiste Villeneuve, creator of *Le Voyeur Royal.*" Penny introduced Andy's companion.

Villeneuve was a thin and pale wisp of a man, with a large nose and sad eyes, and he was as skittish as a feral kitten in a kennel of rabid bulldogs. He ducked at the sound of his name and glanced over his shoulder. "Not so loud, mon ami. Spies are all beside us."

"Jean-Baptiste is a libelliste, a libeler." Penny explained. Villeneuve handed me a pamphlet from a satchel at his feet. Since it was in friggin' French I couldn't read it with any authority, but got the gist. I had seen them before. It seemed like the French expatriates were pressing them out by the thousands and passing out English versions around St. James Square. Even we English got the giggles over those libels, as they called them. Whenever we thought our royals had sunk to new lows of inbred mischief, the Frenchies found a way to top them. The biggest difference, you know, is that the French take their scandals far too seriously. It's all political to them. What a waste of debauchery, I say.

"When it comes to skewering the court in Paris, *Le Voyeur* is unmatched," Penny tapped the cover of the pamphlet.

"And he's been making a bloody killing. Sales have never been better." Anderson said.

"'Tis so easy a thing with the king's new mistress du Barry leading Louis around with her finger up his nostril, no? She is...how do you say, "bitch" in your language?"

This stumped me for a moment. "Bitch, I believe." Oh, well, of course, that *is* our language.

"Bitch. Oui. That she is."

Anderson said, "Mon ami, Frenchie, here, and a dozen other frog-floggers are writing these scandals as fast as they can and slipping them past the censors across the pond. Why, I'd say they're selling better than pornography right now. Isn't that right, Frenchie?"

"You English dogs. You are so lucky to be free. You print what you like. Ta da, ta dum. The king? The court? Write what you want, no worries. Moi? The executioner waits for me at home." Then he smiled and held up a copy of his work. "Instead we send these, and that is the cause of much constipation among the Royals."

"Fine bit of scandalous reading. Jean-Baptiste is never short on material. God, if only III would be so kind to us here. Do you like that? It's starting to catch on. Not His Majesty, nor His Highness, nor King George. We just call him III. And I do wish he would go all French on us all and do something utterly nasty," Anderson said.

Penny ordered brandy. I ordered coffee. "Touch of the gin-flu," I admitted. They nodded in empathy. Hangovers are the price of fine journalism.

I wagged a finger at Anderson Wallace. "So, Anderson. Black-mail. Profitable as ever, eh?"

"You'd be amazed, even you, Leeds, at how much money one can make not from printing what one knows, but from not printing what one knows. More so since III and Queen

Monkey-face put their holier-than-God clamps on the court. No one wants to get on the King's list of shitters. But no one wants to stop fucking around, and my prices have quadrupled since I last saw you."

"I'm proud of you, I think."

"Scandals, Leeds. Scandals are where the money is to be made. The higher up in III's court, the better."

I contemplated the dark coffee in my cup. The bittersweet aroma was a cut well above the sludge they served at most places around Fleet Street. The good people of Westminster, especially those in the theatre district, knew how to crush their beans. And the water to brew it is less likely to kill you than what you'll find in the heart of London.

"Same old Anderson. No scruples whatsoever."

"Show me one man in the news business that has an ounce of moral fiber in his words and I'll show you a man as useful as a pickle in a fish pond."

We all agreed even one solid scruple could be an elusive target when the only target that really mattered was a sizable audience. "So I don't bother to even take aim at the bloody beast," Anderson added.

"So, Monsieur, you are to blame for this patter pittering I have seen?

"Who needs it? It is the same news I find in the newspapers only with interruptions. Je déteste. I hate that." Villeneuve's thin moustache twitched like a dying worm under his beak. "Oui, it is very most true. Though I must add, monsieur, I love your teeth.

So straight. You must give up to me your dentist, no? The mounte-banks of Paris should have your looks."

"I think you're as ugly as my sister's armpit," Anderson said. "But I see Frenchie's point about newspapers. Leeds, do you know how many people can read for themselves today?"

The Frenchman nodded. "Oui. Soon everybody does it."

"And when they do, why, I'll wager you, you'll be out of a job, my friend."

"Not if I do it well."

Mr. Penny banged his glass on the table. "That is precisely what I wanted to talk with you about, Mr. Merriweather. And my friends here agree. Monologue is a dying art form, whether it's news or the theatre. You could do so much more and I told you I can help."

"So what would you suggest?"

"What will you pay for that information?" Penny countered.

"Pay?"

"I told you I am a writer, and I am also a consultant."

"And entertainer's best friend," Anderson tossed in with a wink at Villeneuve.

Penny continued, "Along with my reviews of various theatre performances, I also consult with many of them on how to draw larger, more profitable crowds. I can do the same for your news, for the right price."

A news consultant? Bollocks that. "Give me an example."

Penny tapped the tobacco from his pipe, refilled the bowl, and took what felt like a month of Sundays to settle back with fresh smoke.

"You see, Merriweather, what makes the theatre so lively is the entire experience. It's storytelling for the eyes *and* ears. You have only your patter. The audience needs only ears. You, my boy, are wasting an opportunity and anyone with an ounce of skill in that area can give a news monologue." He cackled as if to make his point laughably obvious.

You try it, you pop-eyed hack. Dash that. Instead I said, "It's not easy to do well. If you had any experience in that you'd understand what I say."

"Granted. But then how is it that so many others have moved to compete with you? They must not find it that difficult."

I picked up and inspected the black knight from the now-forgotten chessboard. He had a point I wasn't ready to admit. I asked him if he had other ideas, but Penny refused to reveal more without some agreement on compensation. "I have already given away enough."

Yes, he had. Penny ignited in me thoughts that blended neatly into a plan of action that was becoming more solid with the clarity of brandy on my lips. "I believe I can do just fine without paying for your advice. After all I have managed to create this without consulting you or anyone. We shall survive just fine." I was sharp in tone and not willing to give the man a farthing for a fart.

"Now, Mr. Merriweather, I meant no disrespect. If you take the advice given here and advance your performance without me, you have my whole-hearted support. I look forward to it. In fact, I look forward to publishing a review of your venture."

Anderson laid a hand on my elbow. "That would be swell,

Leeds. You know a smashing review could absolutely set you heads above the rest. You'd be turning them away at the door."

Penny's gaze wandered across the coffee house. It was bright, although the cream colored walls were stained closer to brown from too many years of tobacco smoke between decent scrubbings. "I have been known to have some effect occasionally on the success of certain theatre productions with my reviews." Penny had a sly smile as he turned to me and watched that idea take root.

I set the chess piece back on the board. "For a price I assume?"

The pipe in his teeth nodded.

I looked at Anderson Wallace and then at Mr. Penny. "Why is it that suddenly feel like the subject of an Anderson Wallace article? This isn't blackmail, is it? I mean, what you're proposing really comes down to what you publish—or don't publish. Am I right?

No. No. Not at all they assured me.

"And if I decline your most generous offer?"

Anderson began rearranging pieces on the chessboard. He righted the knight I had set on its side like a toppled hero. "No sense getting testy, old boy," he said.

"Not at all, Monsieur," Villeneuve added. "We all agree this very evening that information, she comes in different packages—at a price. I believe you were most agreeable to this very thing."

"Mr. Merriweather, I want to help you. I want to be friends with you, and I believe we can both prosper in collusion, I mean cooperation, of course. Let me help you. If you hire me as your consultant, you will find my price reasonable and my advice invaluable. Not only can I advise on news performance, I can guarantee a series of glowing reviews that will spread your reputation from one corner of London to the other. It works here on Drury Lane; it will work on Fleet Street."

I remained hesitant and annoyed even though I could see certain benefits to a marriage of our talents. "I think there might be something to that. Let me consider it for a day or so."

Penny said, "Hmm. If you must. Though it seems so apparent that our way is the best way. Together, I believe we can make pattering magic."

Anderson was now closely inspecting the rook from his chess game. He held it out before his nose and then to his eye as if it were a spyglass. "Agreed. Leeds, I wouldn't hesitate too long. Even I can see the man has options."

"Options?"

"Well, yes," Penny said. "I wish you no ill, as I said. But my services might be well received by one of your competitors, and I would be compensated handsomely to raise their profile and crush you in the process. Don't take that personally. It's just the nature of the consulting business."

"Be smart, Leeds," Anderson said. His voice was rising. "Good reviews from Mr. Penny will send your stock soaring. But a bad review? Pbfldt! I say, have you heard about the play *Prometheus Rides a Pony* at the Haymarket theatre? It was there last month."

"No," I replied.

"My point exactly." Anderson pounded the table. "The play failed miserably after one day and only one article from Mr. Penny. That could happen to you."

"Plus certainement, most certain," Villeneuve said. Penny, my one-eyed expert in the newly created industry of news consulting—bloody rot, he was the entire industry—waggled his pipe up and down. It was three against one. They were full of zeal that curiously bordered on religious fervor. How could I have imagined that?

Theatre of the news? Consultants? I was not opposed, not entirely, mind you. But pattering is an art. It is the heart and soul of a master storyteller with a unique perspective on the world and the freedom to share it with his audience without being packaged at the whim of some consultant.

What really ruffled my wig, though, is that they demanded a commitment on my part immediately, so I resisted just out of spite. It was playful resistance at first, but seemed to throw a chill over what had been a fine evening. In my head I counted the revenue I might achieve with such a performance turn at the Shrew, and applied, against that, the sum that Mr. Penny suggested I pay for the privilege of his guidance. So when I questioned the viability of their proposition in the long run, they questioned my commitment to success. Anderson reminded me of the influence Mr. Penny wielded. Mr. Penny wondered aloud how anyone could doubt his success. Villeneuve went so far as to suggest, by doing so, that I was a heretic. A heretic? Good Lord. I will tell you straight out, that's the kind of stinging rebuke you'd expect from the bloody Spanish Inquisition. But then, nobody expects the Spanish Inquisition.

Chapter Nineteen

By Sunday morning the fears of competition fueled by too much gin and paranoia of Thursday had fully subsided, and I was fortified by the bitter medicine of advice served up by Mr. Roland Penny on Friday. I spent Saturday sampling various thoughts that simmered right through our news performance of which I have absolutely no recollection. Mrs. Fullbright told me it was one of the most eloquent patters she had heard in some time. Credit Mr. Penny, that one-eyed bastard, he had a point—up to a point, and perhaps I should have been more accommodating. But no, I had to get as defensive as the Earl of Suffolk at the siege of Orleans. And we all know how that turned out right? Right? Yeah, that little French wench Joan of Arc kicked his blooming arse.

So I set out Sunday morning intent on fully realizing the ideas that I had alternately conjured up, rejected, and resurrected since this whole adventure began. Now I was sure of my recipe for success to appeal to the broadest audience, the largest share of eyeballs and bums on the benches of the Tamed Shrew. First stop? London Bridge.

"A news actress, you say? Ha. Like, I am not falling for that old line again?" Veronica tugged at the long, loose strands of blond hair that splashed over her shoulder. "First it's, like, men want me to perform news for them, and that is so weak, then they won't stop until they get me in their bed? Oh no, I won't be fooled like that *again*. News actress? Total ha!"

"Beetle, I'm serious," I said. "And who ever asked you to be a news actress before? There aren't any others. We're inventing the job right now."

"Really? Oh then, in that case, like, I'll do it?"

"That's what I'm asking."

"No, that's, like, my answer?"

"What's your answer?"

"I'll do it?"

Frustrated. I said, "Why are you asking me?"

"I'm not asking? I'm telling you, right?"

One less dim than myself would think I'd have gotten used to Veronica's patter, ending every statement with a question mark. I had known her several years by then. She was "Little Beetlebug" to those of us who watched her mature on the streets selling sheet music and singing ballads in that rich, sugar-coated voice of hers. But when she wasn't performing you could put a blade through her heart and push her off a cliff, and her agonizing death scream would echo all the way to the bottom sounding like "Aaaaaaarh?" A question to the end.

"Beetlebug," I said as I took her hands in mine. "Don't say a word. Just nod your head. Yes or no?"

She nodded. Then she gently stroked her finger along my cheek. "You are like, so totally handsome, Mr. Merriweather. Would you dare to come back to my place and let me audition for you properly? I have a couch we could cast about on?"

Now that was quite a definitive question as ever I heard. I consulted the shiny new pocket watch I purchased that week. "Some other time." I told her to join us Monday morning at the Tavern to prepare for our first co-news performance.

Veronica went about her business on the north steps of the bridge. I stayed long enough to admire how she stopped the foot traffic with her melody. She sang *The Ballad of Queen Eleanor's Confession*, a tidy little song of royal snockering and betrayal that was a full fourteen broadsheets long.

She sold sheets for other, more manageable ballads to several in the group that had gathered, and a small book of songs to a middling lady in a workingwoman's cap. She took coins and made change while continuing to sing, never missing a beat or fumbling a line. Veronica owned mastery of the story and an ability to memorize the long ballads and sing them unfailingly through every form of distraction.

It didn't hurt that Veronica was quite striking, though her complexion was tainted by too many hours in the sun. That might have been a deficit on most women, but on Veronica it enhanced the soft gold color of her hair. She was not much more than a girl, but a substantially shaped one with pleasingly large hips and a sufficient bosom. But it was the ever-present twinkle in her eye and infectious laughter that closed the transaction for me. When she laughed, it was musical like the final uplifting note from one of her ballads.

News, weather and sports were to be the pedestals on which our news performance would be grounded, to be sure, like a three-act play. It occurred to me that every play worth a farthing has a strong female part. It would certainly jones the gentlemen and give women in the audience an excuse to get catty. They would so appreciate that. Well, then, I needed a co-presenter. But like an alchemist obsessed with finding a potion to turn lead into gold, I was certain it would take just the right mixture of ingredients necessary to create the perfect news mate.

This I knew: She had to be female. She had to be pretty. She need not be intelligent as long as she could project a measure of credibility about the topic at hand. She had to be equally comfortable immersed in the details of both blood and lust. They do make the world go 'round, I say. And speaking of lust, she had to stand before the audience and be inviting enough that a man might risk everything to bury his head up her skirt, while respectfully keeping his distance. And she had to be blond. In other words, she had to be Kate Jasper. Or as near to that ideal as I could draw from the streets of London. Beetle would fit the bill nicely.

With one member of our cast now neatly tucked in my pocket I set foot to chase down the second.

"I'll be a pig's liver before a January snow," Professor William Nye the weather guy swore. I tracked him through several leads

I got from costermongers as I searched about the streets. I found him in Westminster, near the Royal Stables, where he and Doppler camped on the edge of an open field.

Securing the services of Professor Nye had been on my list of items to do since not long after I encountered him, all energy and elbows and full of weather prognostication. It took a bit of doing to convince him to give news acting a try, for he said he had a life that was already full of activities to keep him busy on a given day.

"Chasing clouds from the sky is just part of it, Johnson," he told me. "Have you ever tried to count all the bees in a hive? Now that takes some doing." He began ducking and swatting buzzing insects that only he could see. I couldn't imagine how the number of bees in a hive could affect the weather, but then I had never encountered anything like Doppler the weather dog either. I passed off bee counts as one more of the professor's eccentric scientific methods and thought nothing more of it.

"Think of the wretched, uncovered heads you'll save from a downpour or brighten with sunny forecasts," I replied. "It seems a shame to keep all that useful information to yourself. Selfish, actually."

"Selfish, you say?"

I smiled. "No, not really. Everybody talks about the weather, but when you talk, people will do something about it."

"Say no more." He nodded his head. "Say no more."

I shook his hand, but the arrangement could not be completed until I also shook paws with Doppler. "He's all in as well," Professor

Nye said. "Whether it's hot or cold, we shall always weather the weather whether we like it or not, Johnson."

And so I had secured two-thirds of what I conceived to be the elements necessary to join me in creating a spectacle of theater, a true news performance to replace my one-man patter. News and now weather. But the idea of adding a sports figure to appeal to the growing class of tradesmen who had more time to follow the travails of local cricket and rugby teams, boxing, and the horses was a bit vexing. Ideally he would be a man who is, himself, accomplished and endowed with reputation in at least one sport that he would patter. A former athlete. My brain had taken a wild flight at one point mulling the odds that Thomas Waymark, England's most notable cricketer, might take up that role. A true celebrity. The man could sock the snot out of an ant and hurl a ball the way Zeus tossed lightning bolts. He retired from the sport and would have been an excellent choice if not for the fact he was spending his days in prison for gambling on games that he personally bribed players to set the outcome in advance. Flog the frog. That dashed my dreams of benefiting from his celebrity status on our stage.

It was nearing two o'clock. The morning fog had given way to skies full of wispy clouds that mixed with a week's worth of factory smoke. Combined, they were thick enough that the sun was a solid white spot in the grey sky, dabbed there at the point of some unseen painter's brush. So I walked along Piccadilly. I purchased some cheese, nuts and a bottle of wine from a cart along the road, paid my admission to Hyde Park, and settled down beneath a young oak tree on the edge of a meadow overlooking The Serpentine. I reviewed notes I had made to myself as I munched my lunch.

A boxer? Never met one who could string more than two decent sentences together without losing a tooth. A jockey? Too short. Cricket players were generally well educated but aloof. I was perplexed. I couldn't come up with the name of someone with knowledge and passion for the latest sports and the ability to patter with the ring of authority born of experience.

That is, until Lady Kate Jasper stepped up and answered the bell.

Chapter Twenty

Boatmen rowed lovers and families back and forth across The Serpentine's waters. Other folk shared their leisure in the meadow with me. Some watched the progress of a game of cricket. I was far enough from London's center now that patches of blue conquered the clouds, making it a fine afternoon for daydreaming. My compliments to Professor Nye. And Doppler.

At that point I was quite content to dismiss my worries for an hour or two until I heard a rustling over my shoulder. A properly dressed urchin was timidly rubbing his shoulder against the tree trunk. We stared at each other wondering who might break the silence first.

"Do I know you, lad?"

He shook his head.

"Do I need to know you?"

He shrugged. The boy traced a line in the bark while stealing glances at me. He was long limbed and rail thin and appeared to be about ten or so, about the age of your average chimney sweep without the nasty soot. I pried from him a name.

"Thomas."

"Grand to meet you Thomas."

"Come with me."

"Is that so, Thomas? Where?"

He pointed to a knoll in the corner of the meadow, not far to my right. A stand of trees guarded the knoll from behind. A picnic was in progress, and there stood my brother Lancaster beckoning me to join them. Thomas and I were almost upon them when a woman hidden behind a parasol turned as I approached. There could have been a hundred others in that party or none at all; I saw only Lady Kate Jasper.

"Leeds, you remember Sir Ian Jasper?" My brother clapped a hand on my shoulder and drew me into the crowd.

I nodded. "A tavern in the company of Ben Franklin. Of course, Sir Ian."

"And this is his charming wife, Lady Kate Jasper." I took her hand and kissed it gently, respectably, and if my heart were to give me away, with a good deal of lustful civility.

Sir Ian made no move to greet me. Instead he poured wine for one of the guests. "Merriweather, of course. I believe you already have made the acquaintance of my wife. Kate usually keeps better company than that."

Jasper let that stand for a half measure and then laughed. It was high pitched and annoying. He glanced around, encouraging the others to laugh along. He took the wine he had just poured for his friend, handed the glass to me and said, "But then, since that old sod brother of yours is one of my dearest friends, I am now convinced that her choice in associates is no better than my own—Merriweather-wise."

"This is my sister, Jillian, and her husband. And the children," Kate Jasper began a round of introductions to ease the tension created by Sir Jasper. I tried to greet each in the party with sincere pleasure, but, in truth, my mind had latched onto Kate Jasper and heard little else. I do remember two brothers, twins with a forgettable surname like Goodwin, Goodrich, Gadzooks or Gawdaffle. Kate Jasper introduced me to the fiancée of one of the Good-Gawd brothers and her female companion who appeared to be attached to none of the above. More than a dozen of London's finest upwardly mobile set had gathered there.

A tall, handsome man with a fine bearing stepped forward. "This is Mr. Bakerstreet," Lady Kate said. "My husband's business partner."

"Ah, another Merriweather. Welcome to our group." Bakerstreet had been the first to rise when I reached them. Now he shook my hand.

"A fine day, I must say." I offered the bottle of wine I had carried from my private picnic and found no takers. I placed it carefully with the label turned away next to a basket full of much finer and much more expensive French wines.

"You don't think those clouds look like rain?" Kate Jasper asked. The entire group turned to face where she pointed to a line of what could have been cauliflower floating above the horizon. Although they were tinged with grey, they seemed none too threatening.

Ian Jasper pooh-poohed her. "Now, now, my little dodo bird, must you always look for the storm behind every silver lining? Anyone can tell you those have not enough rain in them to wet a parched tongue."

Sir Ian said this with a smile just as he had with his previous verbal darts, and the undercurrent of contempt was obvious. Kate Jasper's right eye ticked ever so slightly.

I said, "Madam, I have absolute, irrefutable and otherwise convincing evidence to believe this glorious weather will stay with us."

"And how is that?"

"I have it on the authority of none other than Doppler the weather dog."

"Weather dog?" They all laughed.

I pointed in the general direction of Professor Nye. I could imagine the tip of his mobile cabin on the road jutting just above the tree line. I gave them a short and animated version of my first encounter with Professor Nye. "This tail-wagging oracle's record, I am told, of predicting changes in the weather is unerring."

Again they laughed politely. I caught an exchange of looks between Ian Jasper and his wife, which I read as "See? Even a damned dog is smarter." That silent exchange only worked to solidify my belief that this was one fool I was most certainly not going to tolerate any better than a toothache.

"A dog, you say?"

"That is something I would like to see."

"Yes, I'd pay to see that."

"Worth at least a pence or two."

"You will have that chance," I said. "Professor Nye has agreed to become a regular member of our news performance to provide weather predictions. You should visit us some time."

"Ah, so it's not all scandal and crime," Bakerstreet said. "It seems that is all that concerns the newspapers, and now these performances that are popping up all over London."

"Blood and lust, I say. But no, I have done quite a bit with politics for good measure. Parliament provides some of our most comic stories. Always good for a laugh."

My brother Lancaster sniffed. "I would argue that point, Leeds, if it wasn't so spot-on. You should see it from the benches. There is a reason the house debate is closed to the public."

Sir Ian looked less charitable. "Too often I find that those who are most foolish amongst our ranks are the twits quoted in the news most often. Shamelessly and namelessly of course. How does a newspaper get that information, I wonder. Treason, I say." And then he added, "Unless, of course I happen to agree with them."

"There is no better gossip than a politician with a motive to assassinate a rival, promote himself, or protect his hind part," my brother said.

"Sources," I suggested. "It's all about having good sources." I turned my head toward the cricket match playing out a hundred yards below us to avoid any temptation to steal a glance toward Lady Kate.

Someone asked about other elements of the news performance. "You provide current events and weather; would we find society news, news of the court if we attend a performance at the Tinned Screw?"

"Tamed Shrew," I corrected.

"I would very much like to have a wide appeal, covering topics of interest to all." I explained my current struggle to make sports a part of the program. "It takes a certain combination of experience and natural ability, like the best of those cricket players there."

"Why, that would be the Goodwill brothers," Lady Kate Jasper exclaimed. "Buck, you boys wrestled at Cambridge, if I'm not mistaken."

One of the twins nodded. "Barney boxed."

Bakerstreet offered that the young men had also championed the rowing team two years running.

The Goodwill brothers were strapping young men, though not that much younger than me. They poked at each other playfully, suggesting a competitive fire.

Lady Kate asked them to perform for my benefit a scene they had shared with the others before my arrival. "You really should see this," she told me.

With a proper amount of encouragement from everyone except Sir Ian they acquiesced. Sir Ian wandered to a tree where he sat against the trunk to watch from a distance. Was I paranoid? I was certain he spent more time watching me than the antics of the twins.

"I am Fancy Jack," one of the Goodwills waved. Then he punched his brother with a smack that hit more pride than flesh. His brother bounced lightly with his fists raised in a classic pugilistic pose. "And I am O'Malley. Come now, old man. Show your mettle."

They danced to and fro, circling each other and tossing fists with no real conviction. Goodwill number one use the flat of his palm to knock his brother's wig onto the ground.

"Merriweather," he said as he weaved to his left and then to the right, ducking under a punch. "Boxing. Now that is something worth reporting, wouldn't you say?"

"I am as game for a match as the next man."

"Will you be there this evening, then? Fancy Jack will make short work of The Irish Ape, I am certain of it." With that he gave his brother a true wallop, sending him to the seat of his pants.

"Uncle," Goodwill number two cried. Then he sat up. "And that is how Fancy Jack is going to beat O'Malley in Green Park tonight."

Our group applauded them. I asked them if they would report to the Tamed Shrew and describe the match just so during Monday's performance. "If you can replicate the bout as you just performed there, I say it would be a bruising success." My pun drew a round of chuckles, and the men agreed.

"You see? Your problem is solved," Lady Kate said.

"And you, Merriweather, the brother." Jasper pointed a finger at me. "A fine physical specimen such as yourself. Do you partake of contact sport? Surely you must race or grapple. Cricket? Now there's a sport. Do you play?"

Again I shook my head. "I am quite satisfied as a spectator."

"No stomach for competition, eh?"

"I find life, itself, is competition enough."

Lancaster said, "In truth, Leeds here is quite accomplished in many sports. He's just tweaking your thigh, Ian."

"No I'm not."

"Yes. Leeds was always the most athletic of us. Father made him so."

"Is that so?"

Lancaster described Father's effort to make a military man out of me with the hikes and horseback riding, wrestling, boxing and calisthenics. The mention of cold river baths in January still makes my bones ache.

"Leeds was to be father's legacy," Lancaster finished.

"So what happened?" Bakerstreet asked.

I paused more for effect than to actually formulate my answer. "I chose a different career path when father died."

"A common streetmonger? That's not a career path; that's a mere footbridge over the stink in the gutter," Jasper scoffed.

"At least it's an honest bridge," I returned. "Unlike the thieves in Parliament." And I made of show of batting my eyelids at Jasper with a dippy grin. Mock me? You dimwitted prat.

Jasper took a step forward, but I stopped him with a laugh that mimicked the one he used to prop up his own insults. "My word, Sir Ian. You are such an easy target. No wonder my brother is fond of you. Well, now you have two Merriweathers on your side. I hope that doesn't double the damage to your reputation."

The group laughed at this, and Jasper joined in, though there was menace in his eyes. "Well played, Merriweather. See? You do have a competitive streak after all."

With oohs and ahs the other men sensed that and flanked us as they might surround Fancy Jack and O'Malley in the ring. They jeered and jested and goaded us with suggestions of some good-natured test of skill to settle the matter.

"Since Mr. Merriweather the brother is fearful of physical contact, what do you propose?"

Bakerstreet took command of the situation at that point. "Right. Well, we brought pistols for some practice this afternoon. I would assume Merriweather the Legacy here was trained to shoot."

My brother Lancaster vouched for that. "He's quite good, actually."

"I have not handled a pistol since my younger days at Witt... ehr, at home."

But Lancaster stuck up for me. Damn him all. Shut your bleeding trap!

That settled, I found myself with a pistol in my hand, twenty paces from a target carved into the bark of a large oak. The women gathered in a semi-circle behind us while Bakerstreet and one of the brothers made sure there were no stray children or meandering couples in the area behind our target.

"Whatever shall we wager?" Jasper challenged all.

"A pound sterling."

"No, five pounds," someone said.

"No, ten sterling."

"What say you, Mr. Merriweather?"

I gulped. "Best make it only a single pound. I am but a poor patterer."

Jasper frowned as if I had offered him a snake. "A single pound?" He sighed. "So be it. If I've said it once I must have said it twice or more. It's not the size of your coin that matters, it's how you get it and where you put it. After you, Legacy."

The others set about wagering amongst themselves while I took aim. The pistol was finely balanced with a weighted ivory handle and an etched barrel. Father would approve.

Considering the years that had passed since I last exploded a pistol I was pleased to strike the circle on the tree. The shot kicked up bark several inches from its center.

"Good shot." It was, indeed. The women clapped. The men cheered. I took a bow.

Jasper took his position and angled his shoulder to the target. He used his left hand to cock the hammer with slow deliberation and then raised his right hand with the pistol. He took aim and then lowered the pistol.

"It hardly seems fair. It is such a good shot." Jasper's shoulders slumped as he turned toward us and looked down at the pistol in his hand. "Bakerstreet, have you the money to pay Mr. Merriweather for me? I don't believe I have lesser coins in my purse today."

Before Bakerstreet could reply, he said, "Well, perhaps that won't be a problem." He quickly raised the pistol again and fired his shot. The ball exploded in the tree trunk precisely halfway between my shot and the circle's center.

The women gasped. The men buzzed. And I died a thousand deaths.

"Well made, Ian."

"Most excellent. Fine marksmanship."

As I begrudgingly congratulated Jasper and counted out to him my hard-earned shillings, I was acutely aware that Jasper was not one to take lightly. He had the fire in his eyes of a man not to be denied anything. Anything.

I felt a hand on my shoulder. It was my brother. As if reading my mind he said in a low tone, "He's not one to trifle with, Leeds."

"I don't understand."

"I'm just saying..." Staring straight ahead, he gently turned so that I could see over his shoulder. Lady Kate Jasper stood several yards away sharing a parasol with her sister and chatting. But her eyes were on us. Lancaster took no particular notice. "I'm just saying..."

I declared that having been bested, it was the most opportune time to withdraw. Protests of my departure came from one and all out of respect but no conviction. I nodded to Ian Jasper one final time. "It was an exceptional shot, sir. I am quite impressed."

And then, with words that plunged like a knife in my heart someone behind me said, "And imagine how much better a shot he would have done if he used his natural hand."

Jasper raised the glass in his hand. His *left* hand to be sure, not the right hand he had fired with. He smiled like a patronizing piss ant and shrugged, "Fucking shucks. 'Twas nothing, really."

I will tell you that in this world some men are triflers and some are triflees. I don't need to say which one I had been made that day. Bollocks on a bulldog! I'd been poodled.

Chapter Twenty-One

"What in the name of sweet Jesus are you doing? It is not a question, my dear, it is a fact." Mr. Roland J. Penny wagged his finger at Veronica.

"But that was, like, you know, the facts? I mean, yeah, it's what I said, okay?

I walked in on a tempest when I returned from my rounds loaded down with the Monday morning newspapers. My new news consultant stood there raising his voice in frustration at my new news co-actor. It was an inauspicious start for Team Merriweather.

"Mr. Merriweather, do you understand this child?"

"Of course."

"Look at me, Miss Veronica. Now say it again."

"Society's most awesome courtesan is at it again? Kitty Fisher created another made-for public scandal in St. James Park when she, totally bared her unmentionable parts before a sizable crowd?

She..."

"No. No. No." Penny nearly spit out his pipe. "Kitty Fisher is at it again. Full stop. There was a sizable crowd. Full stop. Those are statements; don't make them sound like a question. In what foreign land do you grow up to hang a bleeding question mark on every sentence?"

Veronica did a fabulous job pouting. With a quivering lower lip, she toed the edge of the stage. Only Penny's hard heart could fail to melt. "Up near Hereford, sir, in the Valley Wye?"

"Why? I'll tell you why. Because I just can't imagine..."

I stopped Penny there. "Trust me, Mr. Penny, that is a conversation that will only noodle your brain. You'll never win. Veronica, just nod your head dear. You were raised in the Wye Valley, correct?"

She nodded sweetly.

"See, Mr. Penny. It's Wye, not why? And why that matters I can't fathom."

"Because she may be only a woman, but she must still project some authority if she is to patter the news. What were you thinking when you hired this empty-headed piece of work for us?" He snatched a broadsheet from Veronica's hand and shook it at me.

"Us? I don't remember us being an "us" when I made that decision. And Veronica is not only a woman. She has 'It'."

"What is 'It'?" he asked.

I still hadn't quite figured that out. "You'll have to ask Doctor Franklin for that one, Mr. Penny."

Penny swiveled his head and glanced at the ceiling. "What is that I hear? Surely it must be the wind." Then he stepped up next to Veronica, brushed her hair from the side of her face and leaned in like a surveyor lining up his one eye to her ear. "Ah, yes, here is where the draft is coming from. And, ho, I can see Aloysius on the other side through the valley between her ears. Hello, Aloysius."

Veronica spun away as Penny waved to A.P. on the far side of the stage. Penny held his pose as A.P., who was hidden to Penny's sight before Veronica moved off, returned the wave.

"I've been giving that considerable thought," I said. "Let me show you."

First, I asked Beetle to sing one of her ballads.

"Perfect," I said. No questions asked. Then I picked up the *Daily Advertiser* and instructed her to read a story about our most infamous courtesan Kitty Fisher. It seems she had drawn a large crowd to watch her ride her horse at St. James Park Sunday and took a tumble. Speculation was the "accident" was quite contrived, for she wasn't hurt.

"But as with all things Kitty-esque, it was a shocking affair." Full stop. Veronica read it with a twinkle in her eye and no question on her lips. "The lady's skirt turned up to her head as she landed on the ground in plain view before the assembled crowd, revealing to one and all that she wore no under garments." She finished with a full stop.

Veronica delivered the article with authority and relish that would have made the author himself stand up and cheer. And not a question in the performance.

"Can I add that it was a Lady Godiva moment for the celebrity tramp?"

Now that was a good question. "A dash of your own fine wit, Beetle. I don't see why not," I replied.

Penny turned to me and moved his pipe from one side of his mouth to the other while audibly sucking the smoke. "Remarkable. She patters quite well when she has the words memorized or written for her. She reads well. But every thought of her own, every extemporaneous bit of babble, comes out like a bloody inquisition. What do you intend to do? Surely, you don't expect to have her stand there and read the news account from the paper?"

I told Penny about my plan to manipulate Veronica's talent. "We simply need to prompt her."

"Prompt her?"

"Exactly."

I called to A.P. and told him to fetch some poster boards I had left near the back of the Tamed Shrew. I took the *Advertiser* from Veronica and made several notations in the margin next to the Naked Kitty account to shorten and sharpen the story.

"Beetlebug, I want you to write this story down with these changes. Make a few of your own, I adore that "tramp" line you suggested." I then instructed her to use large print on a series of poster boards. She got right to it, pausing only to stick her tongue out at our news consultant as she passed him.

"You see, Mr. Penny, our problem is solved. We will prompt her with those cards by having Mrs. Fullbright's boy hold them at the foot of the stage. Veronica only needs to read what she's written, just as she pattered the story straight from the newspaper."

"And this boy with the poster cards?"

"The prompter?"

"Yes. Is he so reliable that we needn't fear subjecting our audience to Miss Veronica unleashed if he fails?"

"I give you my word as a scoundrel and a rogue. It will work."

"Ingenious."

With that, Mr. Penny moved to a table at the far side of the tavern where Professor Nye the weather guy, Doppler, and an artist were creating maps full of smiling suns and menacing thunderbolts.

The Goodwill brothers were playfully knocking about on a corner of the platform. I gave them a few suggestions on how I wanted to see them recreate Fancy Jack's appalling and unexpected defeat at the hands of O'Malley.

"Ten pounds, that one cost me," Buck moped. Or maybe he was Barney. I hadn't yet gotten the two properly identified in my head.

"Good, then. You take on the role of Fancy Jack." And we discussed two other items of sporting interest for the news performance.

I found Mrs. Fullbright and A.P. sharing a pot of tea in the kitchen. A.P. was reading aloud to her the morning *Chronicle*.

"Well, we certainly have Miss Kitty to thank for a nifty story tonight," I said as I joined them at the table. Mrs. Fullbright poured a cup for me and rolled her eyes.

"Love, when can we pick up a newspaper and not see her splayed across the pages of one tattler or another? Believe you me, that woman is famous just for being famous. What has she done to get so much attention, I ask of you?"

"Well, she did work her way up the ladder of married nobility from earls to dukes and back again."

"And made a spectacle of herself and them men's wives in the process."

"Ah, God love the little tart. The public loves to hear about her, and as long as they love her, I'll patter about her all day long. Now what else will we be on about tonight?"

A.P. laid down his newspaper with a poo-eating grin. He said nothing.

"Well, something else there to report?" I asked and pointed at the *Chronicle*.

He shook his head and just went about grinning.

"All right. Out with it, you muppet. What is it that has you so cocked up?"

"Miss Beatrice Post."

"The barrister's daughter they caught sneaking out of Draper's hat shop with a bonnet under her skirt? One she didn't pay for?"

A.P. nodded and then pulled two beautiful gold guineas from a pocket. "She's pleading her belly next week."

"Ape, you seed spewing fountain of luck. How many visits did it take you?"

"Just two. Her father was willing to pay for more if necessary."

"Better to have your daughter disgraced with a bastard child than to hang for theft, I imagine," Mrs. Fullbright said.

It seemed reasonable that English justice could hang a woman for petty theft but consider it inhumane to keep one in prison when she was heavy with child. And that had spawned an industry of which A.P. took advantage. He was living proof that for all the effort to keep the women separated from the general populace, a minor bribe could arrange a conjugal visit. The offspring of a well-timed poke in prison would guarantee a get-out-of-jail-free card.

"Well done, Ape. This is what, number three now?"

"The midwives confirmed it last week. She'll get her pardon in a few days."

"You're getting quite the reputation, Love. Stay away from my daughter or I'll grind you into my next meat pie," Anna warned him.

A.P. admired the coins. "If you change your mind, Mum, I can be had for a price." That was quite obvious.

I said, "I daresay you'll never get rich being paid on contingency, but if this keeps up you may choose a professional life of paternity over the news business." With three victories under his belt, it appeared that when it came to rescuing maidens from prison, if the family was willing to pay, my young friend was money in the bank and sperm in the…well, you could bloody well bank that, too.

"That gives us two stories for tonight. Maybe three." I tapped the upside page of the newspaper. It screamed about a collision of foot carriages on Westminster Bridge that sent one carriage over the edge and into The River Thames, killing the young boy inside who was riding home from school. A.P. raised his hand like a student in class.

"Tragic death."

"Very good, Ape. What did Mr. Penny tell us? Every death is a tragic death. No other word will suffice." Penny had advised us that even the timely death of an ancient family patron or untimely death of a gin-abusing guttersnipe should be described as tragic. All death is tragic for the sake of the audience, he instructed. Though my personal preference was horrific, or possibly, anguish-inducing calamity of death. But then, I get a bit wordy when motivated by blood. And lust. In the case of the lad who splashed to his death in the river you could double the emotion with another of Penny's thoughts.

"Every parent's nightmare," Mrs. Fullbright offered lesson number two without prompting.

Right. Couldn't have a story of harmed children without that phrase, now can we? Until Mr. Penny came around to school us on the proper formula for a news report, it never occurred to me that stories would be better with clichés of tragic death that would be every parent's nightmare. Who knew? I thought that was just poor writing.

"I never dream of my children in a foot coach. And I'm a parent three times over." Anna said. "No, that's for the rich. Give me being tied to a stake and chomped apart by a pack of snarling hyenas. That's a real nightmare, Love."

"And for Kitty Fisher, it would be torn apart by hyenas whilst inexplicably wearing last year's fashions."

I suggested they conjure up three or four more news items for the evening performance. "After all, Mr. Penny says we must keep our stories short and more numerous. We must keep our audience engaged." Penny the news consultant introduced me to a chart he created that timed the length of scenes in your average play.

"Audiences simply don't have the length of attention they used to. Sad that, really." Penny had explained that he had made quite a study of the matter and found that the average audience length of attention was drastically reduced to a mere three minutes these days. Not like the old days when you could patter up a storm just warming up the crowd. No sir. "If you don't hook them immediately, in that first three minutes, why you've lost them for the entire story. They'll be up and off for another drink or slipping out back for a piss before you know it."

I challenged him with my belief that proper execution might outweigh his rule, but he countered with a fistful of charts and graphs and reports of scientific study. With what I was paying for his expertise, little be it for me to contradict the consultant. I would give it a try. We were, after all, improvising as we went along to create this new form of news entertainment. I had my own thoughts on improving our news performance. One of my best was under thunderous attack when I returned to main room.

"You've made the vagina much too large, you fool!"

Chapter Twenty-Two

Mr. Penny leaned heavily on a poster he trapped on top of a table near the stage and slashed at it with all his might, using a lump of artist's charcoal to deface the offending drawing. The artist, an angular fellow with thin bones and thick glasses, grabbed at Mr. Penny's arm but failed to stop him.

"Do you want to get us arrested for smut-mongering?"

"What is the problem, Andrew?" I asked.

Andrew Worall was a street sketcher of fine repute. He dabbled in paint when he had the time, but spent most of his days working in pencil and charcoal, sketching caricatures for shillings. I hired him to create illustrations for our news stories. He had the fastest pencil on The Strand. More importantly, he was cheap.

He wrestled the poster away from Mr. Penny and held it to his chest like a wounded child. Then he turned the drawing to me.

"This is Kitty Fisher when she fell from her horse."

I admit I was quite taken by the amount of detail Andrew captured on paper, based only on the account he had read in the newspaper and the mental image it created in his mind. Even through the scratches Mr. Penny inflicted on the work, Andrew's perspective, from the crowd's point of reference looking up the lady's skirt, as they were, was remarkable.

"So, she really does have a tattoo of a beehive way up there on her thigh, huh?" A.P. wedged his face between Mr. Penny and myself. I swatted him on the nose with the back of my hand. "Yes sir. Some honey pot that," he said.

"Andrew," I said. "Since you will need to draw the scene again perhaps a bit more, uhm, distance from the subject matter is in order. And possibly you might consider a slightly different body position to conceal…well, let's just leave a bit to the imagination of the audience, shall we?"

"Pornography is what that is," Mr. Penny said. "He'll have us all arrested with that one." He shook the stem of his pipe at the artist.

Andrew's face flushed. "But this is really what the story is all about. This is realism. Don't you prats understand anything about art?" He cradled the drawing to his breast again. I thought he might cry.

I pulled Mr. Penny to the side and said in a soft voice, "Work with him, but be kind, Mr. Penny. He's an artist, remember, and you know how they are."

He grumbled. "Artists. Actors. You're all barmy. I don't know why I put up with it."

I swept my palm across the scene. "You put up with it because I'm paying you to turn all this into something that will keep them coming back for more."

At that moment the Goodwill brothers were in one corner tossing little people, trying to determine which of them could fling a midget farthest across the room for their report on a dwarf-chucking competition. Professor Nye was trying to placate Doppler the weather dog who was barking up a storm—literally. Veronica had a mirror in one hand and applied makeup while scribbling changes to her prompts that she posted on the far wall. Andrew sat with his head against the tabletop, wailing over the death of his creative effort.

"Monsieur Patterer." I turned and our favorite libelliste, Jean-Baptiste Villeneuve burst through the door. He waved a pamphlet at me as he crossed the room.

"What have you there, Monsieur Villeneuve?"

Villeneuve slapped a palm upon his pamphlet, *Le Voyeur Royal*, so fresh I would swear I could smell the new ink on it. He said, "Something most scandalous for your pitter. You will appreciate, no?"

I must say I was relieved to find it in proper English, a version I am certain our French friend printed specifically for the audience around St. James. But the scandal appeared quite mundane by the froggies' standards. Louis XV seemed to be torn in choosing which of his three mistresses he would trump privately after a long evening of cards. So he simply decided that a full house was the winning hand and went to bed with all three.

"For you, mon ami, only shillings six."

I shook my head. "No, my friend. I see little here that warrants much more than a minute of attention. And while I agree it is quite salacious, I doubt our audience will give it more than a passing thought. One shilling's worth at best."

Villeneuve snatched the pamphlet and licked his ink-stained thumb. He rolled his narrow black eyes and turned the page. He sidled up to me and directed my attention to one short, incendiary paragraph.

"Did he say that, truly?" I asked.

"The libelliste shrugged. "It is reported in more than one correspondence from Paris. If it is not true, it should be. Is there a difference?"

I handed it to Mr. Penny. "It seems his Royal French Royalness doesn't think much of our Queen Charlotte."

Indeed, he had hurled quite the insult on her beauty, or lack thereof. Reportedly, on his way to the boudoir with the three French tarts on his arms and their husbands trailing behind like befuddled hounds cut from pack, Louis XV remarked on *our* monarch's inability to attract anything better than Queen Charlotte.

"So he called her Queen Monkey-Face?"

"That just ain't right. It ain't proper, no sir." It was A.P. who piped up with that one. "I say it's an insult to all of us. Maybe she is, maybe she ain't. I'm just saying nobody but a proper Englishman should be allowed to call her that."

"But you see, little pitter-patterer, you *do* call her such. For it is, most certainly, how we French have come to understand. It is how we hear you. And, frankly, I must say in our defense it is obvious your king's taste in women is, generally, no better than your food. It is fact most certain."

"Well, if anyone is going to insult our queen, it's for us to do it. Not some frog-flogging French arse."

A.P. attempted a swing at Villeneuve's beak and missed by a nose. I stepped between them. "Three shillings, Frenchie." The anger he ignited in A.P. seemed easy to spark our crowd with. This could play well.

Villeneuve hesitated.

"Perhaps, I may interject?" Mr. Penny said. "What if we were to offer Jean-Baptiste, here, the role of foreign correspondent and report this in person as part of the news performance. We might add a shilling for that."

"Foreign correspondent?"

"He is French, after all. Nothing more foreign than that. Imagine it. News reported from around the world."

I was not as certain as Mr. Penny of the idea's merit, but it would provide one more bit of content, and with a certain flair. That is if the audience, likely to be insulted itself, doesn't rise up and flog the poor frog on the spot just for being French.

"Moi? Upon your stage? There?" Villeneuve pointed. He hesitated. I could see in his eyes he was intrigued yet wary, torn between two mistresses. His nervousness returned. "But spies, Monsieur Patterer. I should not expose myself such." He shook his head but then gazed longingly at the stage.

I said, "Monsieur Villeneuve, you have acquired such acclaimed recognition for your work since you have come to London, you are already a célébrité. Imagine how much more of an impact you can have upon the stage, and your célébrité shall be the shield that protects you."

I patted Mr. Penny on the back and picked up my hat. "Mr. Penny, you negotiate the details. This is your area. I'm going off now. I believe I know where I can find a witness or two to Miss Kitty's unfortunate display." I thought for a moment, and then I grabbed one of Andrew's paintbrushes sitting in a pot of black. I stroked a wide swath of paint across the drawing of Kitty Fisher, leaving plenty of thigh but not much else visible in that region. That was risqué enough. I picked it up and said, "I'll patter a few stops with this to promote tonight's performance. We should fill the tavern."

As I paused at the door and looked back, from the flying dwarf landing with a profanity-laced thump in the corner, to the sketch artist crying at his table, I could only come up with one way to describe what saw there: Bloody fucking barmy. This was supposed to be easy. This was supposed to be cheap. But as I was now sharing profits from the newscasting with Mr. Penny and the rest of this cast of characters, my expenses were growing. And that made filling the seats more critical than ever.

That evening Saint Kitty of Debauchery turned the trick for us unlike anything before. And Kitty was known to turn a trick or two for the gentlemen of note who facilitated her meteoric rise to celebrity in London. Veronica stayed perfectly on script as she read of Kitty Fisher's Lady Godiva moment. Mrs. Fullbright's son Aaron was perfect as he squatted at the foot of the platform and shuffled through the cards to prompt her. Andrew Worall stood behind Veronica and held a much more discreet illustration of the infamous fall where the audience could see it over our news actress' left shoulder. As she continued to read, dividing her attention from Aaron the prompter to the audience with the smooth grace of a ballerina, Andrew held up a second poster over her shoulder—a drawing of a horse with the bold inscription "Tosser." When he flipped the poster, the backside displayed a caricature of Kitty Fisher's face wearing a devil's smile and the caption "Tossed!"

When Veronica read of Lord Robert Duke of Blingwood—Kitty's current patron—Andrew held a poster of just the horse's arse with the caption "Duke." The joke was such a success that Veronica paused reading and strutted across the front of the stage, hands spread, encouraging more laughter and shouting. One drunk in the crowd misinterpreted that gesture as his cue to join her on the stage. Fortunately, A.P. got between him and the news actress and steered him back to his seat.

As it turned out, we had blood a-plenty that evening. Two murders, a slum fire and the foot coach accident that turned into every parent's nightmare. In addition, just before we began our newscasting I got word that the Bow Street Runners had tracked down and killed a mugger.

"This just in," I cried out as I took the stage after our first commercial break. I made up the story on the spot with the fragments of information I gleaned from a couple of the bounty hunters who had stopped in for a gin after taking part in dispatching the Mercy Lane Mugger. While I pattered, A.P. crawled along the foot of the platform with a hastily drawn sign: 'Breaking News.' And then he crawled back in the opposite direction just in case anyone in the audience couldn't appreciate the immediacy of our report.

"I think that sums it up quite nicely, don't you, Mr. Merriweather?" Mr. Penny joined me near the kitchen door after I turned the stage over to Professor Nye. I watched the professor sell the audience on a sixty percent chance of rain for the following day. He supported his case with maps painted with bright circles and arrows, and perky suns peeping over the tops of clouds. He smacked the maps with a willow switch to emphasize his points.

"I said, this sums it up," Mr. Penny repeated. He handed me a sheet of paper. He finished his review of our newscasting before the performance began and would have it in the hands of publishers at three different newspapers in the morning.

I glanced at Mr. Penny's report. "A brand new form of news, emphasizing visual displays of the day's most engaging stories. It's a brilliant marriage of theatre and news that is one of a kind and certainly not to be missed." While not mentioning his own role, it was clear from the examples he cited that Mr. Penny was quite taken by the contributions he made to the performance. I dropped a gold piece in his palm. He never mentioned to the publishers that he was being paid handsomely for those words of praise. Although on a cost-per-word basis, I think I got my money's worth.

"This will bring them in—in droves," he smiled.

I smiled too, later that evening, long after the performance had ended. I leaned back in my chair against a wall, my feet propped up on the table in front of me. It was a late hour for the tradesmen, but not too late for at least one more round. The tavern was still half full, and I couldn't be more pleased with the evening's profits.

Mrs. Fullbright joined me at the table, bearing a most beautiful bottle of Portuguese Madeira and two glasses. "I have been saving this one for the proper time."

"I believe the time is right."

We sat there in contented silence. I motioned to Mrs. Fullbright's daughter Andrea, and told her to pour gin for Charlie and Pepper, the two Bow Street Runners who had given me the story of the Mercy Lane Mugger. In due course they joined us.

"Ya dun us right proud," Charlie said. He was a smallish man about fifty. A former sailor, Charlie was fit enough for a man his age that only a fool would fool with him.

"Yep. A good tale it was," Pepper added. Pepper was much younger, tall and lean with long, bony fingers that suggested he prospered as a pickpocket in his youth. "A shame the fellow got shived when we tried to pinch him."

"Yep, indeed," Charlie nodded. "Cost us, that did. We'd be a few more shilling to the richer iffn we brought him in with a bit of breath left in him."

I was feeling generous. We had a good night so I pushed two shillings a-piece across the table at them. "It was better for us that he got what he had coming. Makes a better patter. I thank ye for the tip, boys." I poured more wine. "Anna, suppose we could provide one last nip for our friends here before we call it a night?"

As the bounty hunters watched Anna retreat to fetch a bottle of gin, Pepper turned back to me, leaned into the table and whispered, "D'ya always pay so handsomely as this?"

"What? For news? If it's good enough."

"Well, me and Pepper, we can keep you full up. We've got a million stories in this city."

"Yes, well, I will listen. But to be fair, there are a million thief-takers like you out there, now isn't there. Sort of a buyer's market, I say. So what you bring me has to be fresh, and it has to be special. And it really must be something exclusive, something that no one else can have but us until we can beat that horse to death."

Charlie and Pepper mulled that idea while Anna poured them another round of gin. Pepper scratched the three-day stubble on his chin. "Special, you say? You mean like a secret?"

Charlie slapped Pepper, gave him a dark look, and then turned an imaginary key in his lips.

"You have a secret, Pepper?" Pepper nodded yes. Charlie shook his head no. I looked from one face to the other. "I don't know who to believe. You boys really should come to some sort of agreement."

I asked Mrs. Fullbright what she thought. "Most definitely." She swatted my hand as I reached under the table and into the pocket of her apron where I knew she stashed the tavern's portion of the evening profits. Then she relented and passed four coins into my palm. I placed them on the table between the bounty hunters and me, considered them for a moment, and then pulled them back and placed them in my pocket.

"No, I wouldn't ask you to betray a trust for any amount of money. I can see you gentlemen are men of integrity."

"But, my loves, if you get it in your heads to change your mind…" Anna added.

What a show it was to see their eyes brighten with hunger when the coins were on the table only to have their faces fall faster than a prisoner through the gallows' trap door.

"The molly houses are going down," Pepper said under his breath. He glanced over his shoulder as if expecting spies to pop out from under the tables. He shushed me with a finger to his lips.

"When?"

"Friday night. Me and Pepper and a few of the other runners have been hired to do a spot of moral cleanup," Charlie said. "But we ain't talking about it 'cuz if word gets out, they won't be nobody to pinch."

So The Societies for the Reformation of Manners was staging for war on the homosexuals beyond the usual complaints from the tradesmen and the public sniping that was growing to a fever pitch in the business districts. "They must be serious if they're paying the bounty hunters to help."

"Th' man, head of the R-and-Mers says they wants at least two raids, and they're paying right good for every head we collect. They wants us on hand Friday evening because it's some kind of homo holiday. Festival of the Jolly Molly, I think."

Oh the drama. The depravity. The jaw-dropping details we could add to appeal to our smut-starved audience. The sponsors should pay us double for such titillating exclusive news as this.

"And nobody outside you thief-takers and the R-and-Mers know?" I asked as I slid a single shilling in their direction." I knew it was a story that would boil the blood of our kind of audience. They nodded. I increased it to two shillings. "Let's call this an advance, then. And more if you make sure my little friend over there—his name is A.P.—make sure he is with you when you go. What time do you think it will happen on Friday?"

Charlie and Pepper exchanged a glance and grinned.

"Sir, what time would you like?"

Chapter Twenty-Three

By the time The Societies for Reformation of Manners sprung its raid on Mother Clap's Coffee House Friday night our newscasting team could barely contain itself. A.P. and I had crisscrossed the parish for a very good part of the day, running from one street corner to the next to promote "special reports of depravity" without tipping our knowledge of what was to actually take place that evening. The tavern filled early; several familiar evil faces I recognized as scouts from our rival news taverns and two newspapers tried to blend in. I pretended not to notice. Bloody hell, if they thought hades is miserable, they were about to find out what it is like to be burned by a hot story like this.

"They will use what they learn here tonight for their news tomorrow." Anna Fullbright leaned over the bar. Her voice was almost lost in the buzz of pre-performance crowd.

"So? That's as it should be. Let them follow our lead; we'll be yet another step ahead with our reporting tomorrow night."

"If."

I nodded a bit nervously. Yes, if the R-and-Mers follow through and create the scene I anticipated. If they raid at the pre-arranged hour. And if A.P. comes through and arrives with an exclusive account in time.

"Let us interrupt this performance for an important announcement," Ape shouted as he burst through the door a little less than an hour later. His timing was perfect. I was in mid-patter, delivering an account of a thief-taker who miraculously survived (Mr. Penny says all survivals must be "miraculous") the severe whipping he received after a case of mistaken identity. It seems the scoundrel he arrested, and hauled through the streets amid jeers and a hail of stones from spectators on his way to the magistrate, was none other than the warrant-issuing magistrate himself.

A.P. shouted from the doorway, "Public lust of the most lewd kind. Riots and suicidal blood flowing in the streets." He bounded to the stage followed by Veronica who towed a tradesman so round he practically rolled to the front of the tavern. The tradesman had a red, bulbous nose with dark blue veins, a belly that spilled over the waistband of his breeches and an attitude of self-righteousness that comes from having never been wrong about anything.

His name was Thurgood. Thurgood was a deputy general of The Societies for Reformation of Morals. He gave his own colorful testimony to support A.P.'s description of how patrons of Mother Clap's bailed from the windows and doors like rats deserting a sinking ship when the reformers burst through the door. All Veronica had to do was ask questions to interview the fellow.

A.P. declared the doorkeeper managed to slash one of the invading parties before being subdued. One patron, an aide to a minor duke, took a knife to his own throat rather than be found alive associating with the mollies at Mother Clap's.

"Is that, like true?" Veronica asked.

"Yes ma'am."

She turned to the audience with wide eyes and paused a beat as if making a transition from the chorus of a ballad to the next verse. "And was he with his employer the duke engaged in despicable acts there? Who is this duke?"

"We don't rightly know. Not yet, leastwise. There was a man who escaped our grasp in that very private room at the coffee house, so distracted were our troops by the bloody corpse blocking the doorway."

Yes, blood and lust. Could it get any better? Indeed it could. The catch of the evening was the arrest of Charles Derby, the bear wrestler. Derby was known far and wide across London as Britain's foremost bear-baiter. Nearly as hairy and every bit as savage as the animals, he was a crowd pleaser at Green Park each Sunday. Andrew, our quick-draw street artist, captured the arrest of Charles the bear wrestler quite nicely and held it high for the audience. That provoked such a wonderful barrage of jeers, cheers and jovial thunder that I nearly cried. Celebrity in chains. No, it couldn't get any better.

With so much advance warning before the Friday night news-casting, I had hired several scouts to follow the pack of reformers as they knocked down the door of two more locations suspected of harboring homosexual activities. It paid handsomely for our news performance on Saturday night by providing additional sordid details and witness accounts of the night's mayhem, including an interview with one of the R-and-Mers' informants who had spent the evening inside Mother Clap's. He answered Veronica's questions while wearing a mask to protect his identity. As an added precaution he stood in the shadows, a silhouette at the rear of the stage. Though he claimed not to be homosexually bent himself, the growing number of violent attacks upon the poof community in the past year made even talking to known buggers a capital offense for vigilantes who had taken up roaming the streets spoiling for a molly to "reform." The man gave the audience a first-hand account of the debauchery going on inside that was so explicit, the crowd jumped up and nearly formed a lynching mob on the spot.

Exclusive. First. Best. We were the envy of every news patterer and printer in London that weekend and beyond. By Monday I salivated over details of the raids in the morning newspapers, details that could have come only from our newscasting. They quoted witnesses in verbatim accounts of the testimony given on our stage. Two mentioned the Tamed Shrew as their source, most ignored giving credit where credit was due, as if they were enterprising enough to be on the scene of the raids.

"Respect," I told Mrs. Fullbright as she poured the morning tea. "It's amazing how quickly we have become their equal. Though I do wish these rags…" I tossed a handful of publications into one pile, separating them from the "likes." "I wish these had at least given mention to us as the source of their information."

"Leeds, it's not as if you haven't done that very same thing to them, eh?"

"Only for inspiration, my dear. Only for inspiration."

"Odd, duck. It didn't sound that way to my ear."

"Ah, well, payback is indeed a bitch, I say."

Anna put her fists on her hips and rained down her most stern look upon me. "Speaking of that, I expect you to make the final rent payment in full. You *are* still planning to move your things out tomorrow? My accountant Mr. Ledgerhammer says we are doing well enough that you can afford a place of your own."

"Since when did you acquire an accountant?"

"Since we started doing well enough. Since you've been daw-dling in your rent payments. Since you started seeing that anony-mous harlot of yours." She sighed. "Just the usual, y' know."

She drew little circles on the table. I took her hand and patted it. "With all my heart, I appreciate you, Mrs. Fullbright, and I shall miss your bed."

She brightened and waved a finger at the tavern walls. "Well, at least we still got all this, Mr. Merriweather, you and me. You have created something here, for sure. I don't claim to understand it rightly, but it sure is a sight to see the tables full at night."

I pointed to the far wall that the tavern shared with the laun-dress' flat next door. "Say, old girl, if this keeps up, we'll need more space to expand and make room for even more customers. Don't suppose the old hag would be willing to make room for us."

Old Mrs. Campbell had been living with one foot in the grave for nearly a decade, to hear her complain about it. She could die any day but lived on, mostly to aggravate her children who saw inheriting the half of that building she owned as their quickest route to retirement. Mrs. Campbell lived off the rented rooms upstairs and the slow but steady income of taking in laundry from a storefront below.

"Knock down that wall, and we could increase the number of heads for our newscasting."

"Hmmm. I'd have to hire on another or two. Would your sponsors pay more? It seems you have them quite tied up now."

I told Anna I had been giving that some thought, though it still seemed as distant as a ship on the horizon. I smiled. "More to come; stay with us."

Chapter Twenty-Four

It was a very good week. A marvelous week. A week made for a minor god or a major mortal. The weather was perfect, though Doppler the weather mutt suffered from some tropical depression with so much sunshine and not so much as a cloud to bark about. Even Mrs. Fullbright's food tasted better.

Tuesday I found myself a quaint little flat just right for a bachelor. An unruly mob, incited by our reports, was kind enough to burn down a suspected molly house in a ne'er-well-to-do neighborhood on Oxford Street in time for Wednesday's newscasting. And the Lord Mayor promised public whippings of the guilty—that is, the sodomites responsible for causing such behavior. Indeed, not a day went by when someone wasn't on display in the pillory for real or imagined crimes against morality. Anti-sodomitism spread over the summer and ran so hot you'd think a stroll down The Strand was like walking on a river of lava.

Growing unrest in America? Blame the homosexuals. Poor economy at home? Blame them for that as well. Even the weather and Abercrombie-Cross' upset loss in a critical cricket match were all blamed on that community of morals-busting, unsavory characters. Buggering was still mostly a capital offense, but while juries were quick to convict, they were lenient with the death penalty when a good whipping could do just as well.

The R-and-Mers and their surrogates, decrying what they felt was the softening of proper punishment, staged even more brazen acts. That generated more news to report. Which generated more anger and backlash, public floggings and protest. Which gave us more items to entertain our audience. I called it the news cycle. It just kept spinning, and appeared to be spinning out of control some days.

Now, as for Thursday of that marvelous week of riotous behavior? Ah, sweet Thursday I spent the afternoon in the arms of Lady Kate Jasper on the bed of the private hidey-hole she had acquired overlooking The River Thames.

"Leeds, sweet Leeds. Whatever could I do without you?" She said as we lingered naked and sweaty on the bed.

"I love you, too, my dear."

"Do you truly?" Lady Jasper stroked my cheek with a gentleness that turned her question into a confirmation of the fact. I did love her.

"I'd give all that I have if you were not so, so…married."

"That," she said with a kiss, "is the romantic in you."

"Yes, I suppose it is, now isn't it?" That was no comfort.

She said, "Though I would suggest that it is far more romantic to be star-crossed lovers than a fuddy, wrinkled pair of old-weds."

She studied my gloomy puss and then rolled to straddle my hips. Her long golden curls tickled my nose. I could barely see her eyes, but I knew they were shining just for me. "Don't be such a sweet, silly boy. I have just the thing to cheer you up."

Before I could protest that I was quite spent already, she bounded from the bed and crossed the room to where she had set a basket of wine and nibbles for an afternoon snack. She pulled out a letter that she had hidden beneath the cloth there and handed it to me.

"It's a letter to Ian from Miles Rutherford."

"Rutherford, the banker? The King of Lombard Street, himself?"

"Yes, and see how the letter is singed by fire? Ian started to burn it and then must have thought better."

I held it to my nose and sniffed the blackened edge. The smell of ash, the scent of secrets preserved at the last moment, brought on a scandal-laced euphoria that I felt down to my toes. And when I read the letter, it was obvious why destruction might have been a more prudent fate for it. Rutherford wrote to thank Sir Jasper for his expert advice on exactly who in the House of Commons needed to be bribed and to what extent in exchange for government investments that Rutherford would oversee.

"And trust me, sir, there will be profits a-plenty that the government shall never realize even exist. I will gratefully forward your commission. Forget buying yourself a title. Buy an island, so sure I am of our success."

Lady Jasper took the letter and tucked it beneath the napkins in her basket. "Ian mentioned last evening that Mr. Rutherford had secured a very large contract this past week, and we are to attend a dinner party with the Rutherfords and several others to celebrate his good fortune. It will apparently make him very rich."

"He already has more money than God."

"But not as much as the King. I believe that is his goal."

I took up my notebook to capture the names mentioned in Rutherford's letter. Ian? No, I couldn't possibly mention him, I told Lady Jasper.

She shook her head. "No, everyone would know where this came from in a heartbeat's time. But this should still rock them solid."

"But, Lady Jasper, it would seem that to stick one's thumb into the eye of Rutherford's plans could, even without revealing Sir Ian's role in the affair, affect your welfare. It sounds as if quite a bit of money will change hands which you are sure to benefit from. The trickle-down economics of it all? Are you willing to forego the gains gotten no matter how ill-gotten they may have been gotten for you?"

"Pish! Ian is a clever enough fellow. This is not his only spoon in the pot. Money is nice; it comes in handy when bartering for a duke's title or this year's fashions. But I never cared a whit for the Rutherfords. Susan Rutherford has no title at all. Miles is lower than Ian; he hasn't even made knight, and yet she thinks she is so much better than those of us who are clearly her superiors."

Something to patter other than the blistering rage against the homosexuals was a good thing to my way of thinking. Made me feel less opportunistic. I tried to include stories such as the successful financing of a new hospital for children, a small reduction in taxes on tobacco from the Americas, and the coalman's parade to honor the Lord Mayor for negotiating a raise in wages. But each time I pattered good news, the tables became noisy and the crowd restless. If no news is good news, then good news is no news and I eventually ceded this point to the audience at large.

"But what does Sir Ian think about the molly house raids and all this publicity?" I asked.

She thought for a moment. "I haven't spoken to him of it. And we shall not either. Just mentioning him and whatever it is that makes him so...well, it simply makes me blue."

I made a few notes more not daring to look up. "And Rutherford? Am I to patter this for your sake or mine?"

"For us, darling." She came to me and tilted my chin up so I was eye to navel with her. I swear it winked at me. The fragrance of her perfume, residual sweat and lust filled my nostrils, and I buried my face in her body. "Now let me give you what you really deserve," she cooed.

An hour later, as I strolled back to Fleet Street, an old sailor man leaned over and shared a mumbled observation with a woman in the doorway of the lottery office. I was certain their eyes were on me as I passed. The old sailor even pointed in my direction. I tipped my hat, and that seemed to please them thoroughly though we exchanged no words. A few more strides and from across the street I noticed a law clerk stopped sweeping the grime from his master's step to leer at me. At first chance I turned briefly into an alley to check for some stain or other telltale sign on my breeches, some noticeable sign screaming out to the world, "Yes! I did indeed diddle the fair Lady Jasper. Yes, yes! I admit it." I found nothing there on my clothes to reveal our assignation and moved on.

A block further and a total stranger nearly broke his neck as he whipped his head around to confirm that I was, apparently, "That Fellow." I felt as if the entire world had witnessed the adulterous bit of pecker polo Kate Jasper performed so exquisitely upon my person that afternoon. I drifted along and reentered the city past my favorite pattering corner. I was lost in my dreams and navigating by habit only. Lady Jasper still dismissed even the dream of a real and honest relationship with such a cavalier attitude that discouraged me. The thought of carrying on without Kate Jasper tore at my heart like ink-smudged waste paper ripped from the printing press, wadded up and discarded with the morning trash.

"You really flogged the frog with this one, Merriweather." I said that to myself, though it was loud enough to turn a head or two.

By and by I came upon A.P. still some distance from my flat and the Tamed Shrew. He was affixing a poster to the wall of Mr. Howard's cutlery shop:

Come Experience the Foremost News Performance in London!
Exclusive Details of Events of the Day!
Four Nights Weekly at the Tamed Shrew Tavern Featuring London's Favorite News Actor, Mr. Leeds Merriweather, esq.!
With Shocking True Events and Celebrity Buffoonery, the Tamed Shrew Tavern Is London's Number 1 Source of News and Information!

Performances at Six and Ten on the Clock.

So there you have it. Once a magnet for advertisers, we had now become one ourselves.

"Ain't that lovely?" A.P said.

"It does seem a bit heavy on exclamations."

"That portrait there looks keen, don't you think, Mr. Merriweather?"

Indeed. Our news performance artist had captured my likeness in a reasonable, even flattering way.

"And what is this about news at six o'clock and ten o'clock?" I asked.

"Mr. Penny says we can increase our income if we are newscasting twice each night instead of just once." He tapped the page. "He paid for the advertisement. I don't argue with a man who pays. Especially if it puts coin in my pocket."

That's when it hit me. Literally. A solid punch at my right shoulder spun me sufficiently that I found myself half turned and confronting the puncher. He was a short and squat fellow with spikes of dirty grey hair sticking out from beneath his top hat like the straw of a scarecrow, and side whiskers fanning out from brim to chin on a face so broad that, had the whiskers been wings I'm certain this man could fly.

"Yor that news actor fellow, ain't you, sir?" he said as he punched an equally short and round woman next to him. "See, Hazel? I told you so. I 'umbly admire yor work. What's the name again, sir?"

"Merriweather. I..."

He grabbed my hand and started pumping. "Good to know you, sir. Damned good to know you."

Whisker-face continued to pump away as I looked past him and encountered stares, glances and gawking eyes full of recognition from both sides of the street. Amid the whispers, another finger pointed in my direction. Faces tilted, heads nodded and I realized everyone seemed to know me as the patterer from the Tamed Shrew Tavern. So, it was not the stain of Kate Jasper's passion that had been turning heads that afternoon. No, the only sin I seem to have committed was dispensing news in public. That biscuit of realization nourished my guilty conscience. I stood straighter, shoulders back, and flashed my most dazzling smile.

Whisker-face went to the wall and tore a corner from Ape's handbill and asked me for a signature.

"For Hazel, here," he said. She nodded with such vigor one might suspect her neck was really a spring causing her head to bobble above her shoulders. The man continued, "Hazel has quite the collection of celebrity 'graphs, don't you, Hazel? Why, she has a card wit' the 'and of the Duchess of Hilton, she does, and a snack bag with most of them that act at the Theatre Royal, and she's even got the prison executioner to put his cross on a death warrant. Although it's just a "x" but it's his for sure. Authentic, that it is."

I nodded politely, as if every man aspires to be held with the same lofty esteem as the likes of the Newgate hangman. I agreed to put my signature on the handbill he pushed against my chest, thus adding my celebrity status to Hazel's collection.

"I wonder if Kitty Fisher started like this," I mumbled with wry amusement to A.P.

"You ain't got the tits for it, Mr. Merriweather," he whispered back.

I retrieved my inkpot and pen from my bag and signed for Hazel, "May all your news be good news—L. Merriweather, esq."

Several bodies milling about the street joined us out of curiosity. One pointed to my portrait on the handbill Ape had hung and then to me.

"He is indeed The Mr. Leeds Merriweather, London's Foremost News Actor," A.P. bawled. "Favorite of his majesty and winner of the Crown's prestigious Golden Gab Award."

The last proclamation drew nods and ahs. Yes, they agreed. I leaned in to A.P. "The golden what?" I whispered.

Keeping his voice low A.P. answered, "I dunno. I just made that up. Impressed the snot out of them, and that's all they'll remember."

"Shave my head and paint me blue, Ape, if you don't make a fine patterer some day."

Someone asked what news did we have for them.

As if slipping comfortably into a familiar coat, I replied, "Blood and Lust."

"Murder and Mayhem," A.P. cut in.

I continued, "Victory at sea and victims of fraud in the name of charity at home."

"Citizens in Fear. Could this happen to you?" A.P. asked.

"Full details with visual interpretations."

"Visual interpretations, ladies 'n gents."

"Tonight, live reporting with stories you'll find only at the Tamed Shrew," I finished with a flourish.

The group clapped. We bowed and A.P. issued a few handbills to them as we left. "Share them with friends. Plenty for all."

It was both amusing and flattering to become aware of one's mark on an entire community in the vein that I had encountered that afternoon. I was being recognized and admired for no reason other than I was a man who stood so often before the public and could be recognized. Famous for being famous. Great actors like David Garrick and his troupe at the Theatre Royal would know this. But me? Well, Mrs. Fullbright was right. I had created something special. Heady stuff, that.

"Well it isn't donkey dung," A.P. said.

Balancing on one foot, A.P. steadied himself. He stretched out his arm and placed a hand against the brick wall while inspecting the sole of his boot to identify some rather large and unpleasant gob he had stepped in. While he tried to cleanse his sole at the corner of the building, I drew a kerchief from my pocket and patted my brow. With a thin layer of clouds overhead, the day had turned humid, just as Professor Nye and Doppler the weather dog had predicted. Sweat was collecting along the headband of my new felt hat. Too bloody expensive to ruin so soon with sweat of the brow, I say.

A newsboy crossed the street from the far side struggling under the weight of unsold copies of the *London Advertiser Daily*. "Read all about it. Coffee house raids. Sodomite witness reveals all."

A.P. reached out his pinky to me. I locked mine in his and we pumped once and smiled. It had become our little victory handshake. We had pattered that very story at the tavern days earlier.

"Boy! Here." I flipped him a coin and purchased the news.

"Anything there?" A.P. asked.

"Hold on. Hold on." I leaned casually against the brick wall, not minding the soot I would have to clean off later. The clattering carriages, the animal bellows, from both human cattle and livestock that traipsed along the street faded into a dull hum while I read the story. It didn't take long to find exactly what I hoped for.

"Hell-oh? Here it is," I said. "As reported at the Tamed Shrew news performance, the witness said blah blah blah."

Those were words of respect. I sent A.P. to fetch two or three additional copies from the lad. "As reported at the Tamed Shrew." Two editions of the *London Chronicle*, two *Advertisers* and even a copy of my former employer McNabb's broadsheet the *Tattler-Tribune* sat on my writing desk now with those words and references to our reporting circled in ink.

"And I have some excellent material for tonight," I said.

"Seen your anonymous friend as usual? She must be one plump goose," he snickered. "You tickle her ovaries, and she gives you a golden egg."

I slapped the cap from his head. Laugh if you will and stuff your morals but the Tamed Shrew was filled every night. "No one else has this story. It's a hummer."

Every news performance that week attracted faces in the audience I recognized as representatives from the local newspapers. I was collecting a good four pounds a week with my efforts. Trust me, I had no illusions it would last forever. The reading public was growing at a furious pace in civilized society, and the value and reputation of print journalism ever assured. Still, bugger the bear, I say. The pen may be mightier than the sword, but in our corner of London that summer the patter was mightier than the pen. I had arrived.

Chapter Twenty-Five

My Dear Ian;

Was it intuition or spite that kept you from the coffee house Friday night? I stayed longer than usual hoping you would come to me one last time. I miss you and the firm slap of your hand that brings out the naughty in me. I have been a complete wreck since you tossed me over for that Lord...Lord, I can't even write his name it makes me so seriously miffed at you, you tosser. Just last week I tried matching my green pearl shoes with a lavender coat and almost made it into public before realizing my grossly tasteless faux pas. See what you've done to me?

No, I hear your new paramour has already brought his influence to bear on the King and his counsel. That title you want will be yours soon. And when we are both dukes, will you still shun me as you have these past intolerable weeks? Two years of bliss destroyed by my misery of missing you now.

You have always worn the pants around here so tell me, are you man enough to stand up to that hag you married? I know she was the push that toppled you into the arms of another. It will serve her right when you toss her aside like the filthy stone around your neck that you have had to bear. When that Lord-of-Your-Heart's-Desire facilitates your elevation to peerage and you finally shit all over that woman as you have proposed so many times before, then I, the Duke of Earl, will be first in line to spit in her eye and inform her about rank—it does indeed have its privileges.

Lady Kate Jasper paced across the room from where the sunlight spilled through our single window and illuminated her naked body, bright, white, and so inviting. Then she moved to the shadows on the far side of the room, almost disappearing into the deep oak panels in the far corner. It was as if she stepped into a cave that hid the rage inside her.

"Ha! I am not a hag. That Duke of Earl. He has more hag-ness in his little finger than I have in my entire body. Do I look like a hag?"

"You definitely do not, my dear," I said.

Lady Jasper snatched the letters from the dressing table and shook them until I thought the incriminating words would fly off the pages. I wanted nothing more than to reach out and hold her, to soothe her in this hour of distress, but the gold velvet cords from the window curtains that bound my wrists to the headboard of the bed had much to say against that.

"Uhm, my lady. If you would be so kind as to release me now?"

Lady Jasper turned her head and wrinkled her nose. Obviously, the timing wasn't quite right for that. Bollocks.

For once she arrived before me that Thursday at our secret flat. It was one of the few pieces of property her father still owned but never visited. Its window looked out over the Thames back towards St. Paul's and the city center. Lady Jasper pounced on me immediately upon my arrival and slapped me with a packet of love letters from the Duke of Earl to her husband. Several included graphic descriptions of activities between two men that most men should never hear. God in heaven! They were liable to imprint an image in the mind of even the most ardent wench-hound, the kind that would shrivel a fellow for life, I say.

"Take a deep breath," she advised herself. Lady Jasper went to the dressing table and performed a snuff job on her nostrils. First the left and a sneeze. Then the right and a sneeze. Then a slow inhale until she could smile. Happy again, Lady Jasper tossed the letters aside as just one more trivial piece of evidence defining the scope of her scoundrel husband's infidelity. She actually laughed and began undressing.

"That's quite a kick in the head," I offered.

"You know where I'd like to kick that wretched piece of peerage. He looks down his nose at me and steals my husband while I am supposed to be the dutiful wife, dull and uncomplaining? Ha!"

"Turn the other cheek." I smiled as she raised her shift above her head, revealing her body. She dropped the shift on the floor.

"Turn the other cheek? Never."

"No," I replied. "Turn the other cheek so I can admire the rest of you. You are so stunningly, totally, exquisitely beautiful."

She came to me and put her arms around my neck. "Oh, love. You are my saving grace." Then she gave me that come-hither glance that suggested something exotic. "Would you fancy a bit of interesting foreplay? For me?"

"You know I would do anything for you, Kate."

That foreplay involved the restraints that held me in check as she proceeded to have her way with me culminating in a shrieking climax—hers, not mine. Though I must be candid it left me speechless, breathless and spent, and I'm sure her passionate cry turned heads throughout the district, right down to the sailors on the docks half a mile away. There is something to be said for restraint in situations like that, for once I was bound, Lady Jasper had none. Anger was an amazing aphrodisiac for her that left me satisfied, sore, and walking gingerly for a full week to follow.

Lady Jasper's amazing ride of pleasure upon my person only calmed her for so long. After a brief rest she jumped up and began her rant about the aforementioned letters while I watched, still the captive audience.

"Really now, Kate," I said as I raised my wrists pleading for release. She ignored me, plopped on the corner of the bed and sat for a moment. Contemplating revenge? I wondered.

"It's not the affair. I've known about it from the start. That is bothersome enough, just as with your brother Lancaster. At least Lancaster respected my station."

She turned her head and then laughed at me. "Leeds, you are a sight. How silly of you, you naughty boy." She kissed me and lingered over the decision to unbind my wrists as if leaving me in such a vulnerable state would make good the humiliation of her husband's affront to her honor. Little be it for me to suggest the irony in our affair at the moment. She untied the cords and curled her beautiful body against my side and fingered my chest.

"Swear that you will never trifle with me."

Never. I noted that the shadows were getting long and that our afternoon was growing short.

"Let me rest here, just a moment more, in the arms of someone who does really love me," she said. "You do love this hag, do you not, kind sir?"

"Until the day I die," I said.

She kissed me again, brushing her tongue against my lips in long light strokes. Then she rose, gauged the shadows on the dome of St. Paul's that told her we had stayed too long in our love nest, and dressed.

"I would get my revenge on them if I could. Stand at the top of the Tower of London and shout out for all the world to know what kind of buggers they are. That would destroy them. They would be lepers, shunned. Serve them just," she said.

Buggers? Such language from a lady.

Revealing the Duke as a wanton molly would cast light upon her husband. That would only serve to make her a social pariah by association. "Unless it could be done without making that connection. That would be most delightful," she said.

"It seems possible. Sir Ian obviously has no need for the duke. He could be comfortably removed from any association if this were to gain public attention."

"But if Ian were implicated, life would be ruined. Even Lord Biffing couldn't sway the king in our favor, and there would be no title for us. It would end all that we've worked for."

"We?" I asked. I suddenly felt as if I had been subtracted from the equation of this messy three-way relationship. And it was not lost on me that implicating Sir Ian had advantages that Lady Jasper couldn't yet fathom. For my sake, Sir Ian needed a good buggering. A disgraced husband gave Lady Jasper no incentive to stay in that smothering relationship. She would be happier with me, there was no doubt. She would see that, wouldn't she?

"Run away with me Kate."

She laughed and laughed. She paused, looked at my face full of earnest, and broke out laughing even more.

"And to where shall we run, my addled but adorable Mr. Merriweather?"

"America."

I explained the offer that Doctor Franklin graciously extended a month earlier. "With Doctor Franklin as a supporter, success is assured." I launched into the details that had worked their way into my dreams of late. Too many details and she stopped me.

"Oh. Oh, you are quite serious. I thought… well, never mind what I thought. I have never been honored by such an honest proposition."

"Then you agree?" I raised both palms and beamed with hope.

She donned her hat and picked up her gloves before tapping her chin with her forefinger in a pose that was either contemplative or counterfeit. "Well, to quote my most beloved news patterer," the lady said with the pitch of her voice as low as she could manage to mimic me on my stage at the tavern, "The answer to that and more still to come. But first a word from our sponsor."

Except for the waggle of her bum as she exited with a flirtatious parting glance, I could not have said it better myself. And yet it was no answer at all, and that left me scratching my chin.

I dressed slowly, mechanically as she had done. In due time I lit my pipe and settled into a chair at the window to further study the letters. When she first showed me the letters, Lady Jasper said her husband had left them in the most obvious location. "As if he wanted me to find them just to torment me," she said.

Surprised, I asked, "In the open? Just like that?"

"Well no. In a locked drawer. In his private room. He doesn't know I have a key. But what more obvious location could there be for such filth? How could he think I would not be curious as to what required such security?"

Good point. A locked drawer to a noted snoop is like waving a red flag in front of a bull. He should have known better. I should get them back to the lady before they are missed. But then again…

There were five letters in all, dating back several months. Together they created quite an intriguing and revolting picture of two men in lust. Quite damaging. But it was the contents of the most recent letter that set my soul ablaze. While Lady Jasper was so offended by the Duke of Earl and his rumination of Lady Jasper's hagification, I was struck by the duke's personal account of the raid on Mother Clap's coffee house the week previous. To wit:

As for Friday's raid on the coffee house, you were so fortunate to have missed the excitement; we might have both been caught up in the chaos. It was exhilarating and terrifying all at once. No amount of wanking by you or at my own hand produced the prodigious orgasm as the one I experienced when they burst in on Constable Murphy and myself in the chapel.

I might have been mortally compromised if my trusted aide Phillipe hadn't slit his own throat and fallen at the feet of our attackers. As that bloody mess distracted them, I slipped out the window. Oh, laugh if you will at the thought of me as I tumbled out and landed awkwardly in the primrose, naked as the day I was born.

By now you will have heard all the stories, and by now, since my name has not been mentioned in various circles, I feel confident I will remain just one more anonymous client who got away. And I know I can trust your confidence.

And so I write this only to inform you that I am willing to forgive and write this off as another of your confounding dalliances. I ask only that once your peerage is assured and the time is right, that you consider what our relationship has been and what it can be again. For I am today, and always,

Your Snookie Bear.

And there it was. If Lady Jasper wanted a measure of revenge nothing would eviscerate the Duke of Earl more than the publicity that would come from such testimony in the public domain. I was master of my domain and this account, directly from a nobleman caught up in the raids, would rekindle the spark of the original story. Anti-sodomitism was still at a peak. Passions were inflamed.

Politicians were stepping forward in a bloody competition worthy of bare-knuckle boxers to see who could pummel those vile homosexuals in public most. Indeed, I reasoned the public wanted to know about the Duke of Earl, and I certainly had no right to keep it from them.

Some might see it as ugly journalism.

Lady Jasper might see it as revenge.

It was simply news to me.

Chapter Twenty-Six

"In the clearing stood a boxer. A fighter was his trade," Buck Goodwill declared. Buck stood on the left side of the pitch at the Tamed Shrew, while his better-looking identical twin Barney had stripped to the waist and struck a pugilistic pose.

Goodwill continued, "His face carries a reminder of every fist that had mashed his mug, or cut him 'til he cried out."

"I am done in!" Barney roared after staggering about his side of the stage, absorbing blows from an invisible opponent. "Let us go-ooh to the highlights."

With that the brothers squared off and recreated the bout that drew quite a crowd just the previous evening in Covent Garden between Mad Jack MacGuinn and Hairy Harry Sullivan. Tin reflectors at the oil lamps along the foot of the stage created shadows on the wall behind them like larger than life puppets copying every move they made.

The audience was ready for them, sotted and whipped up into

a conflagration of righteous energy. The Tamed Shrew was bursting to capacity, and the mood could not be better than if we had filled it with a crowd out to witness a Saturday hanging. They craved violence after my newscasting patter of that bung-holing Duke of Earl's narrow escape from the molly house raiders.

"According to an anonymous source of impeccable character, the Duke of Earl was caught with his pants down at the climax of the raid on Mother Clap's Coffee House. Yes, it was he, the Duke of Earl, interrupted in the midst of a heinous act that is an affront to God and every decent citizen."

"No! The Duke of Earl? Hang the bugger!" When I revealed the identity of Mother Clap's most notable client, the audience went into a state of enmity that rivaled the first night of our reports. Mr. Bachman the candle maker stood.

"I told ye, those nobles are all corrupt. Ye can' fix something that bent, I say." Only the assistance of the few cooler heads among the tradesmen there and a round of free beer kept them from marching out at that moment to lynch the duke. Well, that and the fact that they had no idea where to find the bastard.

I played on every man's natural disgust with the homosexual culture and their fears that it was easing into decent society. I did it with one hand behind my back and fingers crossed. For my brother Lancaster could just as easily have wound up in the web of The Societies' war on the morals of London. I had sent him a letter to warn him away from the district late in the day before the first raid. He wisely scampered off to Wittyglib for the duration of the morals outbreak, and I was thankful he wasn't in the audience as

I scorched the Duke of Earl. Nothing personal, mind you, it was just business.

I held up both hands to calm the crowd. Andrew the sketch maker stood at his position behind me, holding an illustration over my shoulder of the duke's aide in anguish. In a fit of inspiration Andrew had splattered a gob of watery red paint upon the drawing so that it dripped when he held it up for the audience.

I said, "The splattered blood and writhing body of the duke's trusted companion at the doorway stopped the patrol as it would stop each of you. And the duke, being not only a molly, but a scoundrel of the first degree, took advantage of his dying employee's last act of courage to turn tail (if you'll pardon my pun) and snake out the window to freedom."

"Here are the exact words the duke himself used to describe the situation, his words as a willing participant in the debauchery that evening." Then, I quoted from the duke's letters and assured the audience that while I could not reveal more, they came from an anonymous source intimately connected to the situation. "They are impeachable in their truth and accuracy."

It repulsed them, and they rewarded me for it with thunderous applause. It was everything they wanted. Well, perhaps everything but a hanging on the spot. Feeding off their energy I was in a sweat by the time Veronica stepped up and read her prompt cards to introduce our foreign correspondent, Monsieur Villeneuve, with a tale of similar debauchery during a gathering of French noblemen at an estate outside Paris. That seemed to ease the crowd's anger, for that kind of activity is just expected of the French. Not really news, they'd say. Then the Goodwill brothers stepped up for their sports report in order to channel what fury remained into a lesser form of violence.

I stood off to one side toward the back of the tavern, admiring the fever I had created, when I felt a tap on my shoulder.

"Wot d' you mean your charging now for noses?" Mr. Felton the apothecary whined at me. "Doesn't quite seem fair play, now does it?"

"Call it noses if you will, my good medicine-maker." I said casually. "I call it opportunity. My good Mr. Felton, each and every one here tonight will see you pitch your apothecary shop. Each one is your opportunity for a sale; each one could be—how shall I phrase this—each one could be a unique visitor to your shop. That's what you will pay for."

"But I'm paying now, Mr. Merriweather."

"No more pay for play, sir. Didn't you tell me just last week that business has never been so brisk at your shop? You seemed quite grateful at the time. You are a most sought-after man these days, a celebrity in your own right, my friend. The top pattering dealer of drugs in the district."

"I am?" This fact appealed to him. "A celebrity? Me? No, you are mistaken."

"Indeed. And much admired by the ladies if my sources twittering like birds amongst the fairer sex are correct. Your name is on more tongues across London than those croup pills you sell. And much tastier, no doubt about it, sir. How many of your sales do you think are a result of your most exquisite and compelling salesmanship here at the tavern?"

"I have no way of knowing." Even in the feeble light far from the stage I could see his eyes narrow and his brow furrow. Felton had a streak of white in his ink-black hair and with his pointy nose he looked very much like a disgruntled skunk. I turned my shoulder to him and faced the stage without much thought. But surely I must have hoped to avoid being sprayed with his displeasure, should he actually raise a stink about the matter.

"Make no mistake about it, sir. Your good fortune is a tribute to our good work together. And for that, my friend, you must pay."

"Th' hell you say."

I pointed to my barber sitting in his customary spot near the door. "Mr. Browne tells me he purchased eucalyptus ointment for his sliced fingers the day after you spoke so highly of it here one night."

"Mr. Merriweather, if Browne's your barber, I fear mightily for your safety. I tell you I've patched many a shaving customer of his unsteady blade."

"Ah, well, he does charge a cut-rate price, now, doesn't he?" I laughed.

Felton didn't.

So I pointed in the opposite direction. "Mr. Jones-Riddley there. His neck was acting up again. He tells me that upon applying Snidely's Do-Right Whiplash Salve, something you recommended here, he has been pain free all week. Shall I continue?"

The crowd roared. Go on! Like the sea coming in at high

tide, they collectively surged in their seats toward the stage where Barney Goodwill recreated a block that Hairy Harry Sullivan had used on Mad Jack. The crowd surged back away from the stage as Barney laid into his brother just as Sullivan had obtained the upper hand the night before. Buck Goodwill dropped to the stage.

"Let's see that again!" Barber Browne shouted. The crowd hooted and clapped in agreement.

Buck bounded to his feet. "Certainly. And this time for our highlight we will perform the exchange in motion that is slow enough to reveal the quality of the impact." And the twins pantomimed the blow again with such deliberation as to leave no doubt the punch was a rocker. Buck Goodwill's snail-paced and tortured twist down, down, down to the ground drew a wild applause.

"Wot if I refuse?" Felton asked.

"I have many others in line to take your time on the stage," I lied. "Mr. Cardinal over there, your competition, would give a penny a puss. A penny, can you believe that? But Felton, my good man, as one of our legacy sponsors here, I would give you a better price though it goes against every fiber of the businessman in me."

Still, he waivered. "Take the damned Mr. Cardinal, if ya please sir. I can do just's well at Moose and Squirrel or the Firkin Inn. You see, you have competition yourself. Ha ah! Hadn't thought of that now did ya, Mr. Merriweather?"

In truth, yes, I had anticipated just such a push back as Felton attempted. I beckoned a small man sitting at a table to our right. With a high collar and plain grey jacket he looked every bit the bookish clerk he was. "This is Mr. Magid Nelson," I explained.

"Nelson, how was the crowd at our favorite Russians' tavern tonight?"

"A mere single customer more than half the audience here," he replied.

I inquired about the Firkin.

Nelson inspected his notes, holding a ledger up to the soft glow of the lamp hanging above him and adjusting his spectacles. "Seventeen fewer. A good night for them."

Cheshire Cheese? Old Nun's Head? How about the Dog and Pony show? In every case Nelson reported a lesser number than we had drawn that night.

"And you should have been on stage Wednesday," I told Felton. "The audience was packed in here like five pounds of sausage in a two-pound sack."

"That we did," Nelson confirmed. He held his ledger out to Felton as proof.

"We have retained Mr. Nelson here to be the arbitrator of attendance records. A ratings system we have begun, Mr. Felton. All the taverns will be doing it soon."

"Come 'gin?"

"A simple way to rate the success of our news performance as it applies to the business of creating those unique visitors we discussed earlier. And you can see from Mr. Nelson's numbers, the Tamed Shrew is by far the performance with the best rating. That means more customers. And *that* means more money."

I told him he could easily take his commercial pitch to one of the other venues. "But why pay the price for fewer customers?"

"Yeah! That's what we be talkin' 'bout." The crowd was standing now as Buck Goodwill regained the upper hand and delivered a knockout blow to his brother.

In my corner, I had delivered one of my own. Felton sighed, "Is this what it has come to?"

I nodded. "It is the way of the future. But it will pay handsomely for you, Mr. Fenton. I promise."

We quickly settled on a price that I hoped would be sufficient. I had no way of knowing for certain. I was creating my own little silk purse from a sow's ear, and Mr. Felton was the first little piggy who went to market at the Tamed Shrew. But as I hopped to the stage I knew he would not be the last. In fact, I felt for all the world the stars were aligning on our side of the ledger. Nelson's ratings ledger.

Chapter Twenty-Seven

The room had a thin cloud of dust floating about. Particles danced a slow, country round in midair, caught in the sliver of sunlight that streamed from between the shutters of the window. The light slanted through the room creating an irregular box on the ink-stained floor at our feet. I touched the lady's arm.

It was late in the afternoon. It was a Sunday. The shutters were closed to prevent attracting notice from spying eyes. I had cracked the shutters open only enough to provide some help for the two lamps in the otherwise dark room. Secrecy was paramount. We were alone, the lady and I, though I still glanced about fearing we may be found out. Hush.

"There is no finer woman in all the land," I whispered. I stroked her gently. She was lubricated and ready to put out. She was lovely to the point that the mere sight of her, and the scent that filled my nostrils, were more intoxicating than two-penny gin.

I pulled firmly on her arm, turning the spindle pressing the paper against the type blocks slathered with ink in her carriage. Moments later I extracted the newborn page we created.

The printing press exhaled as I released the pressure, and she creaked from every joint. The Lady Typography 1690, a duel-frisket wetvac, print-o-matic ratchet blogger model, was showing her age, but she still could out press most of her rivals. When I had finished with her I found myself craving a smoke, so I fished my pipe from a pocket. I laid our latest handbill on the table to dry and stood there, savoring the moment.

This was not my first flirtation with that duel-frisket print-o-matic since I took a room above her. After moving from Mrs. Fullbright's apartment I found residence a block away in a clean but ramshackle flat over a mapmaker's studio. The rent was reasonable, and I could afford it now. Most days I was awakened by the sound of rattling type trays, the shouts of the two apprentices, and the printing press starting its work. The smells of turpentine and the ink that fed the machine were constant in my nostrils these days.

I turned back to the press. My heartbeat was slowing. Until then I hadn't noticed how it raced as I worked, and how it continued to thump after I carried the handbill from the press carriage to the drying station. This was every bit as intense as the first time Lady Jasper dared to touch me in that marvelous way she dared to touch me. Love or lust, these two ladies elicited the same response in my beating heart.

"She may be easy, but she's not cheap."

Master printer Robert Kearning stood in the doorway. He used one hand at shoulder height to steady himself against the doorframe. He was not a happy fellow.

"She's in fine form today, Mr. Kearning," I said as I spun to conceal the handbill drying on the table behind me. "Back from church so soon?"

"Not soon enough. And what in the name of Hades do you think you are doing?" He crossed the shop as briskly as a three hundred pound bear with gout could. He tapped his walking stick on the floor about him to confirm the path was clear of obstacles. "Are you trying to get us arrested? This is the Lord's day, for Christ's sake." He used his cane to slam the shutters closed.

Kearning was not a spiritual gentleman. But being a regular at church was good for business, since so much of it came from this and surrounding parishes. Being a law-abiding citizen and obeying the Sunday Observance was prudent, though painfully unprofitable.

"Merriweather, I should take you out and whip that smile from your insolent face."

"Can't do that, sorry, sir. It's Sunday, remember?"

"Don't be cheeky with me, Merriweather. I know you. I know your type. I told you to watch my shop while I was gone, not treat it as your own."

I pointed him to a bowl on the shelf behind Lady Typography. "One pound-fourteen and two penny," I said. "That should make good my use of your press, I'd say."

Mr. Kearning huffed. "Thomas has apprenticed here five and some years, and I would not let him print alone yet. How is it that you will ignore me? And on the Sabbath, no less."

I shrugged. "Authority issues, I suppose?"

Kearning tapped his walking stick on the floor again as he went to the drying table. He pulled thick spectacles from his coat, lifted one of the lamps and bent over the drying paper to inspect my handiwork. His nose was so close to the paper, you might imagine he could inhale the line of ink right off the page. Kearning was not much beyond middle age, but his eyesight was dying. I suspected they had not many good years left, but Kearning seemed not to be troubled by their limitation. He said, "I must admit you have taken my lessons to heart. You are doing well."

"Quite the compliment coming from the Master of the Guild."

Kearning nodded, conceding that under his tutelage even a blind monkey could accomplish as much as I had, given enough time. "Merriweather, I am more than a little annoyed at you. Pushy. Quite pushy, using the press without permission." He straightened himself. "That said, on my journey home this morning I had more than adequate time to ponder my future. And lately I have been pondering that it is about time to move back to the family estate."

"Soon?"

"Nothing firm, mind you, a year or so. My recollection is that, on the day you settled upstairs, you said you were drawn here by a certain desire and I ask: are you still set on acquiring a publishing business?"

"Nothing firm," I replied. My words were slow and measured, though my mind was racing through the door that appeared to be opening before me. "But, yes, that is my intention."

"Then our discussion here could not have come at a more fortunate moment," he said quickly. "I've begun thinking that all this might be had for a proper price. I hear you are making quite a name and a bit of income from your news pattering these days. Now you've been thinking that you might venture into this profession. It's a marriage made in heaven."

"Well enough, sir. But I don't have the dowry."

Kearning raised his cane and thumped me on the chest. "Nonsense. A lad as bright as you should have no trouble finding a pocket to pick, a bank to rob, a patron to befriend, or a rich uncle to tap."

It was an amazing coincidence, I thought, for I had an appointment the following afternoon with my new best friend forever, Benjamin Franklin. BFFBF. Doctor Franklin had promised an introduction to colleagues who had associates who had access to investors who knew people... Well, in business as in life, timing is the whole ball of wax, now, isn't it? And he who hesitates is, well, he's up a creek without a map.

"I must remember that," I said to myself, and searched out a pen and paper to write it down. Possibly among my first published works I should produce a collection of my wit, pithy aphorisms exactly like that. I should call it Poor Melvin's Almanack. Could Melvin do for me what Poor Richard did to make Benjamin Franklin's career? Time will ultimately notify us in the end, most certainly. I scribbled that down as well.

I struck a deal with Kearning on the spot. The sale price of his fully equipped establishment was a king's ransom.

"Four thousand pounds?" I choked.

Kearning took the spectacles from his nose and placed them gently in his pocket.

"I will include your first year in rent for the space and the contract of my apprentice Thomas as well. You'll find no better deal in all the kingdom, I guarantee it."

Kearning gave me six months to raise a down payment and suggested a sizable sum of my profits in the following years that would guarantee his retirement until my debt was paid in full.

"I won't include much more than modest interest. You think a bank would be so generous?"

In my eagerness to close the deal I agreed to a price that may have appeared excessive to some, and it seemed ever more so after Kearning strolled from the shop in a very jolly mood, indeed. I began to wonder if I had set myself up for a very short honeymoon in this "marriage made in heaven," as Kearning had described it.

I looked at what I was about to acquire with fresh eyes. I hadn't noticed before that a thick volume of the Parliamentary Digest, years 1706 to 1750, propped up one leg to keep the printing press only relatively level. And spilled ink stained hundreds of cracks in the floor that were suddenly more noticeable than before. Corroded buckets of turpentine seeped. Rolls of unsold parish maps and government proclamations, ordered but never collected upon, were now just relics collecting dust in their racks.

My eyes took all that in, and I could only think of one word for what lay before me.

Chapter Twenty-Eight

"Magnificent."

Doctor Franklin could have been a bit more thrilled, but magnificent seemed to capture the spirit. "You are well positioned now, my friend."

I protested. "Not so," I replied. "In my haste, no, make that reckless leap into this agreement, I neglected one tiny but significant ingredient. Money."

"Posh! I had none when I started."

We sat at a broad table near the open French doors and we could see the courtyard from here. Although the weather was warm that afternoon and the fireplace was cold, smoke clung to the wooden beams and paneled walls, and it soaked the sawdust on the floor of Ye Old Cheshire Cheese. It had been that way for a century. Because of that, to me the Cheese always smelled of chestnuts roasting on an open fire. Even in the middle of summer, one whiff would put images of Christmas dancing in my head and Jack Frost having a nip at the bar.

Two associates of Dr. Franklin sat with us. One of them, a round, pasty man named Pillsbury said, "Sam will be along shortly, I assume. He has a room right over there on Gough Square."

"Sam?" I asked.

"Doctor Johnson."

Yes, of course. *That* Sam. Samuel, Sammy, the Sam-ster, Sam-I-am. Author and poet, he was the same Samuel Johnson who wrote the book on the English language, literally. That was his now famous dictionary. In other words, Sam was just another typical, run-of-the-mill underachiever in Franklin's universe.

"I'm looking forward to the pleasure of meeting him," I said.

"Rest assured, that pleasure won't last long." That snarky assessment came from Thomas Gray. He sat at the end of the table nearest the open doors, taking advantage of the daylight to converse and scribble at poetry. "Sam never met a word or a sentence he didn't like. No one will get a word in with him at the table."

Gray was a dark man, rather gothic, I'd say. Dressed in black even as it was summer, and his thick, black hair had little to show for aging. Gray also had a dour spirit he wore like a winter frock.

I suggested, "Well, Doctor Johnson has an entire dictionary of words he catalogued. No doubt he will want to try each and every one in a sentence at least once before he dies."

They laughed. I felt rewarded. "He will have to outlive us all."

"Well, then, there you have it, Merriweather." You can publish his next edition," Franklin said. "Your troubles are over."

"Believe that, and I have a magic key to the crown jewels I will gladly sell you," Gray said. "Do you know how long he took to produce his dictionary? Merriweather would certainly starve waiting on him."

"Then what say you, Thomas? Certainly you and your fellow professors at Cambridge have important papers to be published all the time," Franklin said. He turned to Pillsbury, his rotund companion, and said, "And you, Pillsbury? You are a republican in need of a voice. Opposing the crown always makes good print. Always the opportunity to stir up the masses."

"Ben, you may be right; my optimism is still strong, but my frustration grows. Will we ever rid ourselves of this monarchy and have a truly representative government?"

"Education, that's the answer," Gray the Cambridge professor said. "And we are making progress, even among the dirty masses such as, such as, well, such as Merriweather there."

"I am more of a blood and lust man, myself," I replied. "I am not so keen on wading into the war of politics. My brother is in Parliament, and he says it may be the greatest circus on earth, but taking sides is something only a fool would attempt."

Gray had barely looked up from his writing and now dove back into the page in front of him with that large beak of his, looking very much like a pelican plunging into the sea to catch his dinner.

"Thomas makes a point," Doctor Franklin said. "Reading. Now that is where it is. More people read these days."

"A growth industry," Pillsbury agreed.

I nodded and told them it was but one more reason why,

despite my success at pattering, I was intent on publishing. And I asked, where will I be when the novelty of news acting wears thin?

"Broke and living on the street," Gray suggested as he inked out an unworkable line with a frown.

I told them I had been there and done that, and had no desire whatsoever to return.

Gray said, "Bad form, that." Then he dangled one page, gently fanning it in the light to dry the ink. A smile crept onto his face at last.

It was Doctor Franklin who, naturally, made the moment decisive just then for the group. He asked Gray for a piece of paper and pen. "Pillsbury, my good man, you have money to invest and a message to be written. I suggest that we stop dithering and draw up a contract right now on this page and hire our good fellow Merriweather. Our investment will be his pay, and his profit will be our reward. That is how I started."

Pillsbury looked at me with skepticism and asked Doctor Franklin, "Ben, my boy, do you really believe he will be successful?"

Franklin replied that with their connections in business and politics they could direct traffic my direction like fat-bottom barges crowding the Pool of London at low tide. "And next year when you are elected Lord Mayor, Pillsbury, wouldn't it be convenient to have a favorable press on your side?"

We struck the deal. Yes, I had arrived. I now had an official place among the notable citizens who inhabited Ben Franklin's world in Britain.

"But where shall I start?" I asked.

"With this."

Thomas Gray held up the writings he had worked to finish as we sat and socialized at his elbow.

"What have you there, Thomas?"

"One of my better works, I'd say. It's a bit of poetry, the elegy for Horace's pet. I call it 'Ode on the Death of a Favourite Cat, Drowned in a Tub of Gold Fishes.'"

"Brilliant," said Doctor Franklin.

"A certain success," said Mr. Pillsbury.

Nonsense, I thought. Who wants to read of dead cats? But then Gray was a respected writer, and I was in no position to reject him. After all, who would nip at the hand that nourishes them? Chomp the palm? Ah, bite the... I must remember to record that phrase. With a bit of polish it could be memorable one day. Masticate the mitt? What would Poor Melvin's Almanack advise at a time like this? Well, never mind. More wine. I would buy the next round.

Could it really be this easy? Absolutely. This is what the nobility do. They are a private club trading favors and credits and the quid pro quo. That is how they maintain their rank. Franklin and his associates were simply the nobility of the common man. And now, I was about to become a member of that club.

I sat back and relaxed. I mused over what activity or bit of cosmic indulgence on the part of God and his minions I could blame for my success, though one never really should question these things, I say. Especially God. Bad form to question God about anything, but haven't you ever wanted to?

I mean, suppose one day you're walking down Drury Lane

attending your own business when suddenly you find yourself standing at the entrance to the pearly gates. Doesn't matter how you got there.

God himself is working the queue standing next to a sign, "Welcome to Heaven: Reservations Required."

And God is looking over his roster as you step up. He asks, "So what about the four thousand-thirty-six times you took my name in vain? There's a few demerits for you."

And you reply. "Well, right. I suppose that was a little out of place." And then, because you simply have been dying to ask, and now that you really are dead you have no self-control whatsoever, you question, "But what is with all the smiting over the centuries? I read about that. It's in all the bibles. Plagues and boils, locusts and forty year strolls through the desert. And don't forget Noah's frigging flood. Anger issues, have we?"

And you hear a great roll of thunder. You jump when a lightning bolt strikes just a few inches behind your bum.

So God says, "I gave you gardens and summer sunsets, love, laughter and ...beer. Did you think about beer? That's proof I want you to be happy. Even Doctor Franklin will tell you that."

So you answer, "I created the news broadcast. Newscasting, if you prefer."

God shakes his head sadly. "Not much of an accomplishment in the grand scheme of things. Trust me, I wrote the bloody book on the grand scheme. A spot of entertainment? Well, that's just not very useful, now is it?"

Well, there you go. Then you find yourself being escorted down a flight of stairs. "Table for one?" a maître d' asks. The name stitched onto the lapel of his blood-red cloak reads Beelzebub, and he is standing under a sign that reads, "Welcome to Hell's Flesh Roast and Barbeque. No shirt, no sins, no service."

So it just isn't a good idea to question God, or fate, for that matter. I was perfectly willing to let both alone and enjoy the moment. The wine was flowing and my heart was soaring. My spirits were so high I knew that nothing could bring me back down to earth.

Except the heavy hand of the law.

Which, at that moment, heavy with authority, clamped my shoulder.

Like one of Andrew's renderings to illustrate the reaction of witnesses to a crime we reported in our performances on the stage of the Tamed Shrew, Doctor Franklin, Pillsbury and Gray provided a visual of shock and amazement for me as an unseen voice from above delivered the news.

"Mr. Leeds Merriweather, it is my duty to inform you that you are under arrest."

Chapter Twenty-Nine

Candidly, I say being clamped head and hands in the pillory in the square outside Newgate Prison is not all piss and poison as you might imagine. Call me an optimist, a dreamer, perhaps, but I found it had certain curious benefits.

Firstly, there is the fresh air of being outdoors, good for your constitution. Secondly, the inability to move about and conduct any activity besides standing there in public allowed time for useful introspection. And thirdly, conversation with passers-by was often quite stimulating.

"Yo! You there, you scum-sucking navel pus."

Now that was an insult I had never heard before and made a note to make a note of it as soon as I reacquired my notebook. Actually there was quite a bit of mirth, usually at my expense, but nonetheless laughter ruled the day. Yes, it seems a good time was had by all.

"You're that there news-actor. Am I right, or am I right?"

"Oye, Lester. We'z got us a celebrity person here. Fancy that."

Due to the nature of my "crime" as proclaimed, first aloud by the bailiff and in writing on the bill posted next to wooden stocks which held my head and hands in confinement, and the fact that so many of the audience to my situation recognized me as the patterer, it seems no one was moved to sling mud and excrement upon this poor victim as they might a thief or confidence man. No, in fact, some tossed carnations upon the platform. Flowers? For me? You shouldn't have. Some called for a march on the magistrate to demand my release. One nice looking, plump young maid slipped past the constable to plant a kiss on my cheek and pressed a bit of cloth into my palm.

"I seen you at the news performance," she whispered. "Many times." Ah, so that was it, was it?

She blushed and batted her eyelashes at me. And as Constable Hoover pulled her from the platform, she added, "If you're needing of comfort when you get released, come find me. I'll wait for you, darlin'." She pointed to the cloth.

Bound though I was, the hole around my wrist was not so tight that I couldn't manipulate the wad of soft cotton to see she had inked her address upon it. What I thought was her kerchief unfolded to reveal that she had used her bloomers as her calling card. Her name was Sarah, and she had drawn a heart around it.

Writers from two different newspapers stopped by in the morning for an interview. "If you would, Mr. Merriweather, provide some reaction to all this. How does it feel, sir, to be disgraced and plummet from public acclaim to public ridicule in such manner?"

"Bugger off. You can quote me on that."

As I said, the conversation was quite stimulating.

"You have been quite an item on the tongues of everyone along Fleet Street," A.P. said when he arrived with lunch. He showed me a copy of that morning's *London Chronicle* with an account of the verdict and sentencing. The newspaper had even included an illustration. A.P. thought it was a fine likeness of me in the box before the judge, though I would disagree. The artist had exaggerated my nose to cartoonish proportion.

"I hope it's not the same sketch-monger as that fellow over there," I said. I jerked my head in the direction of a fellow who had set up an easel and spent the past hour capturing the pillory scene on canvas.

Constable Hoover allowed A.P. close enough to hold the page up for me to read the story for myself. I nodded as the words registered. The account was mostly fair and even got a few of the details right. But it distressed me. More than the unflattering image of my face on paper, my heart sank to see in print—in print, mind you—a confirmation that after my public display in the pillory I was indeed about to face the next year and months of my life in the cold, stone pit of Newgate Prison. Nothing hammers the truth with more force than to read it in print, and I had been nailed.

Let me take you back, now, to that day of my arrest. You see, it had nothing to do with what I first thought. It wasn't even about what I had thought second. Or third for that matter.

"Let's say we forget this whole episode, boys, shall we?" I suggested.

That was my first appeal to Charlie and Pepper, the Bow Street Runners who had been deputized to haul me in and face Magistrate Bath on the day of my arrest. They made such quick work of removing me from the company of Doctor Franklin and his friends that even the good Doctor Franklin was at a loss for words.

"We'll just drop into the nearest spot for a drink and a laugh or two. We can say you never found me. What d'ya say, friends?" I joked.

Charlie patted me on the back as the three of us hustled out and turned up the street. Then he rested his hand on my shoulder with a thumb discretely yet firmly placed at the back of my collar. "Love to do so, sir. But I has me order, don't you know." Charlie sighed as if he, not me, were the prisoner.

Pepper walked along on the opposite side of me, his grip firmly on my elbow. Thankfully they chose not to use hand shackles. Pepper turned me to face him. "The J.P. done deputized us right properly for this assignment, he did. We're both men of the law now."

"Your loyalty and attention to duty is admirable, Pepper. Then let's have no more discussion on that matter." I looked up at the sign above us. As chance would have it, it was the Moose and Squirrel. I said, "But certainly you can accomplish your goal of delivering me to his justiceness and still sit for one quick dollop of gin before we arrive." I jerked my thumb at the tavern door. "Who knows how long it will be before I see the inside of an ale house. Duty is all fine and well, but don't be heartless, Pepper. Charlie?"

"Well," Charlie said slowly. "There's nothing 'gainst it."

"Of course not. And I'm buying."

"I wouldn't think otherwise, Mr. Merriweather." We paused at the door, pondering who should enter first. Pepper asked, "Say, you wouldn't be thinking to use this chance to scamper off on us, now would you?"

"I give you my word as a rogue and a scoundrel. Cross my heart." Just the same, they pushed me ahead of them into the tavern. Some people have no faith.

Where my bounty hunters were at least genial wardens in my delivery to justice, the magistrate would not be moved so much as to smile at any of my attempts to make light of the matter. I was certain I could buy my way out of trouble for breaking the Sabbath two days earlier. That was the only crime I could assume to have committed. I had probed my two guards about it over the gin that Boris had served us. Charlie and Pepper said they were not informed of the charges, only that they felt it was trivial and work related. What else could it be then? I relaxed even though both remained excruciatingly tight-lipped through three draughts of gin. Then we marched out to meet my fate.

Without his judicial wig and robe, Magistrate Bath was a wrinkled cherub with colic. He had a round face and rosy cheeks; his bald head sprouted a corkscrew of hair that drooped over his brow. Magistrate Bath's demeanor carried not even a hint of childish mirth.

"Mr. Leeds Merriweather?"

"Your Worship."

Magistrate Bath had been newly assigned to the bench; I had no history with him. Yet, I sensed something familiar about him as if our paths had crossed before. We were in the drawing room of a home not far from Old Bailey leased specifically for the purpose of housing magistrates and conducting preliminary hearings. If you stood at the window on the west wall and leaned just so, you could look down an alley to the pillory in the square outside Newgate Prison. The sight of that stole my attention from the proceedings.

"Do you deny it?" Magistrate Bath pinned a cup of tea captive on his desk with one hand as if it might try to escape. He held a distressfully official looking document in the other hand.

"Sir?"

"I asked, you are the news actor of performances at the Tavern of the Tamed Shrew, are you not?"

"Yes, sir. But that is no crime, I trust." I grinned. The magistrate sniffed and let the quip lie there between us like a dead dog left too long in the road. Then he turned again to the report in his hand.

"And would you deny that you are the facilitator, creator and manager of the content in said news performances?"

"Say, what is this all about? Eh, with all due respect, of course Your Worship." A simple case of public nuisance such as breaking the Sabbath hardly required this much attention. Even if the magistrate were a card-carrying parishioner of the Church of England, the prevailing liberal attitude of the church to avoid confrontation would dictate nothing more than a severe reprimand. Though I should've prayed for an atheist justice to get off even more lightly.

In fact, I thought that very prayer was answered when his Worship scratched at his temple and shook his head as if agreeing with me. "Well, it seems not much to this case then," the Magistrate laid the report on his desk and stood. At least I thought he stood, for he was no taller than when he had affixed his bottom to the chair. A midget magistrate with little patience.

I felt cheered by his pronouncement. At least there was no reason to panic. I confessed my confusion for all that had taken place and said so. "But bygones and all that, now that we've cleared up your concerns, who am I to question the reason? If there is not much to all this, I shall be on my way." I turned to the bailiff, who stood like a rigid suit of armor stationed near the door. "Harry? My hat, please."

Magistrate Bath rounded the desk slowly, sipping on his tea while wagging an accusing finger. "No, you misinterpret, Mr. Merriweather. I mean you are most certainly and sincerely guilty. Bailiff? Escort Mr. Merriweather to his cell."

Now it was time to panic. "Sir, what justice is this? I haven't even a clue of the accusations that brought me here."

This stopped the magistrate. He stood within inches of me. I pitied him for the sore neck he must get from tilting up to look up at nearly everyone at that close range. His stare was blank, then turned to surprise. "Oh. Did we not discuss the accusations? Are you certain of that?"

I turned to the bailiff because that was easier than bowing my own neck to look into the face of the magistrate. "Harry?"

"Right you are, sir. No mention of his crimes to my recollection."

"Ah, I suppose we skipped that part. My bad." The magistrate sauntered back until the desk stood between us again. He did not consult the report. "Let's see. There is libel. Seditious libel. Defamation. Uncivil public discourse, while promoting civil unrest by degrading a member of the royal family and propagating ill will against the Duke of Earl." He shook his head. "Tsk, tsk. The royal family, no less. That is a criminal offense."

"Oh, is that all?"

"For the moment. Now to prison with you."

Bailiff Harry was gently tugging at my sleeve.

Fully panicked now, I said, "Prison? This is preposterous. I am entitled to a fair trial."

"Oh, you'll have your trial, Mr. Merriweather. But fairness is not in my job description."

Chapter Thirty

To this day I still cringe with the fear of lice chomping at my scalp when I recall my life as I languished in prison waiting for trial. It would have taxed our sensitive news artist Andrew mightily to capture such an ugly scene from the filthy vantage point of my communal cell.

Reporters from the papers spilled into the cell and begged for useful quotes that they could pass along to their readers. It was their way to keep alive the story of the molly house raids, to take ownership of the story uncovering the Duke of Earl, and to publicly castigate one of their own members of the publishing establishment who had made a name for himself by beating them soundly on the biggest story of the year. Payback is, indeed, the hound's mother, I say.

On the other paw, as a professional courtesy, and more for the promotional support it would undoubtedly give our newscasting, I was a most gracious interview.

"Yes, those words I recited were the actual words of the duke. The evidence is unquestionable," I told one. You can quote me.

"No, I cannot tell you the source of my information. But though the person who provided it must remain anonymous, that person is much more credible than the duke, who has everything to gain in lying." Yes, I told the writer, that is for attribution if you'd like.

To another I said, "No, I did not intentionally disparage the royal family. I was unaware that the Duke of Earl was a distant cousin of a brother or what have you." Yes, you can quote me on that. "In fact, I had no idea that anyone in the royal family was doing it with peacocks in such an indecent way as to produce offspring such as the Duke of Earl," No. Strike that, I was only jesting. Don't quote me.

Of course, he did.

A.P. didn't come to visit until I had been locked up nearly a week.

"We've been laying low, just in case," he said. "But Mrs. Fullbright and Mr. Penny think the rest of us is safe for now." He wanted to glean some description of my condition to use in our news performance. "Keeping the public fully informed," he said. "Be a shame to waste such a tale of woe and misery, given you are a celebrity these days. Miscarriage of justice or tragic blunder? If only we could work a little tawdry sex into it as well." He looked at me and raised his eyebrows, hopeful that I might furnish him with some detail to satisfy that missing element.

"I couldn't have framed it better myself, Ape. You have become quite the patterer."

"Well it may be our last patter. The Lord Mayor's Commission on the Purity of Public Information is meeting tomorrow. As sure as a lemon will pucker your puss, they're gonna order us to shut down to shut us up. So could you attempt suicide, perhaps, to give us a bit of blood for a final bow?"

"Right. I'll consider it and get back to you on that one, Ape."

A.P. seemed quite comfortable in the confines of that cell. "Not that bad, Cap'n. Not really. I lived in worse. Put a few curtains over them bars at the window," he said. He sniffed the rotten air. "Maybe change the chamber pot once a month or so, and it might be right quaint."

"Oh joy. Something to look forward to."

He glanced around, studied the half-dozen men who shared my "quaint little abode," and whispered, "I would suggest, though, Mr. Merriweather, that ye find a better class of roommate."

A.P. handed me a satchel full of newspapers with accounts of my arrest and imprisonment as well as paper and ink so that I could write out my defense as demanded by the court. "You'll like what they're writing 'bout you. Though it's been a couple of days since the last report. I think they're bored with the story by now."

I opened the satchel and poked around, inspecting its contents. "Nothing good will come from this if I can't effect my release. We have important pattering to do, right, Ape?" I tried to laugh.

"But most of the merchants have gone. Few want any part of us right now. Mrs. Fullbright will let me patter the news performance with Veronica until you return, though I'll never be an equal to Leeds Merriweather."

"Did you retrieve those letters?"

"Inside pocket. I found them right where you said they'd be."

It cost me the last shillings in my pocket, but a proper bribe got a note past the guards telling A.P. that my fate depended on retrieving the letters Lady Jasper had snitched from her husband's study. I had hidden them, waiting for the proper time to return the evidence to the lady.

Two days later I crouched in a corner of the cell in a desperate state. I needed to submit a letter of my defense the next day. I was paralyzed with a quill in hand, searching for the perfect words to save my skin. Words eluded me like a fox in a forest of dangling participles, incoherent streams of consciousness and a trail tangled with logic. I needed the patter of my life, knowing that this description of my case and those letters, the bawdy scribblings of a lust-sick bugger, were all the court would allow me. So lost in thought was I, that I did not hear the heavy cell door open.

"I would wish you good day, Leeds, but I can't believe any day in this hell-hole could be a good day."

"Lancaster?" I scrambled to my feet, dusted off my jacket and ran my hand through my hair, most certainly disturbing the lice that had recently taken up residence there. My brother looked twice with a furrowed brow at the hand I offered him. Instead, he rested his upon my arm.

"I'd like to introduce my companion here. This is Crenshaw Hathaway."

Hathaway kept a safe distance. He was thin as a reed with a face ravaged by pox and slits for eyes. He held a handkerchief to his nose and mouth, taking shallow, measured breaths. Despite his obvious distaste for the cell, he moved through the open area, fearlessly inspecting each of my mates and the filth of the blankets on which they sat across the floor.

"Merriweather," he simply stated.

"Sir. I'm honored."

Hathaway nodded as if that was a given.

"Mr. Hathaway has agreed to act as your lawyer advocate," Lancaster told me.

It took a moment for his words to make sense. A lawyer? Crenshaw Hathaway had a reputation in London as a master barrister whose success rate, they say, was exceeded only by his fees.

"But, Mr. Hathaway," I coughed. "While I most certainly appreciate, and would welcome your assistance, there is no way I could afford your services. I fear I must go at the court alone."

Hathaway dismissed me with a wave of his kerchief. He was inspecting one of my cellmates with a practiced eye. He said to the man, "I can tell, lad, that you are as innocent as you claim to be. It's a shame they will hang you just the same." The young man's jaw dropped as if broken by the weight of those words.

To another he shook his head. "You, on the other hand, well, your hanging is already years late. Good riddance."

Then he turned to me and approached. His eyes were as dull and dark as gutter wash. "You needn't worry about providing for my compensation. That has already been arranged." He stole a glance at Lancaster.

I looked at my brother as well. "Lancaster, I don't know what to say."

"It's not my doing." He shrugged. "I've never cared much for the duke. But if what some friends tell me you've been saying and doing in those news performances is true, the trouble you have caused, why I'd wash my hands of you, myself. Perhaps London was right. You have a way of doing what you want with total disregard for the damage it might cause."

"This has nothing to do with London. Why should he care?"

"He is here in town."

"London's in London?"

"I was apparently fortunate enough to miss all the excitement—and the subsequent chaos incited by your pattering. I'd still be at Wittyglib, but London has some business to attend to here in town so we all came back together this week."

"All?"

"Yes, Emily is traveling with us. And you picked the worst possible time to become a criminal and embarrass the family in front of everyone they know here. They are shamed and can't go anywhere in public without facing questions about you and the lies you've been spreading."

I told him they were not lies. If anyone knew exactly which men in London had bent morals and limp wrists, it would be Lancaster. I said, "I am sorry for the trouble I have caused with this. Never meant to. I had no idea."

"You never do." Lancaster removed his hat and scratched a spot above his brow under the white, powdered wig he always wore in public.

"Emily is so upset she has withdrawn from all the social activities she had planned. Won't leave the house. And London is denouncing you to all his associates. He's completely disowned you, but then what would you expect?"

"But who is behind this effort?" I asked. For if not Lancaster, who else is there?

Hathaway said, "You have some influential friends, it seems. So let us just say one of them influenced your brother here to make this effort. Do not cock it up. Unless your benefactor comes forward, and I suspect that will not be the case, then it's best that you simply accept it. We shall all profit by it, and get you the holy hell out of this purgatory."

With that, Lancaster left us alone to discuss matters privately in what the dozen or so inmates in that cell designated as the consultation corner. My cellmates turned their backs on us out of respect for the client and lawyer privilege.

"Mr. Merriweather, I ask you, guilty or not?"

I thought for a moment. "Define guilty."

My reply ignited a serious amount of mirth from the lawyer, but I could hear snickering from the others in the cell.

"Well spoken. A shrewd answer," Hathaway said. "I'm not sure who is the lawyer here. Never admit. Obfuscate when you can. Lie when you must. But never, *never* admit. Yes, it would be a shame to lose such a wit to the gallows."

"Gallows?" I swallowed hard.

"Just kidding." He said that the worst sentence the jury might inflict upon me would be a mere two or three years in prison. "But you wouldn't have to serve that long," he added. "You will most certainly die of some wretched communicable disease inside these walls long before your sentence is served. Most everyone does."

"Another jest?" I asked hopefully.

Hathaway smiled thinly, but he shook his head in the same somber manner he addressed the poor lad who exuded innocence but was pronounced by Hathaway doomed to hang just the same.

Hathaway began a slow, thoughtful pace around me. He circled and thought, questioned and circled, and thought some more.

"We are most fortunate that the Duke of Earl is your prosecutor," he said. "The duke has no more intelligence than my boot. Still, the courts are in the pocket of the peers, and they do not take kindly to people who disparage one of their own." The lawyer proceeded to list the charges as we knew them. Slander, of course, and seditious libel.

"Unfortunately for you, the duke is a member of the royal family, no matter how far removed. Did you know that?"

"Not at all," I replied.

"It's a crime against crown. Your most grievous crime. Bad luck there, but then lucky you weren't charged with treason for it." There were charges of defamation and uncivil public discourse. "One would think you agitated the masses to riot against the king."

"But why would the duke want to stir up even more publicity by bringing this to trial?"

Hathaway shook his head. "You don't know just how delusional the man is. He truly believes he has everyone fooled. You have harmed a reputation that only he believes exists. He wants to make an example of you, I suppose."

He asked me to start at the beginning. "Your brother alluded to the fact that you had advance information to the raid on Mother Clap's. Let's start there."

So I recounted the entire episode in varying degrees of clarity and detail as suited our needs at the moment. I admitted having evidence to support my account of the duke's involvement, but gave him no indication of what it was and, more importantly, the source from which it had come.

"You are quite the storyteller, Mr. Merriweather," the lawyer said. Hathaway neither smiled nor frowned. "And your use of description is quite an aid to your tale. I can see now why you are the most respected patterer in London. You are quite good."

I nodded respectfully.

"You are good but useless," the lawyer barked. "Have you a witness to the duke's visit to that den or his timely escape?"

"None."

"Of course not."

"But certainly others were arrested that night. They would know the truth."

Hathaway laughed. His was a nasal, tinny laughter that I was growing to find quite annoying. He employed it in all the wrong moments, I say.

"And who would bear witness to a duke in that compromising position? They would only be exchanging places with you in prison to admit their own debaucheries, if they are not already here. Now, you mentioned that you recited the exact words of the duke during your…what did you call it? Newscasting? The exact words, you say. What is your evidence? Without proof of poofery going on involving the duke, our case is as weak as yesterday's tea."

I fetched the incriminating letters from my satchel and offered them up to Hathaway with both hands as one offers a gift to a king. I knew this was my only hope.

"Oh, this is grand." Hathaway scanned each letter quickly and held each page up to the light that filtered through the bars on the window high on the wall above us. "They even carry the duke's signature. You are certain they are authentic?"

"Absolutely."

"And you haven't mentioned this to the grand jury, court investigator, magistrate, justices or anyone else yet?"

"No. I intended to include this evidence with my letter of defense. I have not quite finished that yet."

"Excellent. Tear up the letter and submit nothing to the court. And do not discuss these with anyone."

"But why? This is the Duke of Earl's confession, and my case, my fate, depends on them."

"My dear Mr. Merriweather, if these letters are made known to the duke before trial, the court would be obliged to let him access them. And with his influence, they would most assuredly disappear."

"Oh."

Hathaway inspected the letters again, a bit more closely. He found something that tickled him in each one.

"There is the question of where the letters came from, of course. I see there is a reference here and there addressing the person to whom the letters were directed, but the name is smudged beyond recognition. Did you do that?"

I lifted my palms as if to plead no contest. "It can be intentional or unintentional, whichever is more beneficial in court. I felt it was of no consequence as long as the jury believes these are the words of the duke himself."

"Then how did you come by these?"

I paused so long that the lawyer not only suspected my conundrum but also became impatient. "These were given to me by a source very close to the situation. And while I would lay down my life to vouch for their authenticity, I could not possibly reveal the name of that source."

"You are right to say you would risk your life; you just might be doing so. Slander is one thing, but theft, well, Merriweather; I don't have to tell you that theft is a capital offense. So tell me these letters were not stolen."

I laughed. "Of course not." Bravado seemed appropriate even if it was forced.

Hathaway folded the papers and placed them carefully in the pocket of his coat. He patted my shoulder and then vigorously wiped his hand with his kerchief. He cast his eyes about, lost as to where he might safely dispose of the germ-ridden cloth. Finally he simply dropped it on the floor as he waited for the guard to open the door.

He stood there, studying me from afar. "Mr. Merriweather, I asked you earlier, guilty or not. Without a doubt, you are guilty.

But you will be acquitted all the same." Hathaway patted his pocket. "I will see to that. But about your source, you still choose not to reveal it, not even to me?"

I shook my head.

"Ah well, there are always considerations to consider. Not unlike your benefactor, I am sure. She is paying handsomely not only for your freedom but for the anonymity that comes with it."

"She?"

"What?"

"You said she."

"Nonsense, I did no such thing. No you were mistaken. I said 'Thee' as in Thee Benefactor. Nothing more, nothing less."

I knew I had heard the lawyer correctly. The dozen cellmates who had grouped together at a discreet distance to watch us as they might witness actors in a play all nodded in slow unison. They confirmed it.

So that was it, eh? Lady Jasper had undoubtedly interceded on my behalf. Of course. It made so much sense.

With a heart-stopping clang, the door to the chamber opened, and Hathaway stepped out.

He paused. "I have an acquaintance with documents in the Duke of Earl's hand. We shall verify what you have provided is true and see you in court. He turned away and then paused to deliver a parting epilogue. "You are fortunate that I arrived today before you so foolishly surrendered your evidence to God only knows what mysterious fate. Until then, Mr. Merriweather, sleep tight. Don't let the cell bugs bite. I am confident we shall prevail, though I offer you no guarantee. Remember, this is a court of justice. Truth is irrelevant."

Chapter Thirty-One

Trial was on a Thursday at the end of October. As I waited in the box for the accused with the others to be tried that day at Justice Hall, I swiveled my head each time the hall's massive doors to my right swung open to admit some court clerk or prosecutor. I really did not expect Lady Jasper to make an appearance, but the romantic in me prayed for it. A good woman will visit you in prison. A great woman will finance your bail, that's what I say.

Lady Jasper needed to remain anonymous as my benefactor; that I understood. She was a married woman, after all, but flog the frog, don't even get me started on that. Hathaway still maintained that he had not let her identity slip, so it was obvious. That was Kate's way of letting me understand the truth without actually revealing it through admission. We all know she is a strong woman, and Lady Jasper always gets her way.

After the first four trials ended near midday, there was room enough in the defendant's box that I slid to the corner and away from prisoner number six, who smelled of a butchered ox left to rot in the sun.

"D'ya know wot today is?" number six asked.

"Thursday, I believe." I scrunched in the furthest corner of the box.

"Nah. It ain't, ain't it? Nah. It's St. Jude's Day. That's wot it is, sir. You know St. Jude, don't ya?"

Jude? St. Jude? It took a bit of effort but Sunday school lessons seldom vanish entirely. "Oh, yes, I remember. Lost causes, right?"

"Right you are. Old Judie is my personal patron saint. He never lets me down."

A short time later number six was called to stand in the dock. His trial lasted seven minutes. On the eighth minute the bailiff cuffed him and led him away to begin a two-year sentence.

St. Jude was having a bad day, and I was feeling less confident about my chances as the juries slapped every defendant with a guilty verdict.

The prior day A.P. delivered money from my savings so that I could purchase a private cell and a bucket of water with which to cleanse myself. I had revealed to him my hiding place for the newscasting profits, and he promised to be a reliable banker on my behalf. I also purchased a decent meal for what I hoped and expected would be my final night at Newgate. He brought fresh clothes and a proper gentleman's wig, barbered and powdered. I was a fresh man ready to take on justice when trial day started. I was prepared to stand up to, and stare down, the Duke of Earl. I would wave his incriminating letters for all the court to see and proclaim, "The Duke is nothing but a fetid bugger of goose poop."

But as the day wore on and the shadows crept across the courtroom floor, marking each hour like a sundial, each trial that proceeded my own ended the same. Guilty was the only verdict the juries were capable of reaching that day.

"Not a single acquittal? What are the odds?" I mused with my lawyer Crenshaw Hathaway during a break.

"Happens every day."

There were still two cases to be tried that afternoon when reinforcements arrived. A.P., Veronica and Mrs. Fullbright entered Justice Hall together. Professor Nye the weather guy followed them with Doppler on a leash.

Finally, all the other cases had been tried, the defendants sentenced, and no other accused wretch sat in the box with me. At that point the duke blew into the room followed by several grovelers, all dressed in fine clothes that I could not afford in a decade of steady work. Those were just the duke's handlers. The duke, himself, wore an outfit of silk and embroidered gold that made the others look like pikers; it sparkled with embedded gems. His face was a mask of powder and rouge, and he paused just inside the court with open arms and head tilted back to savor the personal bouquet of his own presence.

As he minced across the floor towards the witness box, he stopped long enough to exchange a veiled, telling glance with a tall and muscular bailiff. I thought to myself we would need no witness. His grace was a flaming testament of evidence in our favor.

The bailiff called my name; it was finally my turn in the dock. The little bit of sunlight remaining in the autumn day splashed high across the far wall but left the floor of the courtroom entirely in shadow. A mirror suspended from the ceiling over the dock where I stood and angled to catch the sun from the windows above me, reflected the light into my face. The intent, I am told, is so the justice and juries can see a defendant's facial expressions better. I think it was to make him squint and cockle his face into an unflattering and guilty expression. One up for the prosecution with nary a word spoken.

Chief Justice Harold T. Stone began. He read the charges in turn, and the duke concurred with some elaboration on each one, accusing me of Breaking the Peace in all its manifestations of slander, libel, and all that rot.

The Duke of Earl set the entire courtroom atwitter when he included the crime of "defamation by vigorous oral action" to describe the account of slander. No one took more joy from that than his clutch of hens and supporters. Even Justice Stone raised his robed arm across his face to hide a laugh, peaking out so that all you could see were his round spectacles and white wig. Everyone appeared to take a different understanding of the duke's description of the crime than the Duke of Earl. He seemed truly mystified by their reaction.

It was only as the laughter died and order was restored in court that I noticed in the visitors' gallery, barely in sight, my brother Lancaster stood smoking his pipe. He was relaxed and leaning against a wall as if the proceedings were a mere trifle but better entertainment than nothing at all. The difference between these two was never so apparent to me. Lancaster never once exhibited the duke's effeminate style.

"And Libel? How so, sir?" Justice Stone asked the duke.

At this point, the duke's advisor for the prosecution stood. "The words spoken in public by this filthy pirate of the Duke of Earl's reputation have been reported and repeated in several of London's newspapers, turning this vile slander into printed material."

Really? I had more power than I suspected. Charge them then for the crime, I say. Or, I would say, if I were allowed to testify. No need. Hathaway was on his feet making that point. Show them the letters, I pleaded silently. But Hathaway returned to his seat while Justice Stone took the matter under advisement for the time being.

"We'll hang the defendant for that charge later."

Hathaway objected.

"My apologies to counsel, sir. I meant to say we'll hang that charge *on* the defendant." Then the justice turned to the Duke of Earl. "Are you a sodomite?"

"No."

"Have you ever been a sodomite?"

More emphatically. "No."

"Will you ever become a sodomite?"

"Good Lord, no!" the bugger shouted.

The Duke of Earl's fan club roared with approval, clapping each other on the back, and clapping in general.

The Duke then stepped from the witness box to allow his lawyer to pull testimony from two men who swore in court that they had heard me call the duke a bugger on the night in question.

The justice asked me if that were a true statement.

"No, sir. Not I. Now, the crowd was quite large that evening and someone in the audience may have suggested such but I…"

Justice Stone held up his hand. "Silence. No more."

I gaped at Hathaway. Anger rose to burn my ears, and my face, I knew, was flush. I implored him to say something, but Hathaway stared ahead. A bird that had invaded the hall and flitted across the back wall distracted him. In our final meeting before the trial he had warned me that as my counsel the court would only allow him to respond to the prosecution in order to clarify a point.

"We are not allowed to press our own line of defense."

"But what about the letters?" I croaked as something gripped my throat and squeezed my words like a spent lemon.

"Not allowed unless asked. That is the rule of law."

"What the F…?"

"Just answer the justice's questions. Don't elaborate. Leave the rest to me." He winked, but it was of no comfort.

And so far, the trial played out like my worst nightmare. Justice Stone asked for no evidence and created no opening for our defense. He adjusted his glasses and addressed me again. "Then you admit inciting the public to believe your story and go so far as to display their own malicious assault on the prosecutor's reputation?"

"I admit nothing. I…" Silence, the justice commanded again.

He paused to write. Still scribbling, and without looking up, he said in a loud voice, "It appears certain that the defendant did have influence upon public opinion that is quite negative to the prosecutor. How shall we judge this?"

With that, the Duke of Earl returned to the witness box and called upon Justice Stone for as strong a sentence as possible.

"Death would be appropriate, considering the murder of my reputation and his willful attack upon a member of the royal family. You do understand, Your Worship, that I am a favorite member of the king's lineage?"

"You have made that abundantly clear several times."

"You see, I know there have been rumors, whispers behind my back, of this silly nonsense for quite some time simply because I have flair," the duke said. "Indeed, I do love fine clothes, fine wine, and have even been known to favor singing theater show songs in public. But those are not crimes. It is exactly the sort of public twisting of such pleasures into a vile composite of the sort of man we all abhor that we must address by making an example of this assassin of reputations."

And the duke suggested that to let news mongers such as myself freely and willfully destroy any figure in public, particularly one of the royal family who is a mere trunk, two branches, a twig, a sprig and a leaf in the family tree away from King George himself, must be stopped with a punishment so severe as to deter others from doing the same.

"Hear, hear!" The audience responded with as much enthusiasm as I have ever mustered for a news performance at the Tamed Shrew. Even the justice nodded.

So there it was. My fate was sealed while my defense counsel sat on his bonny arse. Is this what Lady Jasper expected for her money? I tried to protest, but the justice rapped his gavel over and over. The bailiff came over to confront me. I did not take the message well, but I took it like a man.

"Snookie Bear!"

In the midst of my rage and the commotion of the court I had not noticed Hathaway rising to his feet.

"What was that? Who said that?" Justice Stone demanded.

"Snookie Bear!" Hathaway repeated.

Justice Stone scratched his thick wig. "What was that, counselor?"

"Ah. Thank you for asking, My Lord. And since you *asked*, I believe I now have the duty, and the allowable right of defense, to explain to the court."

He pulled the incriminating Duke of Earl letters from his bag and pondered them. "I believe you were quite proper, My Lord, in declining to ask of my client the basis for any accidental interpretation of the matters which he may or may not have uttered. Those words which have subsequently led us here today. But now *you* have raised the issue, so let me respond. Once again, I say simply Snookie Bear."

"Who or what on earth is Snookie Bear," the justice asked.

Hathaway held the letters before the justice. "Perhaps I am not the best source for that answer. Instead, I suggest we ask the prosecutor. I believe the Duke of Earl knows better than I."

Hathaway marched to the witness box and handed the letters to the duke.

Got him by the short hairs, now. Flog the frog! I thought.

If the duke's face could possibly get any whiter under his mask of powder he would put a country snowfall to shame. He hemmed and hawed. He shook and had to brace himself against the edge of the witness box so as not to faint away.

"Do you recognize these letters, and do you recognize the handwriting?"

The Duke of Earl paused so long that the exasperated justice instructed Hathaway to deliver the letters to him at the bench. He read each one carefully. In doing so he sucked the collective breath from the grand hall. I knew by his face when he reached the one signed by the duke.

"Are these authentic?"

The Duke of Earl said nothing. The justice looked at me.

"They are, I believe, as right as rain, sir, eh, My Lord...Your Worshipness."

He asked how I had come to have them in my possession.

"They were left with me by a reputable member of society. One of unimpeachable character, I might add."

"Something you seem to be lacking."

Laughter rolled through the hall, some was pure glee, and some carried a nervous edge that reflected the worried countenance of the Duke of Earl. The justice continued, "And just who is this upstanding member of society who so easily shares notes of a personal nature?"

"The name?"

The justice frowned and peered at me as if my mental ladder was three rungs short of the roof. I replied that the letters were given to me in the strictest confidence. "A confidence I cannot betray."

"Quite commendable. Loyalty. I like that in a man." He noted that the name of the recipient and several references that might provide clues to that person's identity had been smudged beyond legibility.

"And it is a decent enough defense," the justice continued.

"If it were allowed.

"Which it is not. The name, sir."

I stood silent. To betray Lady Jasper, my love, would only lead to more questions about our relationship. I could out the duke, and I had a hope that it might, in turn, ruin her husband by association. But I would suffer prison before allowing a public scrutiny of the fair lady and our relationship that might soil her character.

Whilst this was going on the Duke of Earl was in deep conversation with his counselor. Then the lawyer took advantage of the pause while the justice pondered my fate.

"My Lord," he said. "It appears that any public misrepresentation of the Duke of Earl's position on the matter of such appalling deviant behavior and, or, association with members of such an unholy group appears to be one of ignorance and not born of malicious intent to defame His Grace. As such, the Duke of Earl would like to withdraw the charges."

"Withdraw? At this stage of the proceedings? And just as it was becoming very, very interesting."

Justice Stone asked the duke if this was his wish. "You are the prosecutor, Your Grace. Is this so?"

The duke nodded. His lawyer added, "And with the withdrawal of charges and thus no prosecution, we submit we are within our rights to retain all documents pertaining to and delivered in the course of today's proceedings."

The justice thumbed the letters thoughtfully. He gave the duke a thin and knowing smile that left no doubt it was a wise decision. "Of course you would. Including these." Justice Snow made quite a show of sighing and shrugging, and finally he rapped his gavel. "So be it. The charges are withdrawn."

A.P.'s cheer, my brother's clapping, my lawyer's enthusiastic slap upon the table and my heart's thumping were hardly a rousing chorus of joy to fill the justice hall, but it sounded like a roaring wave of euphoria to me. The rest of the court appeared to be stunned. And then a crashing, swirling collision of random observations, speculation and opinions on what had just happened raised the buzz to an overwhelming level. One of the spectators, a man I knew to be affiliated with the *London Chronicle*, bolted from the room. This would be tomorrow's news.

The justice pounded his gavel to restore order. "People," he said. "People. People. We. Are. Not. Finished." He gaveled them again.

When the din finally faded, Justice Stone turned to me. He made some notes and then said, "In the proceedings against one Leeds Merriweather on the charges of Breaking the Peace, let it be known that all charges relating to said proceeding have been withdrawn at the request of the prosecutor."

The gavel clapped like a gun shot.

Hearing that was nearly as sweet as Lady Jasper's whisper upon a warm pillow.

The justice continued. "But it pains the court that it now has in its possession documents, which you have admitted to acquiring. I ask you again, where did you obtain these letters?"

"From a trusted confidant."

"Can you verify that they were provided to you in a legal exchange?"

My heart fell; I knew where this was going. Worse, I knew where I would be going.

"Absolutely legal, Your Worshipness, Sir, ehr, Lord."

He questioned whether I could verify that the letters had not been stolen and that I was not in possession of stolen property—a crime that was punishable by death, of course.

"On my honor, they were not stolen," I said. If you don't consider Kate Jasper spiriting them away from her own husband, and in the context of joint property within the marriage, that seemed on the up-and-up.

"But you have nothing to offer the court to support your word and do you still refuse to name the source of these?"

I stood there waiting for the worst.

"As I see it, if this is stolen property you could be hanged; at the least you should go to prison. And since you refuse to reveal the recipient of these letters, well they might very well have been addressed to you."

Now that was a thought. I could lie, of course, and claim they were written to me. My reputation was at stake, but my neck would be saved. I started to speak up but Justice Stone stopped me with that scolding, iron hand of his.

"If that is the case, then, as a homosexual and a deviant, you belong in prison at least. Though hanging would not be out of the question."

Oh my, that wouldn't do.

"And if these letters were, as you claim, given to you by someone with a legal right to possess them, then by defying the court to name that source, well, you belong in prison."

I sensed an overarching theme to the justice's thinking.

"I hereby sentence you to eighteen months in Newgate Prison or until you reveal to this court the person or persons from whom you obtained the letters, whichever comes first."

Now it was my turn to slump against the bar.

"Oh," the justice added as a matter of fact, "And a fine of fifty pounds sterling and a day in the pillory for good measure. Court is adjourned. Take the prisoner away.

The bailiff strong-armed me down from the dock to the floor of the court. He clapped on iron wrist cuffs. The weight of my sentence made them significantly heavier than on my trip to court that morning. Walking out of Justice Hall I had to pass the Duke of Earl. His face reflected my thoughts like looking in a mirror. It was the look of the condemned. We shared a sad nod. He had his own sentence to live with now; withdrawing the charges after being confronted by those letters in public was an admission of guilt, and publicity would make all of society his prison. In that moment we bonded like brothers, acknowledging the unspoken the truth. We had destroyed each other over a bit of fluff they call news.

Chapter Thirty-Two

Shackle my socks, that is how I wound up in the stocks.

"Well, I can't say you don't deserve it," my brother Lancaster said. He was the first one to visit me in the pillory and bribed Constable Hoover handsomely for the privilege of a private conversation. He leaned with one arm resting across the top of the wooden clapboard that held my head and hands in place while he ruffled my hair just as he did when we were children.

"Yes, you went a bit off the cliff on this one, Leeds."

"It wasn't personal. It was just the news," I replied.

"Really?" Lancaster tweaked my nose to show he believed that as much as he might believe man might one day travel to the moon. Rubbish, I know. But sarcasm was the dagger of choice in Parliamentary debates, and Lancaster was as sharp as any. "Of course, you never *intended* to hurt anyone."

Well, maybe the Duke of Earl a bit. And if Sir Ian Jasper was harmed in all that without my direct involvement, if that convinced the Lady Jasper she was better off with me than her cheating, buggering husband, I suppose you could count that. But no, it was mostly about reporting the news first, best and live.

Lancaster moved to the opposite side of me and tickled the lock with his finger. "This will all blow over just as it has before. Just as it has since forever."

My brother said he would remain "severely vexed" at me for a while, but at the same time, he would bear his influence as a Member of Parliament on certain contacts to get my sentenced reduced. No promises, but it was a promising start to my day.

Brother London had almost nothing to say. He arrived at the pillory in a fine foot carriage, shouldered his way through the middle of the gawkers, and paid his bribe to Constable Hoover— who now sensed he had quite a payday in store. London circled me slowly with his hands behind his back and enjoyed my public disgrace from every angle. He even squatted in front of me in order to look into my eyes.

"Should have happened years ago." Then he rose, turned and left. That was it.

"Love you, too, brother," I shouted as he walked back to his carriage.

Owing to a long-established friendship with A.P., Constable Hoover charged Ape only half the going rate when he arrived with lunch and the newspapers that covered my story.

The constable allowed Veronica to stand next to me on the platform because she was pretty and that would please the crowd.

"Like, I came here to cheer you up?" She said. "This is such a downer, what with you, you know, being locked up and all? So I thought I'd sing to you?"

And sing she did. Her voice was as soothing as ever. I only wish she had picked a different ballad than *Three Ravens Feast on a Fallen Knight*, but it did make me appreciate the fact that I could not look skyward to see if vultures were circling and discussing whether they preferred a breast or a thigh.

"And what are these?" Veronica asked. She noticed the lady's bloomers that my admirer had left behind with her address in case I required some post-prison comfort. I had dropped them at my feet by then.

"They're not mine, for certain," I joked.

Veronica held them up and showed them off for the crowd, and she winked. "She must be quite a lady? You know, a really, really large lady, I'd wager?" Yes, a good time was had by all with that.

Clouds moved in later in the day and Professor Nye the weather guy with them. He told the constable that they would simply have to release me before my full day in the pillory was done for it would be raining before sunset. Naturally, Constable Hoover didn't believe him, not even when Doppler took a nip at his ankle and barked furiously. Not that it would have mattered. The constable had an umbrella and stood guard for the final hour of my day in the stocks as the rain pelted me with drops the size of peach pits and twice as hard.

Finally, he dragged me off to begin my sentence at Newgate. That eighteen-month sentence was the longest three weeks of my life.

"Wadd'ya infer?"

I sat on the floor in my new cell where the guard had tossed me like sack of moldy rice. I looked into the face of a man not much older than myself.

"I'm Luke," he said. His grin was all black gums and swollen lips. "So wadd'ya infer?"

I thought long and hard. "Defamation by vigorous oral action," I said, quoting the Duke of Earl. I tried to laugh, but wanted to cry, so I lacked the heart to carry it off.

Luke didn't laugh; he simply nodded. "Yep. That happens a lot." He raised his hands to his mouth and blew warm breath into his cupped palms. "Lord Almighty, but me hands are cold."

Our cell was deep inside the prison and three seasons had come and gone unnoticed since the previous winter. The chill there was invading my bones as well. Unlike the large, bright, communal chamber in which I spent my days before the trial, this cell, barely nine feet across, had no window, and the walls were rough and moldy stone. Our only light came from a few candles placed at the foot of opposite walls. I shivered. They say that winter is the worst time of year to be a guest in London's prison, next only to summer, spring and autumn. Winter was coming, and my disposition was sinking faster than the temperature at the onset of a blizzard.

The guard who marched me from the gate had made it clear that for a few shillings he could find me a blanket and candles to help ward off the cold and the darkness. As we made our way down a corridor that echoed with the sound of my feet I swear I could hear in it the sound of a thousand prisoners who had gone before me. And then the guard pulled up.

"What shall it be?" he pondered. Door number one? Door number two? Or, door number...three? We were standing in front of three cells near an archway to the next section.

"What's behind door number three?" I asked.

"Him, you wouldn't like. A thief. Chewed off 'couple fingers of his own hand to show remorse to the court and get out of a hanging."

I swallowed hard. "Really?"

"Din't do no good though. Killed his first cellmate right off for snoring. They'z gon' hang the bastard soon. So you'd have the cell to yourself for a spell after, if you last that long, 'course."

Behind door number one, he explained, a trespasser on the King's forest.

"That doesn't sound so bad."

"Claims t'be a werewolf. Captured running nekkid in the bog. Howls when the moon comes out every night, tho can't say how he knows when it's a-rising from inside here, but he's always right. You'll hear him tonight."

"And door number two?"

"Vagabond."

I waited for the rest of the story. "Got himself fined and refuses to pay it. Told the judge if he had a ha'penny he'd shove it up the old man's bum."

He sounded like my kind of cellmate.

The guard pulled a key from his pocket and tapped it against his meaty palm. "Now, what's it gone be?" he asked. He left no doubt that I would get to choose if the price was right.

"Let's make a deal!" I'll take door number two. I negotiated a right price for a blanket, two candles and a cell with Luke the vagabond.

"Smart choice," the guard said as he tossed me into confinement. He promised to visit Mrs. Fullbright to collect his bribe on my word that she would be paid back as soon as I had the means to do so. Ah, the wheels of English justice run smoother than most industry. Where else can you bribe on credit?

My cellmate Luke was a likeable enough fellow, an Irish Jew with a gypsy mother and a traveling salesman for a father. He kept quiet and mostly to himself. Nights were torture, what with the werewolf howling and barking until dawn in the cell next to ours. It was three days before I was hungry enough to swallow the gruel that was our daily meal. It was another day before I could keep it down.

A.P. arrived on the fifth day of incarceration for my weekly visiting hour. He had the blanket and the candles I had negotiated with the guard and slipped me a few coins in case of emergency.

"This may be an expensive stay," I feared.

The good news was that I got my fine paid. The bad news was it took everything I had saved from our news performances, everything I owned as well that loan from Mrs. Fullbright to cover it. I was buggered and broke again. The Lord Mayor's Commission on the Purity of Public Information had shut down our newscasting, which left Mrs. Fullbright in a sour mood and not likely to be tapped again.

The most precious item A.P. delivered was my notebook and a handful of sharpened pencils.

"Be very careful with those," A.P. told me. "They was very expensive when you consider the tax that the guard charged me before bringing them."

And so I fashioned and sculpted each patter before committing it to paper in order to conserve my meager supplies.

A great many things go through the mind of an educated man who has been discarded into a trash bin made of stone walls and left to rot with a cellmate who slurps his gruel and farts in his sleep. The fire I once fanned with thoughts that I had something to say, to print, to publish, that would entertain and inform and move people to laugh and weep was still there, but now it flickered softly like the candle in my prison cell. I thought of the Duke of Earl and how much damage one can do by simply telling the truth for the sake of a few shillings. Until this whole affair began, I denied that my words would have consequences beyond entertaining for fun and profit.

And I thought of Lady Kate Jasper. Lord, how I thought about Kate. I know I loved her with a passion that was a sin. A sin to hide, I say. I was resigned to stay behind these walls and would never give up her name to the judge, but I vowed that if and when I regained my freedom I would confront the Lady Jasper. See for yourself, I wrote that down.

I simply could not settle for our secret relationship any longer. I would give her a choice, and I hoped that she would make the proper one. No one should ever let a husband stand in the way of true love. We were meant for each other. No money? No prospects? No problem. Surely love would see to that. Am I right, or am I right?

Chapter Thirty-Three

"You see. What we have here... is a failure to communicate."

Crenshaw Hathaway's voice, loud and commanding, burst into my cell the moment the heavy iron door swung open. He was berating some chuckle-headed prison minion in the hallway.

"I am not going to let that young man rot away in this place one more day; your paperwork be damned." Hathaway rushed into the cell, following his words like a wave crashing over a rocky shore and creating quite a splash. He was waving a document above his head. "This is all the paperwork you need."

He continued arguing with the prison processor as he took me firmly by the elbow and marched down the hall, out into the courtyard and up to the armed guard at a gate on the far side. He stopped in front of the guard who was quite confused about what was happening. I was equally mystified, but Hathaway said nothing to me.

"This is the writ from Justice Stone ordering the detention of my client. And this," he shuffled a second document in front of the first. "This is the writ he signed ordering my client's release. You've read it. It does not say 'at your leisure' and it does not say to wait until your supervisor returns to approve it. Now, open the gate and let us be gone, or I will return with another decree from the judge ordering your imprisonment. And that is one writ you don't want to see, right?"

Hathaway drove the two documents squarely onto the bayonet of the guard's musket right through their very heart. The beaten little bureaucrat we dragged along from the cell like a mongrel on a leash looked at me, and I returned his gaze with the saddest, woe-is-me lost puppy eyes I could offer. Then he nodded to the guard, and I was free.

I have never seen such a beautiful sky in November. The air was crisp but had none of the prison's chill that hung icicles from your ribs. I gave no mind to the fact that I had to shade my eyes against the light, for I hadn't seen the sunshine since, I don't know when. Hathaway offered me his hat until we climbed into his coach.

"I am amazed. Am I really free again?"

Hathaway picked at his nose that was so sharp it's a wonder he didn't slice a finger. He chuckled with the practice of a man accustomed to having the last laugh. "Justice is an odd duck, my boy." He told the driver to take us to the Tamed Shrew.

"It seems that Justice Harold T. Stone has decided to retire and abruptly resigned his position on the bench."

"But how does that affect my fate?"

"Stay with me here. It would seem His Worship recently came into some inheritance and purchased a very fine estate just west of Royal Tunbridge Wells. Purchased it from none other than the Duke of Earl, I hear."

"I believe I see where this is going, Mr. Hathaway."

"Just so. Those documents on which the justice was able to hang you have...poof! Up in smoke I believe, they are nowhere to be found since the duke agreed to sell that estate to Justice Stone at a price which is a closely guarded secret."

"I suppose that's a good thing," I said. I could see where information like that could affect real estate values across the kingdom. Whatever would the nobles do? The castle bubble might collapse. It could create economic chaos. Why, the next thing you know, we'd be asking Spain to bail us out.

Hathaway said he anticipated just such an event, that the evidence against me would somehow be lost in the proceedings records and ultimately not be available at appeal. As a last magnanimous ruling from the bench before galloping off into the sunset of a rich retirement, the justice ordered my release.

"But, sadly, the identity of the mysterious Snookie Bear will remain forever that, a mystery."

I sat in silence for another long block along Paternoster Row. "I guess it's true," I finally said. "Someone once advised me that what you *don't* reveal is oft times more valuable than the story you do."

Hathaway snorted. "He must have been a bloody lawyer."

"No, a patterer."

Hathaway left me at the tavern door. I asked him to share a

celebratory drink with me, but he declined, citing an appointment with a client. "He is a well-to-do ne'er-do-well who will no doubt grace the front pages of the newspapers and, perhaps, a featured item on your news performance soon."

"We have not a news performance," I said glumly. "Haven't you heard? They shut us down."

"Haven't you heard? They reversed that action only last week. Pish! And you call yourself a news patterer."

"Well, I have been a bit out of touch lately."

When I stepped in from the cold, the fire was roaring inside the Tamed Shrew and so was the collection of misfits there to greet me. Lovely, they were.

A.P. and our ensemble of news presenters, Veronica, the Professor and Doppler, and the Goodwill twins all raised their glasses and cheered. "Welcome home, you slanderous old sot!" Mrs. Fullbright and her daughter rushed forward, squeezed my body between them and simultaneously smooched my cheeks. My landlord, the printer Mr. Kerning, and two of our news performance sponsors, as well as a few tavern regulars, rounded out the welcoming party.

Mrs. Fullbright stepped back and revealed a table full of meat and cheese, bread and mulled wine. "I even baked a special pot of pudding."

"It's a feast!"

Welcome home. We talked and sang and danced into the night. I regaled them more than once with details on the life of a hardened criminal, such as I was, in the bowels of the prison.

Not long before the evening ended, a smartly dressed young man arrived with a letter for me. My heart soared at the prospect of reading Lady Kate Jasper's words and sharing the joy of my release from prison, of which she played no small role. I could barely wait to express my gratitude in person.

The letter, though not from the good Lady, was hardly a disappointment. Doctor Benjamin Franklin had sent over the note as soon as he heard the grand news.

He wrote, "It is with great pleasure that I received word of your release today, dear Mr. Merriweather. A good friend of mine, and rather smart fellow, named Poor Richard, once said, 'Words may show a man's wit, actions his meaning'. You are a master of both."

Sincerely,

B. Franklin

Well, if that wasn't icing on the mutton. I poured myself another glass of wine and offered a toast to Poor Richard.

When at last we exhausted our celebration I wobbled my way to Mr. Kearning's print shop where he had kept my room for me above "at a reasonable rate of only half a monthly rent, seein' as how you were not in a position to actually use it," he said.

As for the Lady Typography 1690 and all the rest that the print shop held, Mr. Kearning held a going out of business sale in my absence, and the fortunate buyer was none other than my weasel former employer Charles McNabb. The old Scot could never resist a good bargain.

He said, "At any rate, how would it look if I turned all this over to a convicted scandalmonger such as yourself?" Before Kearning departed he informed me that I could settle the rent bill in the morning. As if! Twenty-four hours earlier I was a miserable wretch locked in a cell without a pence to my name. Now I was a drunken wretch with no more money than that amount with which I had left the prison. Zero.

He left me there and after some consideration I carefully navigated past ink buckets, tables, and drying lines with their pages dangling like freshly washed linen, to the arms of the Lady Typography 1690. "You could have been mine, you saucy little word wench." I stretched my arms, bent at the waist, and hugged the dear old printing press about her horizontal frame. I laid my head on to the array of letters lined up there like soldiers waiting for the morning call to battle. Then I fell into a deep sleep with the letters pressing against my skin and a large uppercase "L" imprinting itself prominently on my forehead.

Chapter Thirty-Four

For the fortnight following my release from prison I was as useful as a second shoe to a one-legged man. Dazed and doubting, I watched the world go by with little interest. I sat through our reborn newscasting from the back of the tavern. The Lord Mayor's Commission on the Purity of Public Information had made it clear that our performance could only be staged if I took no active part in its preparation and execution. Not that it mattered, for I had no appetite for the news itself either. Oh, it was fine without me. Under the tutelage of our consultant Mr. Penny, Veronica was beginning to grasp the concept that each sentence need not end with the raised inflection of a question. You know? She still relied on prompters and occasionally fell into her vocal vices, but with a blouse scooping low across her bosom and that gleam in her eye, she just had to look good; she didn't have to be clear.

Professor Nye's weather predictions were quite predictable. It was going to be cold. It was London. It was December.

As for the Goodwill twins, sports took a holiday as winter approached. Not even a decent bear and bull fight recently. I didn't see them for days at a time. Still the tavern drew enough of an audience that with two sponsors I could collect a few shillings in residual payments while my debts rose faster. But, then, I had cut my teeth (and they are naturally straight teeth, I say) living on the streets of London, always a master in the art of negative cash flow.

Every day I wrote a letter to Lady Jasper. And every day there was no response. How could I thank her? If Crawford Hathaway had not been so clever I might be lingering in prison to this day. Even if this were merely a business transaction I could never repay the money she surely spent on my defence. But this was much more. It was urgent that we discuss matters of the heart. Matters that matter, as a matter of fact.

I took up wandering the streets, frequently drawn to the Mayfair district where I loitered on the street where she lived. One day at dusk, just as the watchmen were lighting the street lamps, I saw Kate standing before a window on the floor above me. I scribbled a note; I must see her. I paid a young lad to deliver it to the back door. Presently he returned with my note in hand and word from the maid that no, I had been mistaken. Lady Jasper and the family were away in the country.

I was not mistaken.

After that, I spent days staring at the ceiling in the rented room where Kate and I had shared clandestine coitus. I sent word of my plan to wait for her whenever she could slip away. My hopes were raised on the second day with a gentle rap at the door. Before I could move it opened, and I was squinting up at a fine looking gentleman who appeared vaguely familiar and very confused.

"Who are you?"

"Who are you?" I returned. Disappointment drove my head back upon the pillow. I stroked a bottle of gin that rested upon my chest. That bottle had been my only companion in the sad little room while I waited for the lady.

Inspecting me, sprawled upon the bed as I was passing the time creating mental images from the grain of the wooden beams above me, he turned quickly, mumbled an apology, and was gone.

My patience was rewarded somewhat on the fourth day. A letter arrived bearing Lady Kate Jasper's seal. I rushed it to the light of the window with a heart ready to fly right out of my chest.

"*My dearest,*" it began. My heart soared like a falcon taking flight.

"*You have asked for some resolution to the passion we share for one another. Forgive me; I am woman and ill suited for an act of war. And yet it is a ginormous battle that wages inside me today between my heart and my head.*"

My heart plummeted like a turkey incapable of flight tossed from the loft of a barn.

She continued, "*With the King's recent bestowing of the rank of earl upon my husband, and as a Lady of peers now instead of Lady in name only, I have elevated responsibilities to my husband, myself and my rank.*

"*And yet...*"

"Yet?"

"*Yes, and yet I reminisce of our time together, your charm, your touch, your tongue. With words so romantic, I melted before you a puddle of impropriety. And I say to myself, and yet.*"

Yadda yadda yadda. By George, woman, get on with it.

She concluded, "*And so be patient, dear one. I will come to you soon and this shall all be resolved.*

"*Yours truly.*"

Right so. Was that a yes or a no? A definite maybe.

While I spent the next week perfecting my most patient self, and the good Lord knows the lady was exercising my patience more so daily, I received word that my brother Lancaster had recently returned from another visit home at Wittyglib Manor. He wished to speak with me about something that was of utmost importance.

Lancaster kept a modestly genteel townhouse in a long brick row on the fringe of, and behind, the better homes about Berkeley Square. My brother London's purchase of a seat in the House of Commons came with a stipend for Lancaster to advance and defend the family businesses in Parliament. That kept Deuce comfortable enough without being extravagant. I only went to the Merriweather house on those occasions when I was invited, which until now added up to exactly zero.

"London sends his regards," Lancaster said when he walked into the drawing room where I sat drinking the tea his manservant provided.

"He does now, does he?"

"Not a chance. He still hates you. Always will, I suppose."

I did not rise when Lancaster entered. He came to me and rubbed my head like one pets his favorite hound. With no reason to wear a wig and no money to finance my barber, I had not cut my hair since before they popped me for diddling the reputation of a duke and sent me off to prison, and it was now a soft bristle on my noggin. Lancaster poured himself a cup of tea and picked up a biscuit. He said, "Emily did ask about you, however."

"Not in front of London, I hope."

He shook his head. "As far as I know, your name is never mentioned when they are in the same room." We chatted about home and the weather. I kept my pattering tendencies on a short leash and described, with only a little detail, my time of confinement.

"I wish you had stayed there a bit longer," Lancaster said.

"That hurts." I placed my cup forcefully on the settee.

He waved his half eaten biscuit at me. "Not for any reason you might think. That is why I asked you here. I think you would be safer there."

"Certainly it would be more fun."

"You know the community I travel in. And I have never expressed how very much I appreciate that you have never questioned it."

"What was the stable boy's name? That first one?"

"Jaques. He was French."

"Naturally. Does London know of your...manly interests?"

"He's never said it directly, my dear boy. But I am certain it is why he thought it best to set me up here, far from Wittyglib. Out of sight and out of mind."

I had suspected as much. "Right. So for you he provides a home and income and for me a whipping and banishment with not a pence to my name."

"I didn't diddle his wife."

I protested, but Lancaster disarmed me with a smile and a shake of his head. He found it quite amusing. "Who am I to judge what happened or didn't happen? I can only judge the results."

"If you only knew," I said.

Lancaster stood, sipped his tea and inspected the leaves at the bottom of the cup. Then he drew a long, measured breath. "As I said, you know the society of friends I have here. Before my trip to Wittyglib, and since my return, I have heard some bothersome things that I am compelled to warn you. The Duke of Earl travels in a separate and flamingly parallel community of men. The Duke has endured scorn outside our *family*," he said with great emphasis. "And even scorn from some of us within *the family*. So much so that he is not a happy camper, to say the least."

"I reckon not. Though I doubt anyone would have raised an eyebrow more than usual had he not made a public trial of it."

Lancaster then mimicked the duke mincing across justice hall. He was a flourish of arms and wrists and swiveling hips as he glided across his parlor. "You know the duke never does anything in small measure. Every movement and every thought, it seems, is exaggerated." Lancaster stopped cocked his body to one side and laid a delicate finger on his cheek. He batted his eyelashes at me. Then we both laughed.

"He is an insufferable fop even among us."

"It's the Royals. Inbreeding, I suspect."

"Agreed."

And then he turned serious. "He may be a fop, but he is a dangerous fop when riled, and the aftermath of this experience has left him particularly riled at you. I urge you to take care."

I snapped my fingers; I was not afraid. "I can handle His Royal Foppishness."

"It is those he would employ that concern me."

"A bounty, for me?" I was amazed and now concerned.

Lancaster nodded. "Whether the bounty is formal or not I can't say. I do know there are some who believe it would be in their best financial interest to harm you and please the duke. That said, you must be on the lookout both night and day. London is a dangerous enough town, even without a price on your head."

I turned and stared out the drawing room window. The day was grey and cold and the narrow garden separating us from an identical row of town houses barren of life.

Lancaster went to a drawer near the fireplace and withdrew a box. He was still several feet from me when I recognized it.

"I brought this from Wittyglib. I think you may need it."

I ran my hand across its smooth walnut finish. My father's initials were engraved on a silver plate there. My father's military pistol rested inside. A beautiful weapon, I ran a finger along its long, etched muzzle and walnut handle.

I leaned and sniffed. "The flintlock has been oiled recently."

"I took it to master gunsmith Grayson before leaving Wittyglib. London had neglected it, but restoring it gave Grayson such delight that I had to threaten to shoot him just so he would take payment for the work. London may never notice it missing but would do anything to keep it from you. I know how much father wanted you to have this."

"Since prison, and these past few weeks, I have mused that I wish he had been successful, what with my military career plotted and all. He really did expect me to use it against the Spaniards or French or someone who deserved shooting."

"Well, I think you need it now. And I suggest you carry it with you and at the ready by your side always. Be mindful of your back, and your front, for that matter. And judging from what I witnessed at Jasper's picnic last spring, you are as good a shot as you ever were. I pray you'll never need to prove it."

"So do I, brother Deuce. So do I."

Chapter Thirty-Five

As it turned out I did not need to fear the Duke of Earl or anyone who might do his murderous bidding. In fact, that turned out to be the least of my worries a few days later.

It was mid-December by then, and Doppler the weather hound gave us a light snow. I awoke and peered out the window upon the street below. Since my brother's successful effort to scare the holy crap out of me, I had taken to inspecting the street for unsavory characters at the start of each day. That was a problem of Gibraltar-size proportions because nearly everyone along that street looked unsavory. The snow that day temporarily masked the filth of the street and put me in a more accommodating frame of mind. Yes, yes, Lady Jasper still dithered over a life of poverty with me that would be rich in love or a life of wealth and privilege with Sir Ian Jasper that would be emotionally squalid.

That afternoon I sat in the Tamed Shrew. The Lord Mayor's

commission had rejected my half-hearted appeal, and refused to lift my banishment from the news performance, but I felt the tickle to exert my reach and dirty my hands with the creation of its content. A.P. worked to shape a reflector behind a foot lamp on the edge of the stage while I read the morning *Chronicle* to Veronica as we plundered ideas to steal for our performance.

"We have the dog who was stabbed in the eye by a silk merchant in Covent Garden after he pissed on expensive lace that hung from a table at market."

"Who pissed, the merchant?" A.P. asked.

"I hear Lady Rebecca? Countess of Glenmorangle? is said to be on holiday in France, but, like, you know, has strictly gone off and taken up residence at Doctor Vortmeal's asylum for rehabilitating excessive drinking habits?" Veronica said.

"That reminds me. Mrs. Fullbright, more wine if you please."

I was keen on one story from the morning newspaper. I read aloud to Veronica the tale of an extremely large fellow who was arrested for intentionally sitting on his infant stepson.

Veronica thought for a moment and then recited it back to me like this:

"He tips the scale at more than four hundredweight, and tonight he calls jail his home. The charge? Sitting on a sleeping toddler. The accusations are shocking! Jarring!"

"You left out tragic," I said.

"He's not quite dead, though, right?"

"Write it all down," I said. Veronica began scribbling on her prompter cards.

I continued. "The lad slept right through it. apparently."

Veronica drew a breath for her big finish and summoned the blush of anger to her face. "A year-old baby trapped beneath a hulk of a man. Details on this tragic event..."

"Tragic. Thank you."

"Details coming straight away. But first a word from our sponsor?"

"That shows promise," I said. "Write it down."

"Well, look ye there." A.P. halted his hammering. Three men walked out of the light that framed them in the open door. They stopped once they were comfortably inside. The door slammed shut as if to say, "Wake up, you twits. Trouble is here, and he's dressed as Sir Ian Jasper."

A mousy assistant and a tall, finely dressed companion sidled up to him while he surveyed the tavern. They looked only at me. Then Jasper approached, fanned both sides of his travel cape behind his back and stood with his fists on his hips. I remained in my seat, a comfortable chair near the fire. He glared. I glared back. The fire crackled behind me with flames dancing like devilish little pucks anticipating bloody excitement.

He glared more.

I glared back more.

Please, would someone say something? I feared I would go cross-eyed if we kept this up. Finally.

"Well?" he asked.

"Well what?"

"You surely want to know why I am here."

"Not particularly," I replied. "I am more interested in another question."

"And that is?"

"Are you happy to see me, or is that a pistol in your pocket?"

I grabbed at the crotch of my breeches for emphasis.

His face turned as dark as a storm at sea. "You, sir, are a scoundrel and a blackguard, a knave and a villain." He spit the words at me.

I nodded. "Quite true. And your point is?"

"Are you to sit there cowering? Not man enough to defend yourself?"

I shrugged. I had laid the newspaper across my lap where I could reach my father's pistol that rested between my hip and the arm of the chair.

"Hardly cowering, sir. It's just that I've been called worse. In fact, just the other evening someone addressed me as reprehensible. That was the word, was it not, Ape?"

"Yesser. Reprehensible."

"I am quite good at that."

A.P. chimed in, "That you are, Mr. Merriweather. A steaming pile of putrid reprehensibility. Master of reprehensification. King of..."

"We get the point, Ape."

Ian Jasper demanded that I stand and face him. I did so while strategically placing the pistol on the seat of the chair by the armrest so that it would be hidden to him and where I could grab it in one quick move.

He said, "You have taken liberties with my good name and my honor. I have come to seek remedy."

"Come, come, Sir Jasper. Down here on Fleet Street I hear your name is not all that good, and your honor? Well, that is suspect in most corners of England. But that is just what I hear. I would never report it as such. Not in public at least. Could wind up at the Old Bailey all over again. Made a promise to the judge. Not going to go there. Wouldn't be prudent."

"Do not mock me, you insignificant little shit."

"I don't know what you are speaking of, though I would suggest to you that I have taken no liberties that were not were given freely, consensually, and, for that matter, in an excitingly lurid fashion."

That may have been a bit much, but while I was never aces at maths, I could add two-and-two. Jasper's explosion into the Tamed Shrew suggested the sum would be six, as in six feet under for one of us. Right. Well, you saw that coming all along.

Ian Jasper was a blaze of hatred, and I felt singed, standing a yard away. I struggled to remain calm on the outside, for I was quaking inwardly of my own rage and no small amount of fear over how this ugly scene was to resolve itself. I needn't worry; it came soon enough.

"You have disgraced my good name and shat upon my honor."

"What do you expect? You did after all call me a little shit a moment ago. Didn't he say so, Ape?"

"Insignificant little shit, as I heard it, Mr. Merriweather."

"You are making sport of this? How brave. For the moment." He raised a gloved fist and then pointed his finger at me. You, sir, have defiled the honor of my wife."

"Oh, is that all this is about?" Feigned nonchalance and sarcasm were the best I could offer. I must have suffered pattering atrophy with my arduous stay in prison and subsequent lack of verbal exercise since my release. "And here I thought you had come to protect the honor of your lover the Duke of Earl. But that is not at all what has brought you here, is it, Snookie Bear?"

"I demand satisfaction," he roared. Then he hit me across the face with his glove. It would not have stunned me as much if he had only removed his fist from it before striking. A.P. and Sir Jasper's companion both rushed forward to prevent me from striking back.

I said, "Satisfaction? So be it. How about pillows at 20 paces?"

Jasper moved to the edge of the nearest table. He drew a pistol from his coat and slammed it down on the table. "I challenge you, you wormy little maggot. Tomorrow at Dead Man's Meadow."

I sighed. I was totally tired of this run of luck, being on the wrong end of a dagger, someone's fist, just escaping the hangman's noose. When will it end?

I took the pistol I had hidden on my chair. Jasper looked surprised. I placed it on the table next to Jasper's weapon.

He said, "I shall be there with my second at sunrise."

"Fine," I said. "You do that. I shall be there at noon. Saturday is my day to sleep late."

Chapter Thirty-Six

Dead Man's Meadow was nothing more than a narrow opening in a grove of trees at the northern edge of Hyde Park. It was a popular spot for nobles to get their dueling jollies. The previous day's snow had melted into mud, and the sun had come out for the first clear day in a week. Professor Nye had predicted this one perfectly in what might be the last news performance of my life. Well, if you have to die, I say, do it with the sunshine on your upturned boots.

As we conversed and prepared for contingencies that morning, inspecting the ball and powder I would use, A.P. asked, "What if someone happens upon us? It will be noon, you know. There's bound to be people milling about in the park."

"I doubt they would intervene," I told him. "If they do, we could go to jail. Remember Mr. Siderham? He hasn't seen daylight since." Certainly the law would force some accounting for our act, which was (Wink, wink. Nudge, nudge) illegal in the Kingdom. I was certain that Sir Jasper, with his position as Earl freshly minted, would not face any penalty if he walked away unscathed. I, on the other hand, held no such cards, and should I somehow survive intact I would most certainly be arrested for not getting myself killed. I was clearly buggered, dead or alive.

"And if you're shot dead?"

"Then all my worries will be over, now won't they, my little friend."

"Dead," he repeated. "Dead like some mangled warthog crushed beneath the wheels of a carriage and left to rot on the highway to Islip. Road kill. Or perhaps like some felon felled by a firing squad splurting blood like…"

I stopped him. "If you please, Ape. You are turning into a fine patterer, but you are turning my stomach. Wait until my body is cold before you formulate the details of my death."

Yes, it was a glorious day for a duel, and Jasper's second turned out to be his business partner Bakerstreet. For the record, Aloysius Periwinkle Procter served as mine.

Bakerstreet. I remembered him from the picnic where I had learned of Jasper's unfailing ability with the art of shot. I must have encountered him again, perhaps in the audience of a news performance, for I know I had seen his face more than just that day. And then it struck me. It was Bakerstreet who had interrupted my pining for Lady Jasper in our love nest after my release from prison. But why?

I pondered this while Bakerstreet and A.P. circled the area to confirm we would not be witnessed nor interrupted. The only apparent witnesses beyond the four of us were the two horses on which Jasper and Bakerstreet rode in. We were far enough from the trail that traffic would be virtually nonexistent on a workday.

The reasons for Bakerstreet's appearance at the Lady Jasper's secret apartment could be many. At the top of my list was that Jasper had either suspicions or had intercepted one of the letters I had sent to the Lady. He must have commissioned Bakerstreet to investigate the flat to either catch us in a carnal act or at least confirm the identity of the rogue who dared to lay a hand, a finger, lips, thighs and other body parts upon his wife. Or, perhaps the vacancy sign had gone up since the Lady had no need of it any longer, and he was there to meet his own strumpet. He did, after all, appear more confused than I and a bit embarrassed.

I would have searched my mind for more scenarios, but Bakerstreet and A.P. returned and certified that our weapons were reasonably matched for the duel. I kept my head down and toed the bare earth as Bakerstreet described the rules of engagement. I sucked in my breath. Was that blood upon the ground at my feet? Dry brown now, it had the telltale shape and thickness of once being a puddle.

"To the center, gentlemen," Bakerstreet said. He motioned us into the clearing. "Ten paces each and fire at will. If no one suffers we will repeat at a distance of five paces."

A.P. had never seen or even dreamed of a duel. He kept disturbingly silent through the process, agreeing to every stipulation set forth by Bakerstreet. I confess my own knowledge of "code duello" went no further than what I had read in the newspaper or made up in patter for my audience. It seemed so much more amusing then. Hilarious, I say, when it's someone else's blood you are pattering away.

I abandoned my coat despite the cold. If I was going to shiver before an opponent as skilled as Jasper, let them blame the weather. Jasper kept his coat on and we stood there in Dead Man's Meadow, back to back, waiting for Bakerstreet's signal.

"Left or right?" I hissed to Jasper. I raised my father's pistol shoulder high; the barrel pointed to the sky.

"Say what?"

"Are you using your left hand or your right hand?"

"Left," he said. He chuckled low and with deliberate menace. "This is not sport."

I suppose I could take some comfort in knowing that I was enough of a threat to Jasper that he would not toy with me this afternoon. "It's not too late to consider my offer of settling this with pillows instead. Perhaps peacock feathers, tickle to the death? How's that sound?"

"Coward."

"Bugger."

We began our march to opposite ends of the clearing. At pace one I regretted not following my father's wishes to join the military. Fighting the French in America or the Spanish on the main seemed much safer than this.

At pace three I regretted my attraction to older, married women. It got me banished from Wittyglib to start my journey and landed me in a London prison. Now this. Obviously I have unresolved mother issues.

At pace five I regretted that I had no chance to say a final good-bye to Lady Jasper.

At seven I wished I had written a will. Suppose my brother London, one Christmas yet to come, was stumble drunk and fell face-first into his pudding, thereby suffocating on caramel. If there was any amount of inheritance for me from the family estate, I would like it to go to Mrs. Fullbright and Ape.

And at nine paces I simply regretted that I did not have a life much richer with regrets to wallow in. Better than no life at all, I suppose.

At ten I wheeled and pointed my pistol at the figure now twenty paces from me. Then three distinctive images and bits of understanding converged in my head like runaway carriages, crashing and creating a rush-hour pileup in the middle of London Bridge.

The first was the a figure in a flowing green and white winter frock stepping from behind a tree just over Jasper's shoulder. The second was confirming my instantaneous belief that the figure was Lady Jasper. I did so by leaning to my left and tilting my head to better see who it was. The third was actually a medley of my senses' greatest hits. The crack of Jasper's pistol. The sight of the smoke from its ignited powder. The whizzing of the shot through the area where less than a gasp's moment earlier my face had been. The pain of that ball as it nicked the lobe of my right ear, and the warmth of the blood that it drew. The blood spilled out onto my neck and down over my collar ruining my best shirt. Flog the frog! I had just had it laundered too.

"Hello, Leeds," Lady Jasper waved cheerily as if this sort of happening occurred every day in her household. Time stopped. Kate did not. She crossed behind Jasper and went to Bakerstreet's side. And while I watched her, apparently all eyes were on me as I stood there with the pistol still raised, still marvelously balanced in my hand and aimed squarely at Sir Jasper.

"Well?"

"Well, what?" I asked.

"Shoot," A.P. said.

"I can do that?"

Bakerstreet exchanged a troubled glance at Jasper and raised his palms as if to say, "What can I do?" With his eyes locked on Jasper he explained to me that the rules dictated one shot apiece, and if there is no satisfaction then a second shot each at the closer range. I had not fired my pistol.

"Well, I'm satisfied. What about you, Ian old buddy? Are you satisfied?"

There was no swagger in his spit as he launched a loogie in my direction. Even at twenty paces I could tell he trembled. "Be on with it," he said.

"Well then, it's now or never."

A.P., Lady Jasper and Bakerstreet came to me as I reviewed my options. There were only a few. Shoot to kill, shoot to maim, or shoot to miss. But a miss is as good as a mile, for it would only lead to another round. No, my best option for living a long life appeared to be by inflicting serious bodily harm. Open up a bottle of arse-whupping on the man.

While I contemplated the way the story might be described in tomorrow's morning papers, oh, and the meaning of life and death, of course, Kate Jasper pressed her kerchief to my bleeding ear lobe. Then she leaned up and kissed me long and full.

"I've made my choice," she said.

"If I survive this, you will leave with me?" I asked.

"If you survive this, you won't believe the world that awaits you beyond this bloody field."

Jasper was now tapping his foot with his arms folded across his chest. "Will you get on with it?"

I asked Kate, "Is he always this impatient?"

"Ian is always in a hurry. Instant gratification simply is not quick enough for him."

By now I was no longer aiming at Sir Jasper. I lowered the pistol to my side and put my arm around Kate's waist, pulling her close enough to feel her breath. "I love you."

"I know." She stared deeply into my eyes. "You can't do it, I know. It's adorable, it's admirable and I've never seen anything like it before."

"It wouldn't be sporting, now would it? The poor chap's unarmed. No, I won't," I said. I shook my head sadly.

She looked at me with those big, sad eyes and gently took the pistol from my hand. She showed it to Bakerstreet.

"Cocked," he confirmed. I thought he meant the gun. At least that was my take on it.

Jasper by now came raging at us. "What are you discussing? Why are we wasting time? See here."

He stomped his way across the clearing to within a few paces of our group. Bakerstreet said, "Mr. Merriweather does not have the heart to shoot. Is your honor still at stake? Do you still feel the need for all this?"

"I do."

"Then you shall have your satisfaction, Ian." It was Lady Kate Jasper who said that. She raised the pistol and shot her husband dead in his tracks. His life was gone before he hit the ground. It was as quick and simple as that. So fast that it was several moments before the gravity of the situation penetrated my mind.

She handed the pistol back to me. "Good shot," she said.

"But I didn't, I mean you, I...what the bloody hell just happened?"

Bakerstreet said, "It appears you have just killed the Earl of Diddleshire. He challenged you to a duel, and you accepted. Now, as his second, I can vouch that it was a fair exchange, and the better man won."

I protested. I didn't fire my weapon. You all saw that.

"I know what I witnessed. You fired the shot that killed Sir Ian Jasper," Bakerstreet said with absolute conviction. "What about you, my love?"

Lady Jasper was now standing over her husband's body. "I was never here," she said. And then added, "He's quite dead."

Bakerstreet then pulled a pistol from his pocket and aimed it at A.P.'s noggin. "What say you, little man?"

"I swear, Cap'n. It's hard to know what to think what with that pointed at me."

"Come now, Ape. That is what they call you, isn't it? This is to make it easier. I say it was a duel to the death and a fair shot. Agreed?"

A.P. nodded. "Extremely fair."

My Love? "Did you call the lady 'My Love?'" I asked Bakerstreet.

Kate was leaning over the former Sir Jasper as if expecting it to be a ruse and he might pop up any moment, chuckle, and announce that it was nothing more than a flesh wound. "Now, Leeds, it's not what you think. Well, yes, it is somewhat what you think, but not precisely. We are just friends."

"With benefits," Bakerstreet grinned.

"Well, yes," she agreed. And then Kate Jasper explained it was business. "I told you Ian was not an astute businessman. Between that and his extravagant expenditures on a stable of boys, and his tithe to the crown in order to get the title of earl, I fear we should have been forced to make do without the means to support the estate. Our business concerns were bleeding to death. You simply don't understand the degradation of wearing last year's fashions to this year's parties."

Bakerstreet tapped his considerable chin as if he really had been musing the issue. "Of now you will control the interests of the estate, my Lady."

"With advice and counsel," she replied batting her eyelashes. And benefits. "You see, Leeds, it was strictly business."

I had already reached that conclusion. "Then you set me up. Planned it all along."

Kate shook her head. "Not all of it. You were the one who publicly dissed the duke."

"You left the evidence. You knew I would use it."

"Yes, but I was only trying to get back at Ian for the despicable scoundrel he is. He was. Really, now, it's hard enough in this day and age to compete with every young thing in a tight bustle for a man's attention. But to let a man steal your man, that's unthinkable." She paused and lowered her eyes. "I never imagined they would put you in prison. I know you were protecting me. That makes me feel lower than the mold on last week's cheese. Good Lord, how that sounds like something as you might say. See, Leeds? I am deeply affected by you."

Oh, the lady was good. In my years of pattering and the acting it takes to be effective, I should have been able to see her talent from the start. I was such a twit!

"So did you arrange to secure my acquittal out of remorse, or was it merely to set me free in order to stage this elaborate exchange with Sir Pouty Pants there? For it was strictly business, as you say."

At this, she looked genuinely confused. She asked what I meant.

"I mean you paid the expense of the lawyer I could never afford. He said his fees had been paid by you, my benefactor."

"Did prison make you looney? I did no such thing. I don't know what he said or why he said it; but my darling Leeds, you were deceived."

"I was?"

"Though I should have considered it, it never occurred to me. Hmm. Bit of luck, there. I had already started making other plans once Sir Ian was elevated to Earl."

Now which is worse, I wondered. That she might have thought enough of me to arrange my release just so that I would be shot down in a duel to aid her cause, or that she cared so little that I could have rotted away in prison without nary a thought by her of my welfare? And then, who was the anonymous protector who financed my defense? I was in a twisted scene that would do Shakespeare himself proud. Bile was inching up in my throat, and yet I had to ask, "Did you never love me?"

"Of course, I did," she replied. "Of all my loves, you are special. Why, I'd rank you right up there in the top five or so. Certainly, top ten material. That is why you are still standing."

"I can remedy that," Bakerstreet said. He waved his pistol, though I don't think he meant it. Then he reached out and clapped me on the back as if we were the best of friends, or as teammates who had just won a minor competition. It was obvious now that Jasper and I were both supposed to die that afternoon. He cocked it up by missing his shot. And I returned the favor by refusing to pull the trigger. Bakerstreet assured me that no one would believe A.P. if he went to the authorities, though it appeared temptation was tugging at him to dispatch my friend right there as well. "He is not a threat in any case."

He said he had a "limited-time" offer for me. "You can take those horses and ride as far and as fast as you can away from London. By the time I can report this to authorities you should be far enough away to keep you safe for at least a while."

I nodded slowly.

"But wait. There's more." Bakerstreet asserted. "If you act now, we will tell authorities it was your intent to ride north towards your home at Wittyglib while in reality you shall head south to the coast."

Lady Jasper added, "It's a once in a lifetime offer. Don't wait; act now. And as a bonus, we'll throw in this lovely leather purse with five gold crowns." She held it up by the strings, displaying it smartly above the palm of her other hand.

It was only then that I realized I had been standing in this field without my coat, kept warm only by the heat of the moment. Now every bone in my body ached in icy pain. I retrieved my overcoat and climbed into it. I glared at Lady Jasper and then at Bakerstreet. A.P.'s nose was running like the Thames and he rubbed it vigorously with the sleeve of his coat.

"Do we have a choice, Mr. Merriweather?"

I shook my head and said nothing as I brushed between Kate and the blackguard, Bakerstreet. She pressed the purse against my chest and into my hands. Without breaking stride, I tossed it back over my shoulder. The gold clinked as it landed on the frozen ground.

Chapter Thirty-Seven

Ha, ha! Ha, ha! Staying alive. Staying alive was foremost on my agenda each day. Laughing at those who sought to catch me was just a bit of a bonus. Each day I stepped along in the rhythm of the crowded streets of London, choreographing moves I knew I would need to survive. So I ran with the crowd. When the sun was up I moved amid the crazy dance of foot traffic with well over half a million other Londoners. Where better to hide a needle, I say, than in the haystack of humanity. (I wrote that one down in my notebook for future reference.) When the sun was down I slept under bridges and abandoned basements on the worst side of town, or in better accommodations in the greenhouses and carriage barns behind homes in west London where the residents had gone to the country on Christmas holiday.

I knew only a bit about hiding out in the city. A.P. grew up on those streets and knew the best places to squat. I adopted the disguise of a ragged sailor who might only be in town for a bonk and a beer before heading back to sea. I would have avoided public in the daylight hours, but I had a plan. I had people to see and arrangements to make to pull off a permanent solution to my fugitiveosity. It would be painful and liberating at the same time.

"You are a horse thief now," A.P. told me not long into my life on the run.

"I suspected as much." I refused to accept that fact with gloom and pity. It only strengthened my resolve to resolve what needed resolution. A.P. and I had settled in that night amid the residents of the St. Giles slum. We warmed ourselves at a communal fire in a ring of stone between the high walls of the ramshackle dwellings.

No one seemed to care much about A.P., and he was able to move about town much more freely with the expert eyes and ears that had served him so well at newsgathering. He said, "Bakerstreet let out word that after the duel you rode off on Jasper's horse. He claimed that you had arranged it in order to rob Sir Ian, Lord and Earl of Diddleshire and all that rot. That's a hanging offense."

"That is no surprise at all, Ape." Not much would surprise me anymore, not after Lady Jasper shattered my world by turning on me so completely. She had played me like a cheap lute. Well, maybe I was a lute in need of serious tuning, but no matter. "No one would believe our version of the story now," I said.

I paid a pair of whores a shilling to let us share their lean-to for the night. I paid them an extra shilling apiece to leave us be. I didn't need a conjugal bed; I only wanted a place to sleep out of the cold.

Maybe it was not a coincidence that I chose that sort of shelter for the night, consorting with the workingwomen as it were. In fact, I felt a kinship with them, given the way I seduced and stroked audiences with my patter until they burst with an eruption of righteous passion. For what? A bit of silver per show? And given so much time to ponder all that, I found myself questioning my motives and the cause and effect of my attitudes that steered me down a road leading me to that cliff.

"It's a moral dilemma, that's for certain," A.P. said.

"That it is, my friend."

"What with the girls being paid for and all. It'd be a shame to let that money go to waste. But what'll I tell Liza in the morning when she wants to know where I slept all night?"

"Yes sir. It's a conundrum. That'd be a good word for you to learn, Ape."

Learn it, he did. I waited outside by the fire while A.P. mastered conundrum inside the lean-to, getting our money's worth from the women.

Later, when I could safely curl up under a blanket with my four "roommates," I reluctantly acknowledged how I had been not a master of the news, but its slave and just how powerful a mistress the news business could be. If you treat her with respect she can be elegant and noble, the belle of the ball. But in the hands of a pimp who is only looking to make money from her services, well, she's no better than the over-painted whore snoring beside me that night.

I had much to reflect on about life in general, not just the value of news performing. Lady Kate Jasper taught me only a fool falls in love with a married woman.

And an unfortunate mix up at the apothecary shop taught me to never mistake glue for hemorrhoid ointment.

Life is constantly delivering important lessons. Some are more painful than others.

Two days from Christmas I received a visit from my brother Lancaster.

"It has all been arranged. You will set sail tomorrow at sunset." He turned over a long neglected water bucket and crowded close to the meager fire I had going in the one horse stable behind his home. Lancaster had no horse, of course. Earlier that week he sent word to me that authorities had thoroughly searched the area around Wittyglib Manor as well as his home in London. Everyone assured them that the entire family would rather see me hanged than to give aid and comfort to a black sheep like me.

"I believe London even asked that before you are hanged he be allowed to issue the whipping you denied him so long ago."

I nodded. "You know, Deuce, if ever I write this story I shall work on his character a bit. Far too spiteful and far too one-dimensional."

Lancaster stoked the fire and smiled thinly, wistfully. "No one but you has called me Deuce since father died."

I patted his arm. "I will miss you. I will write from America, and I won't rest until I repay you. Thanks."

"No repayment is necessary. And no need to thank me."

Lancaster went on to deny being the source of my deliverance.

I was out of suspects and stymied. No, he assured me, it wasn't some furtive gesture on the part of our eldest brother. "He's too one-dimensional for that," Lancaster laughed.

I asked him if he knew who had come to my rescue. He dismissed the question with a wave of his hand. Then he said, "Doctor Franklin says he will have that letter you asked about delivered an hour before the tide. He was surprised and very pleased that you have decided to take him up on his offer."

"Certainly he understands how circumstances have changed, though I admit I'm a bit surprised. He sent me a note after my release from Newgate to let me know I haven't fallen out of favor with him. But this? Flog the frog, it's amazing."

Lancaster tousled my hair. I always hated that. Now I'm going to miss it as much as anything. "He believes in you, Leeds. Why, I can't fathom, but maybe that's all part of him being a genius, I suppose."

"I am actually looking forward to this now, and with a letter of introduction from Doctor Franklin, finding work in America will not take long."

With that Lancaster rose. I stood and we hugged. "You'd better get some rest. You have a long journey ahead of you." He pulled back but kept his hands upon my arms. He winked. "Oh, and Leeds, Merry Christmas."

"Merry Christmas to you, too, Deuce."

Chapter Thirty-Eight

The following afternoon I stood on the dock looking up at the mail ship that was to be my home for the next two months, give or take a bit for the currents and all that. A haversack dangled heavily over my shoulder with most of my worldly belongings. Lancaster had provided a small traveling case and some spare clothes. The ship was groaning and creaking, straining against the lines that held her. The tide was rising and we would be leaving soon. The wind was blowing cold, and the sky was grey though not threatening. More than one sailor bumped me as they carried sacks of mail and supplies past me and up the gangplank. One barked at me to get my arse into it and get to work.

I was still wearing the sailor costume I had adopted for my forays around London town. It was absolutely necessary to get past the sentries at the gate. I fell in with a group of similarly dressed mates who were roughly escorting a press gang to the dock. The young men being pressed into service at sea created quite a stir what with bickering and trying to escape. The guards at the gate wanted nothing to do with them and so never gave me a second look either.

I found a narrow gap between the cargo crates and bags ready to be loaded. I changed out of my disguise and into my traveling clothes. It would not do me much good if I were mistakenly pressed into service. And the captain was expecting a gentleman passenger.

"You'd make a fine gentleman if ya could only shut your yap and give up pattering." I turned from watching the activity on the ship's deck above me. A.P. and his girl Liza approached. Liza handed me a small bouquet of pansies.

"Aloysius and I thought these'd bring ya luck on your trip."

I kissed her cheek and shook A.P.'s hand. "And what of you, Ape? I can see you have just the right reason here refusing my offer to start fresh in America with me."

The couple exchanged the look reserved for sheepish young lovers and playful octogenarians. "Liza is with child."

"Well, a hearty congratulations on that." I kissed them both this time.

"If she's a boy we're going to name her after you," Liza said.

"Leeds? No that would never do," I replied. "Let's hope she's a girl. But if not, how about naming the boy Boston?"

"Boston?"

"That is the city where I expect to eventually settle in America, God willing."

"Splendid," A.P. said. "Keep up the ol' Merriweather tradition. As for the newscasting, don't you worry, Mr. Merriweather. I will take good care of her. I believe I was meant to patter. Thanks to you, Mrs. Fullbright and Mr. Penny will let me stay on as your permanent replacement."

"So it's true what I heard. She married the old sod?"

"Indeed. And her daughter Andrea has replaced Veronica who tossed us over for more money at the Cheshire Cheese before getting herself hired away just days later by the Dog and Pony show."

"Remember, though, what is the Tamed Shrew?"

A.P. beamed. "First. Better. Best."

"Keep it that way. Aloysius."

I returned to the ship *Poseidon*. Oh what an adventure this will be. I carried my belongings on board and presented my papers to the purser in command of the deck. A short time later I was on a watch of my own at the port side railing.

"Make way! Make way!" I heard as a sedan chair approached. Two strong footmen jogged through the crowd that crisscrossed their path. I raced down the gangplank to meet them. They carried the coach to the dock and set it before me. Out stepped Doctor Franklin.

"She's a bit worn, but like many women, sometimes the most reliable have a few miles on them," he said as he pushed his glasses to the tip of his nose and took note of the ship. "Mr. Merriweather, I have come to wish you a fair voyage. You will be amazed at the opportunities in the colonies for a spunkster like you. You are just like me in so many ways. Just the sort we need over there."

"I'm honored that you think so, Doctor Franklin. Frankly, I was afraid that the criminal record I seem to have created in my dispute with the Duke of Earl would have you thinking otherwise."

"Nonsense. If anything it makes me feel even more confident in providing you with this letter of introduction. And if it tweaks the king's thigh that you got away, well, all the better. Happy to do it. If the account I received on the cause of your incarceration is true, then you have much to be proud of. It's an honorable thing you did, as a news man and a human being, to keep the confidence of your source in that matter."

"It didn't seem a choice at all. I couldn't have done otherwise." I thought that if Doctor Franklin knew the exact circumstances surrounding my stand he would most likely think it less honorable. Still, who was I to argue with such a distinguished man?

"Bully for you. Not many a news man these days, even the most reputable, would have been so fearless."

Of course, the other bit of spice in that stew, and what I couldn't say at that moment, was that if I had any inkling of what Lady Jasper was up to, I would have turned her like a chicken on a spit.

"When you get to Philadelphia, give this to Mr. Thomas Whitmarsh at the *Gazette*. He'll be easy to find. I have already written to him that the time has come to set up a shop in either Boston Town or New York. As I suggested long ago, I think Boston would the best choice for you."

"Why is that?"

He whistled softly. "Political winds are blowing out of that area. It seems to me the people are more passionate, more radical than in most of the other colonies. Frankly, it is troublesome to me. But the larger concern for us is that where politics are concerned, an energized population has a voracious appetite for news. We must feed the beast."

"Boston, it is."

"I think you will like working there. It's not half as large as the east side of London. But a much more inviting and intelligent community." Before I could say anything he added, "No, don't thank me. Trust me, I am an old professional at this. I arranged a similar franchise for Mr. Whitmarsh years ago, and it has paid quite handsomely."

Doctor Franklin then reached out his hand to me. "Don't think of this as a strict business arrangement, however. It's an investment of faith, or, better still, let's call it a collaboration between friends."

"I will be honored."

We had walked slowly towards the gangplank as we talked. Doctor Franklin was favoring his foot again. "Wait one more moment, Leeds."

As he walked gingerly back to the coach I called after him, "It appears the gout has you today, friend."

"Thank you for reminding me," he said without turning but with an abundance of sarcasm. He limped back from the cab with a package in his hand. "Most days are better than some. Today it feels like the devil himself is gnawing at my ankle. The cold weather does that. Here." He handed the package to me. Something solid was hidden deep within the folds of cloth. It was thick and heavy and tied with a brown ribbon.

"What is it?" I asked.

Doctor Franklin's face lit up like Christmas candles. Even as darkness was settling in over the wharf and lamp men were bustling about, I could tell he was as amused as he's ever been. "It is a parting gift from your benefactor."

I reached for the ribbon but he stopped me. "I know you've been wondering, and have every right to be impatient, but trust me Leeds. You will enjoy this more if it is revealed to you in private."

The tide was cresting, and the purser called down from the rail of the *Poseidon*. It was time to go.

"Safe travels, Leeds. I shall follow you in a month or two. Whenever we can conclude this tax and representation nonsense with the crown. Keep me informed of your progress."

I promised to do so, and my friend Doctor Franklin promised to stop in periodically to gauge the welfare of A.P. and the cast of characters at the Tamed Shrew.

I resisted the temptation to rush to my cabin and open the mysterious package as the guide boats nuzzled us away from the wharf and the sailors began raising sail. Yes, I resisted though the mystery was tugging me like an enormous fish straining the line that was attached to my heart. This was Christmas Eve, for God's sake. No, instead I stood on the deck and savored the breeze and the harbor lights drifting past us, and the glow of London as it receded. The clouds broke, and our journey began like a dream that catches you in that narrow slice of awareness between slumber and wakefulness. I couldn't really tell which was the dream, London, or the ship beneath my feet as we headed for open sea.

Later, after first bells, I sat on my tiny bunk with the lantern swaying above me. I slipped the ribbon from around the package and pulled apart the folds of cloth that I could now tell protected a book.

Not any book, this. It was battered, stained and dog-eared. A well-loved book, I'd say.

Fanny Hill—Memoirs of a Woman of Pleasure.

I buried my face in one hand and shook my head; I chortled until I choked. I opened the book to find a note with the fragrance of lavender and an inscription on the title page. The note read:

Dear Weedsy.

Can you ever forgive me for the innocent bit of intimacy that caused your exile from our home? Upon reflection, perhaps it was for the best. For if you had remained at Wittyglib into full manhood we might have very well provided scandalous fodder for a novel such as this.

You mean we didn't?

Never speak to London of my participation in helping you straighten your legal affairs, nor the source of the funds diverted from household accounts for that purpose. He does not know, and I trust he never will. I simply could not bear the thought that I was somehow responsible for setting you on the path that took you to the doorstep of the gallows. I write this not expecting nor asking for gratitude, but only that you should know if I would have had a say in the matter so long ago, I would still be married to a Merriweather today—just not London. You will always be my favorite.

Emily

Where was my wit? Where was the snide or comical come back appropriate to prevent a total lapse into sentimentality at a time like this? I found only a tear in my eye.

The inscription in the book was simple enough.

"*Life is full of passion. Embrace it. Or embrace the wench nearest you, and think of me.*" She signed it E.,1765.

I reached for the haversack and pulled out my father's pistol. I laid it carefully on the cover of *Fanny Hill,* wrapped them together in the heavy cloth and cinched the ribbon.

Blood and lust.

They make the world go round.

Though hardly ever in the way you expect.

About the Author

Larry Brill spent 25 years as a television news anchor, picking up numerous awards for his reporting and storytelling skills. Free from the required objectivity that comes with being a serious journalist, he has unleashed his quirky outlook on life and offbeat brand of humor on the fans of his novels from his home base in Austin, Texas.

www.ingramcontent.com/pod-product-compliance
Lightning Source LLC
Chambersburg PA
CBHW051329250626
47155CB00007B/2513

* 9 7 8 0 9 8 8 8 6 4 3 4 4 *